WHO KILLED
ALFRED SNOWE?

J.S. FLETCHER

This edition published 2022 by

OREON
an imprint of
The Oleander Press
16 Orchard Street
Cambridge
CB1 1JT

A CIP catalogue record for the book
is available from the British Library.
ISBN: 9781915475015

Cover design, typesetting & ebook: neorelix

For first news of
titles, give-aways and
discounts, sign up to our
infrequent newsletter at:
oleanderpress.com

Contents

Chapter One

IS IT MURDER?

I WAS IN BED, half awake, at the Mitre Hotel at Wrenchester, about half-past six o'clock one fine morning in the June of 1924, when the night-porter came thundering at my door and roused me to awareness of the fact that he was not only there himself, but was accompanied by somebody who was loudly calling my name. Being – after my custom – wide awake on the instant, I recognized the voice of Aubrey Snowe. Snowe was a young medico who had recently set up in practice in Wrenchester, his native town; he was also an old schoolfellow of mine, and after not seeing each other for some years we had foregathered the previous day on the Wrenchester cricket-ground, where I, just then on my holidays, had been playing for the London Roundabouts against the town club. Usually a very phlegmatic and matter-of-fact sort of fellow, Aubrey Snowe was at this moment in an evident state of excitement; he supplemented the night-porter's bangs on my door with blows of his own, and bawled my name loudly enough to wake everybody on that floor.

"Camberwell!" he shouted. "Camberwell! Open your door!" I jumped out of bed and flung the door open. Aubrey Snowe fell rather than walked in, and staggered to the bedside; the night-porter stood on the threshold, staring.

"What on earth's the matter?" I asked.

Aubrey gasped, made an effort, spoke.

"My uncle!" he said. "You saw him yesterday – at the cricket-ground?"

"Well?" I demanded. "What – ?"

"He's dead! Found dead – just now. And I believe – murdered!" he gasped.

"Murdered!" I turned to the night-porter. But the night-porter shook his head. Evidently he knew nothing.

"Pull yourself together, Aubrey!" I said. "Come, now! Tell about it." Aubrey swallowed once or twice.

"I'm certain he was murdered!" he muttered. "I saw –" He interrupted himself, hesitated a little, and then spoke more calmly.

"My uncle lived in Little Straightway," he said. "I live a few doors away in the same street. This morning – about half an hour ago – the milkman knocked me up. He said that when he left the milk on Mr Snowe's front doorstep he saw that the door was partly open. He pushed it open a little more, and saw my uncle lying in the hall. Then he ran for me. I went back with him. My uncle was dead; I saw at once that he'd been dead some time. I got some help, close by – police and Dr Wellsted – and then ran for you. You're a private inquiry agent nowadays, Camberwell, you told me yesterday. Well, come back with me. It's murder, I tell you, murder!"

"How do you know that?" I asked.

"I saw certain marks on his throat!" he exclaimed. "Unmistakable!" While this conversation had been going on I had been hurrying into my clothes; now I was ready. I turned to the night-porter, who had lingered, listening, open-mouthed.

"Better not say anything about this just yet," I said, giving him a look.

"Right, sir, right, Mr Camberwell!" he answered. "All the same, if what Dr Snowe says is correct it'll be all over the town by breakfast-time."

He went off downstairs, and Aubrey and I followed him, and out into the High Street. I knew enough of Wrenchester to know that the queer old street called Little Straightway was close by, only just beyond the old Market Cross, but there was time enough before reaching it to ask Aubrey a few questions.

"Did Mr Snowe live alone, Aubrey?" I inquired.

"Absolutely alone!" he answered. "He wouldn't have a servant in the house. At least, not to live in. He'd a woman who came in the daytime – eight o'clock till six in the afternoon. Lately – since I came here, that is – I've done my best to persuade him to have proper service, but it was no good. He was a bit peculiar, Camberwell – an eccentric in some ways. These clever chaps are, I believe."

I knew something of Mr Snowe – Alfred Snowe – by repute. He was a somewhat famous antiquary, a Fellow of the Society of Antiquaries, and a member of many other learned societies. He had written books, pamphlets, and treatises on the subjects most dear to him, and was well known to historians and archaeologists. And, as Aubrey said, I had seen him the day before, at the cricket ground – a frail, delicate-looking old man of something between seventy-five and eighty, as I guessed, whose hold on life I should have put down as feeble and precarious.

"Was your uncle known to keep money in the house?" I asked.

"I don't know that he was known to do so," replied Aubrey. "And I don't know that he did. He was known to be well off, very well off, and he'd a lot of valuables in the house, but chiefly in the way of books, pictures, and curios. Were you thinking of robbery?"

"If what you suggest is correct there must have been some motive," I said. "But perhaps you're mistaken, Aubrey – he was very old, and he may have died —"

"No!" he interrupted, with emphasis. "There's been an attack on him. I saw the marks, plainly. Wellsted will say so – you'll see!"

We turned into Little Straightway. Little Straightway was one of the oldest streets in this very old town of Wrenchester, so narrow that one could easily have missed its opening in going along the High Street. There was just room for one vehicle to pass between its yard-broad side-pavements; I question if the sun ever shone on the tall houses on either side. They were very old houses, those; built, I should say, in the early days of the eighteenth century; narrow-fronted, high-win-dowed, with acutely sloping roofs, over which ancient chimneys rose at strange angles. Always whenever I walked its length Little Straight-way seemed to be plunged in sleep, and you could not help wondering whether human beings lived within the houses, and if they were asleep or dead.

But on this summer morning there were signs of life in Little Straightway. Mr Snowe's house was Number Five, and before its door several people had gathered, and at the door itself there stood a couple of policemen. The milkman of whom I had heard from Aubrey was still there; his milk-cart stood in the roadway; he himself was talking volubly to the guardians of the door. We pushed through the little crowd and went into the house; one of the policemen shut the door on us.

The first thing that struck me on entering was the unusual narrow-ness of the entrance hall, or, to give it a more proper name, passage; the second, that it was lined with thickly stocked bookcases, on either side, from one end to the other: there was little more than room to pass between them. But at the end of the passage the hall widened out to a square, with double glass doors at its farther side, opening on to a walled garden. There were four men in this wider space, and they were grouped round a table in its centre. On that table they had laid the dead man, and I went up at once and looked at him. I saw immediately what Aubrey meant when he spoke of violence. On either side of the throat there were distinct, unmistakable marks, livid in hue, and on the right shoulder were the clear signs of a grip which must have been savage in its fierceness. From that shoulder one of the doctors had turned back the dead man's nightwear, an old-fashioned nightgown; this and a much-worn old dressing-gown was all the clothing on the body. Evidently Mr Snowe had been roused from his bed by some sound in the lower part of the house, had come downstairs, and – had met his fate at the hands of whoever it was that had broken in.

I had been some days in Wrenchester then – we were making it the centre for a series of cricket-matches – and I knew the four men who were standing round the table. There were Dr Wellsted, one of the leading medicos of the town; his assistant, Dr Compton; Superintendent Bailiss, Chief of Police; and a police inspector whose name I knew as Jervis. Bailiss turned to Aubrey as soon as we joined them.

"Where, exactly, did you find him when you were fetched, Dr Snowe?" he asked.

Aubrey pointed to the foot of the staircase.

"There!" he answered. "He was lying half on the floor of the hall, half on the stairs. When Dr Wellsted and one of your men came we lifted him on to this table."

"Looks, then, as if he'd been seized as he got to the bottom of the stairs," remarked Bailiss. He turned, questioningly, to Dr Wellsted. "You've no doubt about the cause of death, doctor?"

"There's none!" replied Wellsted brusquely. "None whatever! The thing's patent to anybody. He'd gone to bed – he heard some sound

down here – he came down – he was seized at the foot of the staircase
– look at these marks on shoulder and throat – a powerful grip, too,
in both cases. And he was a frail, delicate old man! A brutal murder –
an abominable murder!"

Bailiss made no remark on that. He had turned from the table and
was looking about him.

"I don't know this house at all," he observed. "You'll know it, of
course, Dr Snowe? What is there of value in it, now?"

"You'd better look round," said Aubrey. "Camberwell, look round
with them. Superintendent, I don't know if you know Mr Ronald
Camberwell, of Chaney and Camberwell? – they're in your line, you
know, in a private capacity. Mr Camberwell is staying in the town, and
as he's an old schoolmate of mine I fetched him along. Look round,
Camberwell – on my behalf."

The two police officials gave me a nod, and looked me up and
down carefully. They knew my name well enough – it and Chaney's
had been before the public a good deal of late. But the glances they
gave me were those of the professional who looks at the amateur, and
Superintendent Bailiss's nod was very cool.

"Ah, just so!" he said, almost patronisingly. "Yes, to be sure. Well,
we'll just take a look at these ground-floor rooms."

Leaving the three doctors still talking in low voices by the dead
man's side, Bailiss, his Inspector, and I went into a room at the end of
the hall (they were very narrow houses, those, and the rooms were on
only one side of the hall-passages), and found it to be an old-fashioned
dining-room, small in dimensions. There was some old furniture,
some old pictures on the walls, old china in a cabinet, and on a sideboard some old silver, heavy candlesticks, salvers, dishes, cups – well
worth any burglar's attention. And everything was in order.

"Um!" said Bailiss. "Don't seem to have been in here, anyhow! That silver's worth above a bit. Queer business! I should have thought that would have gone. What do you say, Mr Camberwell?"

"At present, Superintendent, nothing," I answered. "Except that I see nothing to arouse any suspicion – here."

"Neither do I!" he agreed. "Let's try that front room." The door of the front room was half open; when we had pushed it to its full opening we found ourselves on the threshold of an apartment the like of which, I suppose, was not to be found in all Wrenchester. It was about eighteen feet square, and of a considerable height, and its walls, save where they were pierced by a window looking out on Little Straightway, and by a fireplace, were – literally – covered by books, from floor to ceiling. There was not one picture in the place. Nor was there much furniture. An oblong table stood in the centre of the room, and on either side of the fireplace there was set an easy-chair. These three articles, with a ladder for reaching the higher book-shelves, were the only objects in the room other than books. And here, as in the little dining-room at the back, everything seemed to be in order. At any rate, there was no sign of any struggle, disturbance, or meddling with the arrangements of Mr Snowe's very orderly library.

"Well, I don't see anything here!" remarked Bailiss. "Nothing at all. Now perhaps you do, Mr Camberwell?"

"Yes," I said. "I see certain things. I see that Mr Snowe had been reading the evening paper, and had left it by the side of his – probably favourite – chair. I see too that he left his spectacles on his blotting-pad, there on the table –"

"Oh, I mean anything – anything of importance!" interrupted Bailiss. "Anything to show us who it was that got in here last night. We shall have to see about fingerprints, Jervis," he went on, turning to the Inspector. "I don't know whether this'll turn out to be a Scotland

Yard job, but fingerprints'll come in, anyhow. Well, let's have a look upstairs."

I followed the Superintendent and the Inspector upstairs. On the first landing one door was open; it proved to be that of what was evidently the dead man's bedroom, a plainly furnished, simple apartment above the library. Again there were no signs of disturbance. Nothing was out of place. The bedclothes, however, were turned back, and the state of the pillows showed that Mr Snowe had been in bed when he heard something that made him get up and go downstairs – to his death.

We went over the rest of the house. Bailiss said it was merely a preliminary – just a preliminary examination; but I soon made up my mind that there was nothing whatever to see. There might be fingerprints somewhere . . .

Aubrey Snowe and Dr Wellsted were in the library when we went down. Bailiss at once tackled the elder medico with a question.

"Doctor, can you say when this occurred? I mean, how long had the poor gentleman been dead?" he asked. "It's highly important to know that, you know."

"I was called at a quarter past six," replied Dr Wellsted. "I should say Mr Snowe had been dead about six or seven hours."

"That," said Bailiss, "would fix it at about midnight – between eleven and midnight. Your uncle lived alone, Dr Snowe? Yes. Well" – he paused, looking about him as if in wondering search of something – "well, I see no disturbance of what you might call the domestic arrangements, and no signs of a burglar. Of course, I've a theory of my own. I think a burglar got in and was scared from carrying out his plans before really getting to work!"

"An excellent theory, Superintendent!" remarked Dr Wellsted. "You've omitted, however, to mention that your burglar managed to kill Mr Snowe before leaving!"

Chapter Two

WHAT DID MR SNOWE MEAN?

AFTER MAKING THIS REMARK – in a caustic tone which suggested, to me, at any rate, that he had very little opinion of Superintendent Bailiss's abilities – Dr Wellsted drew me aside.

"Take Aubrey Snowe away!" he said. "Go with him to his house and stop with him a while – he's thoroughly upset, and he'll do no good here. But perhaps you're playing cricket again?"

"No," I replied. "This is an off-day; we've no match on, and if we had I shouldn't play. I'll look after Aubrey. But tell me, doctor, what do you make of all this?"

He gave me a knowing look.

"My opinion?" he asked. "Um – well, it isn't Bailiss's. I think there's some very extraordinary mystery about the poor old gentleman's death. My idea coincides with Bailiss's, it's true, so far as to think that Mr Snowe interrupted the doings of somebody who had entered the house for some specific purpose, but I don't share Bailiss's opinion that the purpose was burglary. I think the murderer had already found what he wanted and was clearing out with it when Mr Snowe came downstairs to him. But not ordinary burglary! If it had been, what was there to stop the burglar, after quietening Mr Snowe, from taking that silver in the dining-room away with him? Nothing – Bailiss's theory of interruption from outside is nonsense. However – you're one of the Chaney-Camberwell combination, I understand? Well, here's something for you to exercise your skill on. What was Mr Snowe's assailant and murderer – though, mind you, he mayn't have meant murder – after, in this house? Nice problem! But take Aubrey Snowe and make him eat some breakfast and attend to his engagements – we'll see to things here better than he could."

I got Aubrey to leave the house, and steered him through the increasing crowd of people outside. His own house was only a few doors away; before we reached it a breathless youth came calling after my companion.

"Dr Snowe! Dr Snowe! You know me, sir? Skinner, reporter for the *Wrenchester Journal*. Our publishing day, sir – can you give me an exclusive for the 'stop press,' doctor? Just a few words, sir –"

Aubrey looked at me in perplexity. I drew him out of the enemy's clutch.

"You'd better see the police, Mr Skinner," I said. "They'll give you reliable information, no doubt. You'll find Superintendent Bailiss in Number Five."

Mr Skinner did not wait to thank me; he turned and ran, and Aubrey and I walked on.

"So it'll be in the papers?" he muttered. "Of course it will! But I hadn't thought of that. Poor old Uncle Alfred – he hated publicity! What'll come next, Camberwell? Will – will there be an inquest?"

"That's inevitable," I answered. "But, look here, just leave all that alone for the time being – Wellsted on one hand, and Bailiss on the other, will see to everything. Here's your spot, Aubrey, and I'm coming in to have breakfast with you."

"Breakfast?" he said. "Oh, yes, I suppose it is getting towards breakfast-time! Yes – yes, do! I'd forgotten about that."

He led me into his house – another typical example of Little Straightway architecture – and, telling the housekeeper that I was breakfasting with him, conducted me into his dining-room. There he suddenly turned on me.

"If I seem half-there, Camberwell," he exclaimed, "there's more than one reason for it. Not only this – this awful business, but I've been up all night. From half-past nine last night until just before that milkman chap came to fetch me – I'd only just got in then, in my car – I'd been out at Felbourne with a serious case – pulled it through, though. And I'm half dead with sleep – still, there's a lot to be done, and certain patients to see this morning."

"Couldn't you get one of your fellow-practitioners in the town to take your patients over for today?" I suggested. "What about that assistant of Wellsted's? And Wellsted seems to be a very good-natured sort."

"I'll see – I'll see, after breakfast," he answered. "Some strong coffee – but, by George, there's one thing I must do, at once, and that's to send off a wire to my poor uncle's solicitor, Mr Heyman, in London. He must be told this awful business without delay. He'll be fearfully cut up, old Heyman! They were bosom friends – not merely solicitor and client."

Breakfast came in. I did my best to make Aubrey eat and drink, and even to arouse some diversion of subject in our conversation. But he kept going back to the dismal event of the morning, and finally he rose from the table, saying that he must get the telegram off to Mr Heyman. And at that very moment Mr Heyman himself was announced.

I knew Mr Heyman by sight – an elderly, spare-figured, hawk-eyed man, who had a great reputation in his profession and was well known about the Law Courts and the Lincoln's Inn Fields district. He came in looking very much upset, and I saw at once that he had heard the news.

"My dear Aubrey!" he said. "I have heard the news about my poor old friend on my way from the railway station! There is already a newspaper placard in the streets. But I can scarcely comprehend or understand matters. You wonder to see me here, in Wrenchester, at this early hour of the day? I am here because, yesterday afternoon, about five-thirty, as I was just about to leave my office in Bedford Row, I got a letter from Alfred, asking me to come down here by the very first train this morning. I will read it to you." He paused, glancing over his spectacles at me. "This gentleman," he continued. "Friend of yours, I suppose –"

"Mr Ronald Camberwell – old schoolfellow, Mr Heyman," said Aubrey. "Camberwell's the famous Camberwell of Camberwell and Chaney, private detectives. He's having a holiday in the town – mere chance that he was here, but a jolly good job for me."

Mr Heyman nodded – quite agreeably.

"Oh, yes, yes!" he said. "Yes, to be sure – Camberwell and Chaney? Ah, yes, the missing baronet case, and – and others. Dear me – most interesting! Well, well, perhaps Mr Camberwell can bring his detective sense to bear on poor Alfred's letter, for I'm sure I do not understand it at all. But I'll read it, I'll read it."

He produced a letter from his pocket, and, seating himself with his back to the light, began to read.

5 LITTLE STRAIGHTWAY
WRENCHESTER
Tuesday 8.45 A.M.

My Dear Heyman,

I have accidentally made a most important discovery,
the exact nature of which I need not explain in this
letter, but which must necessarily have an effect of
the most serious sort upon the lives and fortunes of
more than one person. I am desirous of discussing it
personally with you at once, and I shall be obliged if
you will come down to Wrenchester first thing tomorrow, Wednesday, morning: the matter is of such
importance that I beg you will not allow anything to
prevent your coming. I see, on consulting the railway time-table, that if you catch the 6.30 at London
Bridge you will arrive here about two hours later –
I shall accordingly expect you to breakfast with me
at 9 o'clock. I will afterwards acquaint you with the
particulars arising out of the discovery above referred
to – a discovery the seriousness of which your lawyer's
mind will appreciate even more than mine possibly
can.

Your affectionate

Alfred Snowe

Mr Heyman laid the letter on the breakfast-table and turned to us.

"Now, whatever is the meaning of that letter?" he demanded. "What is the 'important discovery'? Has he spoken of any such discovery to you, Aubrey?"

"Never!" replied Aubrey. "I haven't the faintest idea as to his meaning. I have seen him every day during the last few days – I always have seen him, every day, ever since I came to live here – and he never mentioned any discovery to me."

"When did you see him last?" inquired Mr Heyman.

"Alive? At the town cricket-ground, yesterday afternoon. He was quite well then, and in his usual spirits," said Aubrey. "I don't know, Mr Heyman, what he means by that letter. But what I'd like to know is – has this discovery he refers to anything to do with his murder?"

Mr Heyman made a wry face. "Was – was he really murdered?" he asked.

Aubrey pointed to me. I gave Mr Heyman a plain account of what we had found and seen, and told him what Dr Wellsted said. Mr Snowe's assailant, perhaps, had not meant to murder him, but only to prevent him from crying for help; the grip, however, which he had exerted on the poor old gentleman's throat had silenced Mr Snowe for ever.

"That's murder!" muttered Mr Heyman. He remained silent for a moment, staring at the letter. "Whatever can it be that Alfred had discovered?" he said at last. "Something – about somebody, I suppose. But what? – and where? – and how? Shall we ever know?"

"There is one thing certain, sir," I remarked. "If Mr Snowe's murder arose out of this discovery, as he calls it, it is very evident that the discovery was known to the murderer. And now that you have read Mr Snowe's letter to us I am wondering if Mr Snowe was not deliberately murdered – to stop him from speaking."

Mr Heyman nodded his head two or three times.

"Yes – yes – yes!" he said. "Yes – I see your point. I wonder! Some secret? What does Alfred say? 'Must necessarily have an effect of the most serious sort upon the lives and fortunes of more than one person.' Most extraordinary! We are, of course, utterly in the dark. Is anyone suspected?"

"No one so far," I replied.

"I know no details, you know," said Mr Heyman. "A mere paragraph in the 'stop press' corner of the local paper which I purchased on my way through the town stated that Alfred had been found dead and that foul play was feared. You know more?"

"Practically no more than I have already told you," I answered. "I will go across again, and hear if the police have anything further to report."

I left them together and went off to Number Five. But in the street I met Bailiss; he was coming to see me. He drew me aside – there was still a crowd of inquisitives there – with an air of mystery.

"We've found out how the murderer got into Mr Snowe's," he said. "At the end of the hall there's the kitchen. Behind the kitchen is the scullery. And behind the scullery, and opening out of it, there's a sort of greenhouse; it's not good enough to call a conservatory, and all that the old gentleman seems to have kept it for was to dump rubbish in it. Well, Mr Camberwell, the door of that place had been forced! No difficult job, for it's a ramshackle contraption, and could be easily prised open with a chisel. That greenhouse opens on to a yard at the back of the house, and the yard gives on to a narrow alley. My notion is that the man, whoever he is, got in that way, but left by the front door, and left that open. Anyway, that greenhouse door has been forced, and the marks of the forcing are quite fresh. You follow me?"

"Oh, quite, Superintendent!" I replied. "Very clear indeed."

"It's a rum business," he went on. "What was the murderer after? We've had a further look round since I saw you, and hang me if I can make things out! Upstairs, in the old gentleman's bedroom, on his dressing-table, there's a gold watch, chain, and seals – old-fashioned stuff, you know – I'll lay anything they're worth not less than sixty or seventy pounds. Then there was his purse lying there – nearly twelve pounds in it. And a pocket-book with a couple of fivers. And – as you no doubt saw – there's a lot of good old solid silver on the sideboard in the dining-room. A nice haul, you see, altogether! And yet – nothing touched! What can the man have been after?"

"Difficult to say, Superintendent," I said. "But your notion is that he was surprised and went off hurriedly, isn't it?"

He shook his head. "Aye, well!" he replied. "Say my first notion, Mr Camberwell, my first notion! What's the saying? Circumstances alter cases. Now that I've seen more, I'm inclined to think otherwise. I've a man – constable – who comes along this street about half-past twelve. I've seen him; he saw nothing and heard nothing. To be sure, he didn't try Mr Snowe's door, and he can't say if it was closed then or not. And we've made inquiries round about – none of the neighbours heard a sound. No, my opinion now is that the murderer broke into that house to get something – something, you understand, Mr Camberwell! He'd either already got it, whatever it was, when the old gentleman came down, or he got it after he'd quietened him. When he got it he just – cleared out!"

"That seems a very likely theory, Superintendent," I agreed. "On the evidence you've got up to now, a very probable one."

"Yes, I think so," he said, with satisfaction. "But – what was it he got? Who's going to tell me anything that'll help to an answer? Had Mr Snowe got something in that house that was of – of some unusual value? And who's to say? If he had, I dare say it was a secret to himself. But if so – how did the murderer get to know of it?"

"Possibly something may come out before the inquest," I said. "When will that be held?"

"The inquest?" he replied. "Ah, I'll see about having that opened tomorrow. Keep your ears open, Mr Camberwell – we're never above taking in a bit of amateur assistance!"

Chapter Three

MISSING!

ALTHOUGH I WAS NOT engaged professionally in it, I certainly kept my eyes open, and my ears on the alert, in this Snowe case – not with any intention of assisting Bailiss and his men, but from sheer curiosity. I made it my business, at the beginning, to verify what Bailiss had told me, and I came to the conclusion that he was quite right in believing that the house had been entered from the back premises – there were marks to show forcible entry, and they were fresh. And he was right, of course, as to the personal possessions of the dead man, lying about in the bedroom where anyone could have picked them up and walked off with them. Robbery, then, was not the motive of the criminal. So – what was his motive?

To show how interested I was in the case I gave up a day's cricket in order to be able to attend the inquest, which, as Bailiss had promised, was duly opened on the day following the murder. During the thirty hours which had elapsed between the discovery of Mr Snowe's dead body and the beginning of this inquiry the police had worked incessantly not only to get on the murderer's track, but to collect evidence about Mr Snowe's last doings. In the first they had so far met with no success whatever; in the second with very little. The coroner, remarking that he might as well take all the evidence available up to then, before adjourning until some future date, commented on the extraordinary mystery surrounding Mr Snowe's death, and hinted that when he adjourned it might be without fixing any definite date for resumption – the police, he said, were evidently faced with a problem of an unusually baffling nature.

The evidence that we listened to had no new element in it for those who, like myself, had been on the spot and within the circle of first-hand knowledge from the beginning. There was the evidence of the milkman, who had made his discovery in doing his early-morning round. There was the evidence of the medical men as to the cause of death, and of the Superintendent as to the condition of the house and its contents and the means by which the unknown assailant had entered. Mr Snowe's day-servant, a woman who had done his daily work for some years, arriving at eight o'clock in the morning and leaving at six in the evening, testified that when she left the house on the night of his death he was in his usual health and spirits. Then came some evidence as to Mr Snowe's daily customs. It transpired that for a great many years he had gone every night of his life – except when he was dining at a friend's house – to dine at the Mitre Hotel. A special table, in a certain corner of the dining-room, was always reserved for him there. He always arrived at five minutes to seven o'clock, spent exactly one hour over his dinner, and went away as the clocks struck eight. He had dined, as usual, at the Mitre on the night of his death.

But the people at the Mitre were not the last people to see Mr Snowe alive. The very last person who saw and spoke to him on the evening into the circumstances of which the coroner was inquiring proved to be a clergyman of the town, Canon Revington, a great personal friend of the dead man. He had come forward voluntarily – and his evidence was interesting.

"I understand, Canon Revington, that you have informed the police that you were with the late Mr Snowe during the evening before his death?" said the coroner. "That is, on Tuesday evening last?"

"Yes," replied Canon Revington. "I was. I called on Mr Snowe about eight o'clock, and remained with him until a quarter to ten. When I called he had just got in from the Mitre Hotel."

"You were great friends, I believe?"

"Great friends – close friends. Being, as we were, fellow-members of two or three antiquarian and archeological societies, we had much in common."

"And, I suppose, you visited him frequently?"

"At least twice a week. Sometimes he came to see me."

"As you knew him so well, you would be quick to notice anything unusual about him. Did you notice anything on this last occasion?"

"Nothing at all! He was just as usual."

"In his usual health?"

"He was rather better than usual. He was not a strong man – rather feeble, if anything, or becoming so. But that night he was very well indeed, and was very proud of himself for having walked up to the cricket-ground that afternoon, spent two or three hours there, and walked back without suffering any ill consequences. No – he was in very good spirits that evening."

"Did he say anything to you, tell you anything, hint at anything, which could in any way be considered, now, as having some, or any, connection with his death?"

"Oh, certainly not! Nothing at all. Our conversation, as usual, was about archaeological matters. Nothing else."

"And he was quite well when you left him at a quarter to ten?"

"Quite!"

The coroner had no more to ask. But Bailiss put in a question.

"Mr Snowe would let you out at his front door, sir, no doubt. Now, can you remember – did you hear him fasten the door after you'd stepped out?"

"Yes!" replied Canon Revington. "I heard him turn the key. He always did that when I left. I know – from what he told me – that he always went to bed at ten o'clock, to the minute. That was why, when I went to see him, I always left at a quarter to ten. He had rather a fad – he was a faddist! – for doing things at the exact moment."

Canon Revington was stepping down then, but Mr Heyman stopped him.

"As the late Mr Snowe's solicitor," he said, "I want, Canon Revington, to ask you a most important question. In the course of your conversation with Mr Snowe that evening, did he say anything to you about his having made a discovery – a remarkable discovery?"

Canon Revington showed his surprise.

"A discovery? No, indeed he did not! An archeological discovery?"

"We will leave the nature of the discovery out. Did he mention – did he give even a hint – of a discovery that he had made?"

"No! Not a word." Canon Revington was obviously deeply interested. "He always shared any news of that sort with me," he added. "But no – there was never a hint of any such thing that evening." He lingered in the witness-box, as if desirous of being questioned further. But Mr Heyman hesitated. I knew – or guessed – what he was hesitating about. He was wondering whether it would be wise, at that stage, to divulge the contents of the letter from Mr. Snowe to himself which he had read to Aubrey and myself. I was sitting just behind him, and he suddenly turned round to me.

"Camberwell," he whispered, "what do you think? Shall I make that letter known?" The question took me unawares. What should I answer? I thought quickly. Whatever the discovery alluded to by Mr

Snowe in his letter to Mr Heyman was, its nature and secret were by this time, in all probability, known to Mr Snowe's murderer. If Mr Heyman, by reading the letter, let him know that we knew there was a discovery and a secret, but knew nothing of the nature of either, he would feel secure. If, by keeping the letter back, we made him think that somebody other than himself knew the secret, he would possibly make some false step that would bring him into the light. I shook my head.

"No!" I replied. "Say nothing about it – here, at any rate." Mr Heyman gave the witness a polite bow; Canon Revington stepped out of the witness-box, looking a little unsatisfied; the mere mention of a discovery – which he, of course, at once associated with his favourite hobbies – had roused his curiosity. And the coroner too looked at Mr Heyman as if he wanted to know more.

"What discovery do you refer to, Mr Heyman?" he asked.

But Mr Heyman was not to be drawn. He assumed a sphinx-like expression.

"I think, sir, it would not be in the public interest if I said more at this time," he answered blandly. "I merely wished to know if the late Mr Snowe had happened to mention the matter I am thinking of to Canon Revington. As he did not…"

He ended with another polite bow, and the coroner said no more. A few minutes later the inquest was adjourned, without date.

Two days later Mr Alfred Snowe, Fellow of the Society of Antiquaries, and member of several other learned bodies, was laid to rest in the churchyard of a little village just outside Wrenchester. Late in the afternoon of the day of the funeral, as I was changing out of my cricket flannels at the Mitre, I was summoned to the telephone: Dr Snowe wanted to speak to me, if I had returned.

"Yes, Aubrey?" I said, getting in touch with him. "Here I am."

"I didn't know whether you'd got back," he answered. "I say, will you come round to Little Straightway? Not to my place – come to Number Five. You'll find me there. Come now, if you can."

"Be with you in ten minutes," I replied.

I ran up to my room again and finished dressing. Then I hurried round – there had been something in Aubrey's tone which suggested that the business was important. I wondered why he was at Number Five. Mr Snowe's house had been carefully locked up and secured since his death, and I should not have credited Aubrey with any desire to enter it. But he was at the door, awaiting me, and I saw at once that something had happened. Without a word he beckoned me to follow him into the front room – that in which the dead man's library was stored. And there, looking very grave, was Mr Heyman. On the table in the centre of the room lay some legal-looking sheets of paper – I guessed at once that they represented Mr Alfred Snowe's will.

"Look here, Ronald," began Aubrey, without preface, "neither Mr Heyman nor myself have any great faith in that chap Bailiss – he means well, and he's painstaking, but he's no imagination, and can only see the obvious. And now we want somebody who – who can see through a brick wall!"

"Has something happened?" I asked.

Aubrey pointed to the sheets of paper.

"That," he said, "is Uncle Alfred's will. Mr Heyman brought it down with him this morning when he came to the funeral. This afternoon, when we got back from Helham, where the funeral was, Mr Heyman read it to me. I needn't bother you with the details – we knew pretty well what they'd be. Uncle Alfred has left all he had in equal shares between his sister, Louisa, and his sister-in-law, my mother, with remainder – they only have a life interest, you know – to me and my sister Mabel. That's the will – I'm telling you all this so that you'll know all about things – the will, I say – but there are two codicils. And one of them has led us to make a discovery which –" Here he suddenly broke off, turning to the solicitor. "I think you'd better go on with it, Mr Heyman," he said. "Let Camberwell hear what it means, exactly."

Mr Heyman, who, while Aubrey was talking, appeared to be plunged in profound meditation, roused himself and picked up the will.

"There are two codicils," he said. "The first instructs the executors, of whom Aubrey is one and I the other, to offer this library of books, *en bloc*, to Mr Harston, antiquarian bookseller, of Great Russell Street, London, it being the testator's earnest wish that he should acquire them, and we are empowered to agree with his reasonable offer – Mr Snowe evidently had great faith in Harston as an expert, and wanted his books to fall into Harston's hands as a collection, rather than that they should be sold at auction or sold piecemeal. Well, that's all right – I dare say we shall not quarrel with Harston. But now comes the second codicil – and here we are face to face with a problem which we now submit, Camberwell, to you!"

I said nothing. Problem? In the codicil of a will? What could it be?

"This second codicil," continued Mr Heyman, "is virtually an instruction to the executors to hand over – immediately after the testator's decease – to the Bodleian Library, at Oxford, a certain book called *A History of Wrenchester*, by Septimus Flood, and bearing inside its front cover the bookplate of Samuel Garsdale, 'which book,' says the codicil, with all Mr Snowe's love of particularity, 'will be found in its usual place, being the first book on the third shelf of the bookcase standing on the right-hand side of the fireplace in my study.'" I instinctively turned towards the place mentioned. Mr Heyman turned too.

"Just so!" he said. "But the book isn't there!"

That, of course, was obvious. The book was not there. Where it should have stood was an empty space. I saw at once that it was not a very big book – no weighty folio, as many of these local histories are. The shelf on which it should have been found, according to the directions in the codicil, was made to accommodate volumes of no more than eleven inches in height – probably, then, it was a full-sized demy octavo. But I attached little importance to its absence.

"Misplaced," I said. "Mr Snowe must have put it elsewhere."

"No!" exclaimed Aubrey, with a decidedly negative gesture. "That won't do! My uncle was the most particular man that ever lived about putting a thing back in its place. Besides, I've already searched every shelf in this room, and it's not here. And he never allowed a book to lie around anywhere – every book in the house is in this room. If he took a book or pamphlet to his bedroom, to read at night, he brought it down again in the morning and put it in its proper shelf. The book's gone!"

"And the question is – where?" asked Mr Heyman.

Then, during a moment's silence, we all looked at each other. I knew what the others were thinking – I was thinking the same thing myself.

Mr Heyman put it into words.

"Is it possible," he said, "is it really possible that *that* was what the burglar was after? That – a mere book?"

Chapter Four

STOLEN! BUT WHY?

MR HEYMAN'S REMARK MADE me aware of the fact that however clever a lawyer he might be he was not greatly gifted with imagination, nor, perhaps, very well acquainted with the mysteries of the book world.

"There are books – and books," I ventured to suggest. "This particular book may have been of great value."

"Sufficient to make a thief go to the length of murder?" exclaimed Mr Heyman. "Can't think it!"

"We don't know that this was deliberate, intentioned murder!" I said. "The medical evidence shows that Mr Snowe was in such an enfeebled condition that a sudden shock would be sufficient to cause his death. I take it that he came down, found the thief in the act of carrying off the book, and seized him. What happened then we can guess at – in fact, we know. But I think it was this missing book that the man was after – and got away with."

"I don't think there was any particular value about it," remarked Aubrey. "I've seen it – once had a squint at it when I was waiting here for my uncle. Old thing – shabby binding."

"It may have been worth a great deal, Aubrey," I said. "I should say it was. Why, otherwise, should Mr Snowe have made a special gift of it to the Bodleian Library? He attached great importance to it, anyway." Neither of them made any comment on that. Aubrey continued to prowl round the shelves, in spite of his previous examination: Mr Heyman was poring over the sheets of the will. Suddenly he made a suggestion.

"This will was executed about eighteen months ago," he said. "Snowe no doubt had the book, in the place indicated, at that time, but he may have lent it to somebody in the meantime."

Aubrey shook his head.

"He did lend books to his cronies," he said. "But" – he paused, pointing to certain places in the shelving which ran all round the room – "he'd a system. See these open spaces, where a book's been taken out? Well, wherever there's a book missing there's a card – here's one – put in its place, with the title of the book, the name of the borrower, and the date of lending. There's no card where that book ought to be."

"May have forgotten to put one in, in this instance," said Mr Heyman. "We'd better put an advertisement in the local paper, asking anyone – I mean the borrower, if there is one – to return the book to you. If that produces no result I suppose we must conclude that the book's been stolen. You think that's what the thief was really after, Camberwell?"

"I think it looks very much like it, Mr Heyman," I replied. "As I said before, this *History of Wrenchester* may be a very valuable work – I don't know. What I should like to know is – was the book there, in its usual place, the night on which Mr Snowe came by his death? If it was –"

"I see your point! I see your point!" said Mr Heyman. "Well, let's draft an advertisement and get it in the papers at once."

The advertisement appeared in the Wrenchester paper next morning, and as Mr Heyman and I were breakfasting with Aubrey Snowe in Little Straightway Canon Revington was announced. He came in with a copy of the paper in his hand.

And he was obviously a little excited.

"This advertisement," he said. "Do I understand that Snowe's copy of Flood's *History of Wrenchester* is missing?"

"That is precisely what you may understand," replied Aubrey. "Not there! My uncle left it to the Bodleian Library. Mr Heyman and I went to look for it yesterday afternoon, for my uncle had specified the exact spot in which he kept it, and had left instructions that we, as executors, were to hand it over to these Oxford people at once. Well, it just wasn't there! "

Canon Revington gasped and sank into a chair.

"God bless my soul" he exclaimed. "It was there the night of Snowe's death!"

Mr Heyman twisted round from his plate. "Ah!" he said. "You know that?"

"I do know it" replied Canon Revington. "I can take my oath that the book – that book! – was in its accustomed place when I left Snowe at a quarter to ten that night. I put it there – where it always stood – with my own hands!"

We were all so profoundly impressed by this positive affirmation that we became silent, staring at our visitor. Canon Revington went on.

"You know what I said in my evidence at the inquest?" he continued. "That I called on my old friend that night, and that we had one of our usual talks on archeological subjects? Well, in the course of our talk something cropped up relating to some phase of Wrenchester history, and I took down this book in order to check a reference. When I had done with it I put it back. As I said just now – it was there, in its accustomed place, when I left the house that night."

"That settles it!" exclaimed Aubrey. "The murderer stole it! That's what the devil broke into the house for – a book!"

Mr Heyman laid down his knife and fork and pushed his plate away.

"Let us be practical," he said. "We must know more, much more, about this. Camberwell, bring all your detective wits to bear on this problem." He turned in his chair and faced our visitor. "Revington," he continued, "what was there about this book that should make a man go to the length of housebreaking and, eventually, murder, in order to get possession of it?"

"I don't know!" he exclaimed. "I'm wondering."

"Was it of great value?"

"Value? Monetary value? I shouldn't think so. It may have had some little value. Ten or twelve pounds, perhaps. I can't say."

"Was it a scarce book?"

"Scarce? Oh, yes, it was scarce enough! I don't suppose there are many copies in existence."

"Then it may have been worth more than you think?"

"It may have been. I'm not a collector myself. Yes, it may have been worth more, now I come to think of it, because of its scarcity."

"Well," continued Mr Heyman, "you know all about it. Had the book any particular history, interest, significance? What can you tell?"

"I think I can tell you all there is to be known," replied Canon Revington. "The history of the book is this. It is *A History of Wren-*

chester, by Septimus Flood, printed and published in Wrenchester in 1827. The book itself is a demy octavo, of about four hundred pages. Snowe's copy was in a somewhat shabby contemporary binding of full calf, with double lettering labels of crimson leather. Inside the front cover was the bookplate of Samuel Garsdale – Snowe bought the book when Samuel Garsdale's collection of local historical and topographical works was sold, a couple of years ago. I think I have heard him say that he gave a few pounds for it, and that it was, or would be, worth more. It was, as I've said, a scarce book. Perhaps one should say very scarce."

"What made it so scarce?" asked Mr Heyman. "I suppose there'd be a lot of other copies when it was first printed?"

"No, there were not," answered Canon Revington. "I'm going to tell you the book's history. Septimus Flood, the author, was a very wealthy Quaker gentleman, who flourished about a hundred years ago, and was one of the founders of the Wrenchester Old Bank. He had historical and antiquarian tastes, and he spent many years of his life in collecting materials for and eventually writing a history of the town – the book we are talking about. When it was finished he had it printed – very well printed – by a local printer, and it was embellished with some excellent plates – altogether it is a very admirable production. But Mr Flood only printed fifty copies of it! And not a single one was for sale. He presented the fifty copies to fifty friends – forty-nine friends, to be exact. His own copy, sumptuously bound, is in the Cathedral Library. Snowe's copy, as I have already told you, came out of the Samuel Garsdale collection. Fifty copies only – that's why the book is so scarce!"

Mr Heyman turned to me. "How does all this strike you, Camberwell?" he asked. "I mean, in reference to Snowe's death?"

"I want to ask Canon Revington two or three questions arising out of his very interesting account of the book," I answered, turning to the clergyman. "You say, Canon, that Flood only printed fifty copies of his history, and that he distributed forty-nine of them to his friends!"

"That is absolutely correct," replied Canon Revington. "The facts are well known."

"Those friends, one may suppose, lived, for the most part, hereabouts?"

"In the town and district, I should say."

"And they were probably people of substance – well-to-do people?"

"I should think so. People of his own class – and he was a rich man."

"Then it is highly probable that the copies so given away are still in existence," I said. "In the libraries of the descendants of the people to whom Mr Flood originally presented them?"

"I dare say – I dare say they are," admitted Canon Revington. "Yes, I suppose there will be a good many copies in the private libraries around here."

"Then – in Wrenchester, at any rate – the book is not such a rarity, after all," I continued. "Mr Snowe's copy was not at all unique!"

"Not unique – oh, no – certainly not unique!"

"If it had been merely the book that the thief wanted," I went on, "I should think, from what I have seen during my holiday in Wrenchester, that he could have stolen the copy in the Cathedral Library whenever he liked! Couldn't he?"

Canon Revington started and looked alarmed.

"'Pon my honour, so he could!" he said. "Yes – I'm afraid he could, indeed, now you mention it, Mr Camberwell!"

"Nothing to do but take it out of its shelf in that library and walk off with it," I said. "Which makes it all the stranger that he should want

Mr Snowe's copy. But – from all the evidence before us – he did want Mr Snowe's copy. And – he got it!"

"What's this leading to, Camberwell?" asked Mr Heyman.

"To this, sir! The thief didn't want Mr Snowe's copy of Flood's *History of Wrenchester* for itself. He wanted it for –"

"Yes, yes!" interrupted Mr Heyman excitedly. "For what, now?"

"For some reason the secret of which we've got to find out," I answered. "But now I want to ask Canon Revington a few more questions. You're pretty well acquainted with the history of this old town, I believe – recent history, I mean?"

"I have lived here twenty years, Mr Camberwell," replied the Canon.

"Well, who was Samuel Garsdale, whose bookplate was in Mr Snowe's copy of Flood, and out of whose collection Mr Snowe bought it?"

"I can tell you that easily. Samuel Garsdale was a wealthy old gentleman who lived at Marbourne Park, a small country-house –"

"I know Marbourne Park," I interrupted. "I was playing cricket there a few days ago – Harry Garsdale's place. Is Harry Garsdale a descendant of Samuel?"

"Nephew. Harry Garsdale came into the property when Samuel died, two or three years ago."

"How came Harry to sell his uncle's library?" I asked.

"Oh, I don't know! Harry has no taste for books – he's a sporting man. A lot of the old gentleman's belongings were sold – books, furniture, prints, curiosities. Mr Snowe got all the local books."

"Got 'em still," remarked Aubrey. "The Garsdale bookplate is a good deal in evidence across the street."

"Just one more question, Canon Revington," I said. "You were quite familiar with this particular copy – Mr Snowe's copy – of Flood's Wrenchester?"

"Oh, quite! Very familiar. I often took it down from Snowe's shelves."

"Probably been clean through it – at one time or another?" I suggested.

"Oh, yes – from cover to cover! Very useful reference book."

I asked no more questions. The answer to the last question puzzled me. Canon Revington had been through that stolen book from cover to cover. And that book had been stolen by Mr Snowe's murderer – there was no reasonable doubt of it. Why? For what reason? I left Wrenchester the next day; my holiday was over. As soon as I got back to town my partner, Chaney, left for his holiday. He was away three weeks. And the day after he got back, and we settled down to joint work, Aubrey Snowe sent in his card with an urgent message – he wanted to see me at once.

Chaney pricked up his ears when I mentioned Aubrey's name – I had already given him an outline of the case, and he told me, later, that he had exercised a good deal of thought over it during his holidays. Moreover, we both knew that although some weeks had now elapsed since the murder of Mr Snowe the police had utterly failed to find the murderer or to get any clue to his identity. So we both regarded Aubrey with interest when our clerk, Chippendale, brought him in.

Aubrey was not alone. He had a man – elderly – with him: a man who looked to me like a student of some sort.

"Ronald," began Aubrey, without preface, "this is Mr Harston, who bought my uncle's library – you remember the codicil? I want Mr Harston to tell you something."

Chapter Five

WHAT THE SHOP-BOY SAW

I SAID THAT MY partner, Mr Chaney – whom I formally introduced to our visitors – and I would be very glad to hear anything
Mr Harston had to tell us about the late Mr Snowe's books, and
especially if he could say anything about the missing volume. But Mr
Harston, it was at once apparent, had nothing to say about that.

"It's not so much about the books," said Aubrey, "as about a
chap who's manifesting an extraordinary interest in them! Tell them,
Harston."

Harston, a quiet, soft-spoken man, looked at us with a smile.

Wrenchester at the time of his death, I'm a little suspicious, and
I thought it well to tell Dr Snowe what he now asks me to tell you.
As Dr Snowe has just said, I bought his uncle's library – the whole
lot. A great many of the volumes had been sold to Mr Alfred Snowe
from my own shelves – so they were coming home again. Well, after
bringing the library to London, I classified and arranged it in my shop,
and began getting out a special catalogue of the contents. Before the

catalogue was ready, however, a man called in of whom I happen to have some slight knowledge. He's a man named Archer, and I know him as a searcher at the British Museum, and also as I've seen him now and then at important book-sales, such as Sotheby's and Hodgson's."

At this stage Chaney, reaching for his memorandum book, began to make notes in the peculiar shorthand which – so he boasted – he had invented himself.

"Know the man's private address, Mr Harston?" he inquired.

"I don't," replied Harston. "But I know that he can generally be found, any day, in the Reading Room of the British Museum."

Chaney made a note of that too, and motioned our visitor to continue.

"Well," resumed Harston, "Archer, on coming in, on the day I referred to – he'd often been in my shop before, of course – said that he'd called on behalf of a client of his, a book-collector, specially interested in British topography, who had heard that I had bought up the library of the late Mr Snowe of Wrenchester. His client had instructed him to go through the whole collection and to note any items that he, Archer, thought would be particularly interesting to him, the client; I gathered that the client lived some distance out of town, and could not come up to look at the books himself. Of course, I told Archer to make whatever inspection he pleased, and he set to work there and then. And before very long I noticed something that rather surprised me. The Snowe collection had been arranged by me and my assistant in my back-shop. It filled the shelving which covered one wall –"

"How many volumes, now?" asked Chancy.

"Something over two thousand," replied Harston. "Say two thousand two or three hundred. Well, I noticed that Archer began systematically to go through the lot! That is, he began examining every book separately, starting at the top shelf on the left-hand end of the wall, and taking each book down, one after the other, as if he meant to have a careful look through the inside of each, from end to end. I made some joking remark to him about this – to the effect that it would take him from now till Christmas to do things like that, but he only answered that it was a highly important collection; his client didn't want to miss anything out of it, and time was no object. Well, time was no object to me, either, and I let him do what he pleased – I was otherwise engaged. But now and then I was in the back-shop, and I couldn't fail to notice the extraordinary care he was taking in this inspection. A good many of the books had folding plates in them; Archer, whenever he came across anything of this sort, opened the plate out most carefully. Again, some volumes had pockets at the end, containing folded maps or charts; he had every map out and inspected it, and the pockets as well. In fact, I'd never seen a man examine a library so carefully before, and –"

"A moment, Mr Harston," interrupted Chaney. "I want to know something. This Snowe collection, being duly arranged in your back-shop, was, I suppose, for sale – to anybody who chanced to come in? Now, supposing a customer had come in while Archer was engaged –"

"Pardon me," said Harston, "but the collection was not yet on sale. We hadn't finished cataloguing it, and it wasn't – it isn't – on sale until the catalogue's ready. There is a door between the back-shop and the front, and that is kept closed. So Archer had the run of the place all to himself."

"I see," said Chaney, making a note. "Well?"

"Well, he came for several days, spending two or three hours at a time," continued Harston. "I noticed another thing that I thought a bit odd – although he was there, according to his own account, on behalf of a client who wanted a report, he never made any notes. All the books had already been priced, by myself – the prices were stated in pencil inside the front covers. But Archer made no note of prices – nor of anything. One day I referred to this – in this way. 'Finding nothing?' I said. 'I don't see you noting anything down?' 'Oh, I've found plenty!' he answered. 'I carry my notes in my head, Mr Harston. Nothing? I've noted no end – this, and this, and this, and that, and that, and that!' he went on, pointing here and there. 'Oh, yes – some deeply interesting and scarce items here, sir. And I've noted the prices too!' he added, with a laugh. 'Quite reasonable, quite, Mr Harston. In one or two cases I should have put a bit more on if I'd been you.'"

"You believed all that, of course?" suggested Chaney.

"Well, I didn't see any reason not to believe him," replied Harston. "I thought it was his way of doing things. However, I'll come now to the – episode, I'd better call it – which made me acquaint Dr Snowe with the whole story when he called on me this morning. It's something that happened yesterday, and I think it of significance, considering what has taken place. Yesterday morning –"

"Stop a bit, Mr Harston," interrupted Chaney. "What do you mean, exactly, when you say 'considering what has taken place'? What are you referring to?"

"I'm referring to what I referred to when I began," replied Harston. "The disappearance of Flood's *Wrenchester* from the late Mr Snowe's library at the time of his death."

"Ah! You thought Archer might be after that?" suggested Chaney.

"No! Because I knew it wasn't there," replied Harston. "I knew every book in the two thousand odd. What I thought was this – it was evident, from what I'd read in the papers, and had heard from Dr Snowe when I went down to Wrenchester to buy the library, that whoever stole the *History of Wrenchester* did so because of something which he believed to be in it – some document, say. Well, it also seemed to me that the thief didn't find in the book what he hoped to find, and that it then occurred to him that what he was after might have got into some other book! And that the real employer of Archer was not a book-collecting client, but the man who –"

"Who stole the Flood's *Wrenchester*!" interrupted Chaney. "Good theory! I see your point, Mr Harston. Go on, if you please."

"Well, yesterday morning," continued Harston, "I had occasion to go to a sale, and I took my assistant with me, leaving my shop-boy in charge. He is an intelligent, sharp lad of sixteen or seventeen. My assistant and I were out until one o'clock; when we returned the boy told me of something that had occurred which he evidently thought irregular. He said that soon after we went out Archer came in and resumed his task of examining the Snowe collection. Now, I had left the boy with a definite job to do in my absence. That was to address wrappers from our list of regular customers, in readiness for the Snowe catalogue. He did this addressing at a table in the back-shop. From time to time he watched Archer examining the books. Eventually he saw something which excited his curiosity. He saw Archer take down a book at the end of which was a pocket containing maps. Archer set the book down on the corner of the table at which the boy was writing, and proceeded to extract the maps from the pocket. As he was unfolding one, an envelope, which, from the boy's account, I conclude to have been a foolscap size –"

"Nine inches by four," interjected Chaney, always particular as to details.

"Precisely! A foolscap envelope fell out of it, to the floor. Archer, according to the boy, picked it up, glanced at some writing on it, and at once clipped it back into the map, and put the map back in the pocket. He then, after a glance or two at the book, restored it to the shelves. Two or three minutes later he said something about not being able to stay any longer, and, turning to it again, took the book down from the shelf, and glanced at the price marked inside the front cover. He then said to the boy that here was a book he himself wanted, and as the price was marked he'd pay him for it then – twenty-five shillings. The boy – who is quite conversant with the details of my business – said that he didn't think any books of the Snowe collection were on sale until the catalogue was out. Archer pooh-poohed that, said he'd make it all right with me, put down the money, and went off with the book. The boy, however, was sharp enough to look at the title, and he immediately made a note of it. And the title – in view of all I've been talking about – is of interest."

"What was it?" asked Chaney.

"*Addenda to Flood's 'History of Wrenchester,' with Maps and Diagrams*," replied Harston. "Not by Flood, but by Martinson, a local antiquary, who lived some years later."

A brief silence fell on us; I think we – and especially Aubrey Snowe and myself – were all wondering and speculating.

"What did you do?" inquired Chaney.

"I went straight over to the British Museum," replied Harston. "I have a reader's ticket, so I went at once into the Reading Room. Archer, I knew, always occupied the same seat – I made for it. But he wasn't there, and the attendant at the door, who knows him well enough, said he hadn't been in that morning. And, of course, I don't know his private address. And – I think that's all, gentlemen."

"What do you make of it, Ronald?" asked Aubrey Snowe.

I turned to Chaney. Chaney was drawing faces on his blotting-pad. He couldn't draw at all, but he always drew what he called faces when he was thinking and had pen or pencil in his hand.

"I should like to know what my partner thinks," I answered.

Chaney suddenly turned on Aubrey Snowe.

"I suppose there's not the slightest doubt that that book – what do you call it? – Flood's *History of Wrenchester* – was stolen from your uncle's library on the night of his death?" he asked. "There's no mistake being made about that?"

Aubrey glanced at me, looking puzzled. And I answered for him.

"There's no mistake about it, Chaney," I said. "I went into that myself. Canon Revington, who called on the late Mr Snowe that night and was with him until 9.45, a quarter of an hour before Mr Snowe's usual – and invariable – hour for going to bed, saw the book in its usual place when he left the house. He and Mr Snowe had been consulting it, in reference to some point they'd been discussing."

"Yes," said Chaney. "But – when was the book missed?"

"Not, certainly, until the day of the funeral," I answered. "On reading the will and codicils Mr Heyman and Dr Snowe went across to Number Five to get the book, the exact position of which was described in the codicil, and it wasn't there."

"Yes," remarked Chaney. "But between their going there and the discovery of Mr Snowe's dead body four or five – four, was it? – four days had elapsed. The book may have been stolen during that time."

"I don't think so," I said. "From the time of the discovery of Mr Snowe's dead body onward Number Five was under constant, uninterrupted police surveillance –"

"And the library was locked up," interrupted Aubrey, "and I had the key."

Chaney drew another face or two. "Well," he said, "let's take it that the man who killed Mr Snowe stole the book. Now, we want to know why? The supposition is that the book contained something of value. Mr Snowe, the day before his death, had written to his solicitor, Mr Heyman, saying that he'd made a most important discovery. What are we to think about that? There's only one thing we can think, in view of all we know. Mr Snowe, rummaging about in his old books, had found some important document; he wanted to consult Mr Heyman about it. But – had he already consulted somebody else about it – somebody close at hand, in Wrenchester? Had he let this somebody know that the document – we're supposing it was a document – was in that book – had, perhaps, been found there? Now, perhaps Dr Snowe can tell us – was there any solicitor in Wrenchester whom his uncle ever consulted?"

"No!" asserted Aubrey. "I'm certain of that. All my uncle's business and legal affairs were in the hands of Mr Heyman."

"Well, it looks to me," said Chaney, "it certainly looks to me as if somebody knew there was something worth having in that book, and broke into the house to get the book! And it's my opinion that this man Archer has probably been employed by that person to overhaul the books now in Mr Harston's possession, with the object of trying to find the – let's call it document – which the somebody on examining the Flood's History found, doubtless to his surprise and discomfiture, was not there! It had been there, mind you, and the somebody knew that – but it wasn't there when the somebody stole the book . . . because Mr Snowe had put it elsewhere! Mr Harston," he continued, turning to the bookseller, "what time does this man Archer usually come to your shop?"

"About ten to a quarter past," replied Harston.

"Very well," said Chaney. "Then tomorrow morning my partner and I, and Dr Snowe, if he'll be good enough to stay in town and accompany us, will be with you at that time, or thereabouts. I propose to take a direct line with Mr Archer, and to ask him on whose behalf he is examining the late Mr Snowe's library, and what was in the envelope he found yesterday."

Chapter Six

ON THE TRACK

A UBREY SNOWE STAYED IN town that night, in accordance with Chaney's suggestion, and at ten o'clock next morning he, Chaney, and I presented ourselves at Harston's door in Great Russell Street. Harston at once took us into the back-shop, where the Snowe collection was housed – a big, roomy place, separated from the still bigger front-shop by a glass-panelled door, over which hung a light curtain; once in there we were free from the observation of anyone who entered the front-shop. Harston left us to ourselves, saying that if Archer followed his usual practice he would be there in a few minutes, and that when he came in he, Harston, would bring him in to us without warning of what awaited him. But at the end of half an hour Archer had not come, and Harston, coming to us, said he would go across to the British Museum and see if he could find him in the Reading Room. He was going off there and then, but Chaney stopped him.

"No!" he said. "I want to catch this man unawares – to give him a surprise. You think he'll be there, Mr Harston?"

"I've a reader's ticket myself," replied Harston. "It's useful when one wants to refer to anything. And I often go there, and my experience is that Archer, five days out of six, is to be found there from ten o'clock to the hour at which the Library closes."

"Another question, then," said Chaney. "What sort of man is this Archer? I mean – temperamentally?"

"A nervous, highly strung sort of fellow," answered Harston. "Jumpy!"

Chaney got up from his chair; this reply evidently suited him. "We'll all go across," he said. "When we get there you, Mr Harston, go into the Reading Room; we, of course, not having tickets, shall have to stay outside. If Archer is there say something to alarm him. Tell him that something – you needn't specify anything – has arisen out of his purchase of that book in your absence yesterday, and that he'd better come out and explain matters. When you bring him out we'll be there, outside the door of the Reading Room – he won't know who we are, and he'll probably take us for detectives. And, if he's the sort of man you describe, I'll bluff him into a confession."

"I'm not to say who wants him, then?" asked Harston.

"Not a word! Get him out – if he's there," replied Chaney. "Leave the rest to me."

But at that I put in a word myself; it seemed to me that I could improve on my partner's suggestion. If we were going to bring dramatic effect into the business I fancied that I knew better than Chaney what would produce it.

"Stop a bit, Mr Harston," said I, as the bookseller and Chaney were making for the door. "Chaney," I went on, "I think it would be far better if you and I went over to the Reading Room by ourselves. That is, if you want to take this man by surprise."

They both stopped; Chaney turned on me with a question in his eyes.

"What's the game, Camberwell?" he asked sharply.

"Just this," I answered. "We go over – you and I. We find out from the attendant at the door of the Reading Room if Mr Archer has gone in this morning – he'll know him well enough. If he has we send in for him – on urgent business. And when he comes out – I'm going to repeat your words, Chaney – leave the rest to me."

For once Chaney made no reply. But Harston spoke, nodding his approval.

"That suits me," he remarked. "I'd rather be out of it – at least, as regards going over there. Of course – you'll have to bring him back here?"

"We shall bring him back here," I said. "Now, Chaney, come along!" We left Harston and Aubrey Snowe in the back-shop and went – in silence – across to the Museum. The attendant at the door of the Reading Room, eyeing us with some curiosity, said he knew Mr Archer very well, and Mr Archer had just gone in. And within the moment he too had gone in and was bringing our man out.

I took a good look at Archer as the doors parted to admit him into the big central hall in which Chaney and I awaited him. He was a shambling, loosely-put-together sort of man, and when he came close to us, staring at us wonderingly out of a pair of pale, watery eyes, I detected an aroma which convinced me that he was fond of the bottle, and had taken his morning dram before commencing his literary labours. When the attendant pointed us out to him he took a suspicious, speculating glance at us; it lingered scarce an instant on me, but it went all over Chaney, from top to toe, and I read the man's thoughts as plainly as if they had been set up in the biggest type and printed on a placard dependent from his neck – a detective! But he came up – close.

"Mr Archer?" said I.

He nodded, saying nothing. I handed him our professional card, watching him closely.

"We desire a few words with you, Mr Archer," I continued. "You bought a certain book yesterday morning at Mr Harston's, across the way. There is a question arising about that book –"

"I paid for it!" he interjected.

"There's no question about that," I answered. "The question, or questions, relate to something other than purchase. Will you come across with us to Harston's?"

He was still looking from the card to us, and from us to the card. Suddenly he seemed to pluck up some courage.

"What's it all about?" he asked. "This is a busy morning with me – I'd just settled to my work. I don't know you –"

"You'll know us better if you come across," I said. "All we want – and must have, Mr Archer – is an explanation. I think you had better come, because, if you don't –"

I paused there, purposely, to give him a chance. He looked at us sulkily.

"And what if I don't?" he asked half defiantly.

"Then we shall be under the disagreeable necessity of asking the policeman over there to keep an eye on you while I phone to Scotland Yard," I replied. "I think you'd better come, Mr Archer."

I have said that the man had signs of a bibulous inclination on him, but his face paled visibly at the mention of Scotland Yard, and his eye turned sharply on the policeman towards whom I nodded.

"Oh, well, if it's something of that sort," he said grumblingly. "Though what you're after is beyond me. I'll come across to Harston's in a few minutes."

"Not at all, Mr Archer," I replied. "You'll come now – with us. If you're thinking about your work or your papers, I know enough of the

British Museum Reading Room to know that anything you've left on your table will be safe till you come back."

He made no answer to this, and we all three left the entrance-hall, crossed the big quadrangle outside, and went over to Harston's shop, all in silence. But as we entered the shop I slipped in an aside to Chaney.

"Leave this chap to me, Chaney, will you?" I whispered. "He's doubtful about you – but he's afraid of me."

Chaney nodded his acquiescence; he knew what I meant. And from that I took matters into my own charge, ushering Archer straight into the back-shop, where Harston was talking to Aubrey Snowe. The bookseller and the searcher exchanged glances; Harston smiled a little, but Archer looked hang-dog and sheepish.

"'Morning, Mr Archer," said Harston. "You're late this morning? Ten o'clock's been your time since you began showing such an interest in this Snowe collection. But perhaps your interest's died out?"

Archer looked round from one to the other; Aubrey Snowe's presence seemed to puzzle him.

"It's about time I knew what I've been brought across here for," he said resentfully. "If there's something –"

"Take a chair, Mr Archer," I said, motioning him to one near the centre table, at which Aubrey Snowe sat. "We'll soon make you acquainted with the reasons for desiring your presence. Now," I went on, as he mechanically obeyed my suggestion that he should sit, "you came here some days ago and told Mr Harston that you had a commission from a client to examine the collection of books which Mr Harston had recently bought from the executors of the late Mr Snowe of Wrenchester. For some days, under that pretence, you have been searching among those books – searching, I suggest, not inspecting –"

"I'm a professional searcher!" he interjected. "It's my job!"

"At the British Museum, no doubt," I said. "Pedigrees, genealogies, and so on. But you were searching these books – some two thousand odd, Mr Archer – for a certain definite thing. And I think you found it yesterday. For yesterday morning, in Mr Harston's absence, you suddenly decided – although you knew the books were not yet for sale – to put down twenty-five shillings and walk off with a certain volume. That volume, Mr Archer, was the *Addenda to Flood's 'History of Wrenchester'*. There was a pocket in it, and in the pocket a map, and from the folds of the map, Mr Archer, there dropped out, when you were examining it, a foolscap envelope. And that, presumably, was why you bought the book from Mr Harston's shop-boy. That envelope, Mr Archer, was what you were searching for. Now, then – on whose behalf?"

He had sat, open-mouthed, listening intently; for the most part he kept his eyes on mine, but once or twice he looked round. And once, in looking round, I think he noticed that Chaney, behind his chair, was leaning against the curtained door.

"It isn't usual to give the names of one's clients," he answered. "It's – not professional to do so."

"I'm afraid you'll have to break the rules, then, Mr Archer," I said. "Anyhow, you're admitting that the envelope I've referred to is what you were hunting among the Snowe books for? Am I right?"

"Right – oh, yes, right," he answered. "Yes, that's so. But – what is it all about? I'm in the dark. I only discharged a job entrusted to me – to seek for a thing. I found it. Well –"

"Mr Archer," I said, "you want to know what it's all about, and I'm going to tell you. And I'll put it into one ugly word. Murder!"

He blanched again at that, and, gripping the edge of the table before him, looked from one to the other of us. "Murder?" he whispered. "Why – ?"

"Murder, Mr Archer!" I said. "And something very important may turn on that envelope you found yesterday and carried off in the book. Now, where is that envelope?"

"The envelope!" he exclaimed. "I – I sent it away, at once."

"To the man who employed you, of course," I said. "Very well, Mr Archer, then there's just this. Who is he?"

He had been watching me all this time with a certain amount of speculation in his eyes, fingering his mouth with a hand that shook a little, and now he shook his head as if confronting a problem that he found it impossible to solve.

"I should like to know what all this is coming to," he said. "Where do I come in? I've only executed a commission. And, as I said, it's not professional to give away clients' names. Suppose I don't answer?"

"Supposing you won't answer, you mean," I said, correcting him. "Won't is the word!"

"Well, won't then," he retorted. "What then?"

"Then we shall have to tell what we know to Scotland Yard, Mr Archer," I replied. "Just that – neither more nor less. And if I were you I should answer my question."

He shifted about in his seat for a second or two. Then he seemed to make up his mind, and he spoke plainly.

"The man who employed me is named Skrimshaw," he said. "James Skrimshaw." I glanced at Aubrey Snowe. He shook his head. Evidently the name conveyed nothing to him.

"And who is James Skrimshaw, Mr Archer?" I asked. "You know, of course?"

"All I know about him," he answered, "is that he and I were at school together; at Stroud, in Gloucestershire, years ago. We've some-times met, of late years, in town; he's to be found, sometimes, at a tavern near the Law Courts where I drop in now and then. He's – I only know what he tells me – he's managing clerk to some solicitor at Wrenchester."

"What solicitor? The name?" I asked.

"Never heard him mention it," he answered. "As to this job, it was this way. He met me about a fortnight ago, and told me that Harston had bought all the late Mr Snowe's books, and that it was believed that somewhere among them, probably slipped in anyhow or anywhere, there was a sealed envelope, foolscap size. I was to search every book for that, and if I found it I was to send it to him immediately, by registered post. He –"

"A moment!" said I. "Did he describe the envelope?"

"He said it had two initials on it – S. G.," he replied. "Nothing more."

"Well – and you found it yesterday?" I said.

"Yesterday," he assented. "And I sent it to him within the hour."

"You'll give us his address, Mr Archer?" I said. "We must have that!"

"Marbourne," he replied. "Woodside Cottage, Marbourne, Wrenchester." I wrote that down, and got up from the table.

"Only one question more, Mr Archer," I said. "Do you know what was in the envelope?" But I saw he didn't; there was truth in the shake of his head.

"No more than you do!" he answered. "Skrimshaw didn't tell me, even if he knew, and the envelope, when I found it yesterday, was sealed."

Chapter Seven

WOODSIDE COTTAGE

W E WERE NOW IN possession of definite information, the exact nature and value of which nothing but further close and patient investigation could determine. I summarized it, rapidly, in my own mind, as I stood there confronting the man from whom it had been extracted. There down at Wrenchester was a man named James Skrimshaw, of whom we knew nothing except that he was – according to his own account – managing clerk to some Wrenchester solicitor. For some reason unknown to us Skrimshaw believed there was a document of importance hidden in some volume of the late Alfred Snowe's library, and had employed Archer to hunt for it. And Archer had found the document and had sent it to Skrimshaw, in whose possession I now supposed it to be. So the next thing was to see Skrimshaw. But there was something to be done first.

Archer stood watching me, obviously anxious to be gone. The others were watching too – Chaney, who had faithfully kept his word to leave matters to me, with some evident speculation. I let a minute or two go by before I spoke.

"Mr Archer," I said, "I take it that you will be expecting a fee for the work you undertook for Skrimshaw?"

"I've got it," he answered. "He paid me in advance – said it would save time, and he knew me well enough to know I'd do the work thoroughly."

"I'm glad to hear that," said I. "Have you any objection to telling us what the amount was?"

"None!" he replied readily. "Twenty pounds."

"Then – everything between you and Skrimshaw is concluded?" I suggested.

"Finished!" he answered.

"Well, and I'm glad of that too, Mr Archer," I said, "for I'm going to put you on your honour. Just let me remind you that if I pleased to do so I could phone Scotland Yard, ask them to send a man or two here, tell those men what we've learned, and –"

"But what have I done?" he exclaimed. "I've only been employed –"

"In assisting to appropriate a certain document which we believe to be of the most serious importance, and which has probably some relation to the murder of the late Mr Alfred Snowe," I said, interrupting him. "The police, Mr Archer, would want to know a great deal more than we do. But I'm not going to call in the police – yet, anyway. You'll come in later, no doubt, as a witness. You've told us your tale, and I'm satisfied – only I want something more."

"What is it you want?" he asked, eyeing me doubtfully.

"I want you to give me your word of honour – you see, I'm treating you as a gentleman –"

"I am that!" he said, drawing himself up. "I've known other days than these."

"Then give me your word that when you go out of here you won't communicate with Skrimshaw, by letter, or telegram, or telephone!" I said. "That is of the utmost importance. Skrimshaw must know nothing of what has taken place here this morning, between you and me."

"It's given," he said. "I want nothing more to do with the affair – unless I'm forced into it. I'm paid, and I've done the work for which I was paid, and there's an end of it. You can trust me."

"Then good morning, Mr Archer," I replied. "That's – all!"

He went through the curtained door the next moment, and I turned to the other three; they were plainly impatient to know what I was going to do next. But I thought it high time that Chaney should take a hand.

"Well, Chaney?" said I. "The next thing?"

"The next thing is to get hold of this man Skrimshaw," he answered. Then he turned to Aubrey Snowe. "You don't know him, doctor?"

"Not that I know of," said Aubrey. "He may be a man I know by sight, without knowing his name. I can't think, either, which of the various solicitors it is that's indicated. One thing I do know – my uncle never employed any Wrenchester solicitor. All his legal work went to Heyman's."

"Well," remarked Chaney, "it's very evident that this man Skrimshaw knew that there was this document, whatever it may be, among, or likely to be among, the late Mr Snowe's books – and now he's got it! And the only thing we can do is to get down to Wrenchester and tell Bailiss of all we've discovered this morning."

"You can come down in my car," said Aubrey. "We've only to go round to my hotel." But Chaney decided that we would go down in our own car; he also pointed out to me that it would be the middle of the afternoon before we could start, for there were things to be cleared up and arrangements made at the office. So Aubrey Snowe went off alone, with strict injunctions to say nothing to Bailiss until we arrived, and presently Chaney and I left Mr Harston to his books and his business and departed to put our own in order.

It was five o'clock that afternoon when Chaney and I drove into the old streets of Wrenchester, and I saw at once that it was early-closing day; there was accordingly no chance of our finding Skrimshaw at the office in which he was employed, even if we had known which it was. Our ignorance on this point, and of Skrimshaw himself, was very quickly cleared away when we met Bailiss. Bailiss, to whom, in his private room at the police-station, I told our story in every detail and particular, let out a sharp exclamation of astonishment when Skrimshaw's name came out.

"Good Lord!" he said, throwing up his hands. "Skrimshaw – James Skrimshaw? You don't mean to say – well, well! Skrimshaw, why, of course, he's well enough known about the town – he's Mr Clayning's managing clerk. Queer chap, certainly – but I should never have thought he'd have been mixed up in this. Odd that Dr Snowe doesn't know him. I'll bet you've seen Skrimshaw yourself, more than once, when you were here on that cricket tour, Mr Camberwell."

"Not to know who he was," I said. "I have no recollection of him."

"Aye, well," he replied. "You stayed at the Mitre for a fortnight or so, didn't you? Well, you no doubt sat in the old bar-parlour then of a morning, before starting out for cricket?"

"Often," I answered. "Nearly every morning. Delightful old room."

"Very well," he continued. "Did you ever notice a clean-shaven, middle-aged, spare-figured man, slightly grey-haired, and with a very worn face, who came in there at eleven o'clock to the minute, drank a half-pint of bitter ale and mouthed a bit of bread and cheese, never spoke to a soul, and vanished as swiftly as he came? You did? Well, that's Skrimshaw. Silentest, and softest-mannered man I ever came across – bit of a mystery. So – your discovery's about him? I'm amazed. And yet, I don't know – there's a saying, you know, that still waters run deep."

"Superintendent," I said, "we must get in touch with Skrimshaw at once!"

"And there's no doubt about that!" he answered, with enthusiasm. "We will get in touch with him! But you feel you can depend on that man Archer's word not to communicate with Skrimshaw?"

"I think so," I replied. "Archer struck me as being honest."

"Aye, well, you never know," he said. "I've been deceived so often – however, if we're going to look for Skrimshaw it'll have to be at his own home. This is early-closing day in Wrenchester, and even if it weren't Clayning's office would be closed now. Skrimshaw lives at Woodside Cottage, just near Marboume – we'd best go out there in my car. I won't take any of my men with me – I think the three of us'll be sufficient. What's Mr Chaney say?"

"I say that we've got to proceed with great caution," said Chaney. "We're on a mission of inquiry. We want to know why Skrimshaw employed Archer, whose suspicious behaviour at Harston's has led to our forcing information out of him, in the course of which Skrimshaw's name came up."

"A bit more than that, I think," observed Bailiss, with a wink at me. "We want to know what's in that envelope?"

"That'll be led up to," said Chaney. "Leave it to Camberwell."

Bailiss called one of his men and gave an order about his car; within a few minutes it was brought up to the door and the three of us set out towards Marbourne. Marbourne is a lonely village lying on a creek of the sea some six or seven miles south-west of Wrenchester. I had been there, at least at Marbourne Park, playing cricket during my stay at Wrenchester a few weeks previously, and I remembered the district as one of dense woods, solitary farmsteads, great apple orchards; into the actual village of Marbourne I had never been. Nor did we now go to it; at the sixth milestone along the main road between Wrenchester and Kingsport Bailiss turned his car into a narrow lane at the corner of which stood a signpost bearing the one word Marbourne on its solitary finger; this lane he followed for a good mile, until he came to the edge of a thick wood of pine. And there he pulled up.

"We shall have to leave the car here," he said. "Skrimshaw's cottage is on the side of this wood, approached by that footpath. I told you he was a queer sort – he lives all alone in that cottage; they say he does all his own housework and cooking, and won't have a woman about the place. I've been in the place once myself; I called there with some papers for him. That," he continued, when we had gone a short way along the side of the wood, "that's the spot, where you see the tall chimney – a real old-fashioned cottage, hundreds of years old, I should say – I've heard that Skrimshaw bought it, dirt cheap, from an old man whose folks had lived in it since Adam."

I was taking an observation of our surroundings; I wanted to know exactly where we were.

"Marbourne Park, where I came to play cricket, is behind this wood, isn't it, Bailiss?" I asked. "Just behind it?"

"That's right, Mr Camberwell," he answered. "This wood makes a boundary to the Park. At the other edge of the Park is the open sea – you'd notice it from the cricket-ground, no doubt. And Marbourne village is away there to our left, on the east side of the Park, and at the end of the road we've just left. And all out here," he went on, waving his hand northward, "is just nothing but woods and spinneys and apple orchards, and the marshes on the side of Marbourne Creek, so this place of Skrimshaw's is about as lonely a spot as any man could find to live in. And here we are, close to his bit of garden and there's no smoke coming out of his chimney!"

We advanced along the pathway, which ran close by the side of the wood, until we came to the gate which admitted to the garden. And there we were in full view of Skrimshaw's cottage, which certainly seemed to justify something of Bailiss's extravagant estimate of its age. The lower parts were of old, much-worn red brick; the upper of lath and plaster, with cross-beams here and there of oak; the roof was thatched; the chimney at the gable end leaned towards the neighbouring trees as if to invite their support. The garden in which this ancient habitation stood was used by Skrimshaw for growing vegetables; there was an old well in one corner and a dilapidated summer-house in another; altogether, the place suggested itself as the home of a rustic labouring man. And as we approached the door it struck me that there was just one word to apply to it – 'lifeless.' I knew somehow, before ever Bailiss knocked loudly on the paintless panels, that the cottage was empty.

No reply came to Bailiss's repeated knockings. We looked in at the uncurtained and blindless window, and saw a sort of living-room, half parlour, half kitchen. The hearth was black, and there were no signs of any recent meal on the table. And when we walked round to the back of the cottage there was nothing to be seen of Skrimshaw, inside or out.

"He can't have come home," said Bailiss. "He must have stayed in Wrenchester. And I don't know of any haunt of his there."

"How does he get in and out from here?" I asked.

"There's a motor-omnibus runs along the highroad between Wrenchester and Kingsport," replied Bailiss. "He uses that, and he gets off at the signpost, where we turned into the lane."

Chaney pulled out his watch.

"It's seven o'clock," he said. "Camberwell and I have had nothing to eat since one. Yet it's no good coming out here and going away empty-handed, and I suppose this man's bound to come home. Could we get anything at Marbourne? Some supper, now? And then come back again and see if he's in?"

Bailiss replied that there was a country hotel in Marbourne village where we might get some sort of a meal, so we went back to the car and drove on. The hotel was able to give us some cold fowl and to put a fine piece of cold sirloin on the table with it, and we all three sat down and made a hearty supper. And Bailiss remarking that it was no use going back to the cottage too soon, we remained at the hotel till ten o'clock, when we once more went round to Skrimshaw's lonely dwelling, which, in the darkness, seemed lonelier than ever. But there was no light in the window, and repeated knocking at the door brought no answer.

"He must have stopped in town for the night," said Bailiss. "We'd better go back and call at Clayning's office first thing tomorrow morning. Meet me there at nine o'clock."

We went back to Wrenchester, and Chaney and I put ourselves up for the night at the Mitre. Next morning we found our way to Clayning's office in St Michael Street. Bailiss met us there and bade us walk along the street while he made inquiry. He came to us presently to say that Skrimshaw had not arrived. We posted ourselves in a convenient place close by where we could see Skrimshaw arrive – but Skrimshaw did not come. And when ten o'clock struck from the numerous churches in the little town Bailiss bade us follow him, and, emerging from our hiding-place, walked over to the office and asked for Mr Clayning.

Chapter Eight

LAWYER CLAYNING

M R CLAYNING HAD NOT yet arrived, according to the clerk of whom Bailiss made inquiry, and his office seemed to be in some confusion. A couple of smartly attired young gentlemen, obviously articled clerks, leaned, hands in pockets, against a mantelpiece, idling; no one, down to the office-boy, was in any way employed, and on a flat-topped desk in the centre of the room which we had entered lay a great pile of letters which it was evidently nobody's business to open.

"When do you expect Mr Clayning?" asked Bailiss of the clerk who had come forward.

"Don't know, sir," answered the clerk, shaking his head. "Mr Clayning's here at 9.15 as a rule, sharp. He left no word yesterday about being late this morning. And," he added, "it's court day, and we've two or three cases."

"What about Mr Skrimshaw?" suggested Bailiss. "Can I see him?"

"Mr Skrimshaw hasn't come either," said the clerk. "He's always here just before nine. I've never known him late before, never! And I've been here a good many years."

"Perhaps Mr Clayning and Mr Skrimshaw have gone straight to court?" said Bailiss. "The court sits at 10.30, you know." But the clerk shook his head and pointed, first to the pile of correspondence, and then to a heap of papers folded and tied with red tape.

"No, sir," he said. "They wouldn't do that. There are the papers there that'll be wanted in court. And there are this morning's letters to look at."

"When did you see Mr Skrimshaw last?" asked Bailiss.

"Last, sir? Yesterday, at one o'clock – early-closing day," replied the clerk. "Mr Skrimshaw and Mr Clayning left the office together, just before one. Neither of them said anything about being late this morning. And I don't know what to do about these court cases."

But at that moment Clayning himself came bustling in: a big, heavily built man, with bushy eyebrows, a strongly marked face, and curiously watchful eyes. He pulled himself up in evident surprise as he recognized Bailiss; from Bailiss his quick glance turned sharply on Chaney and myself. In the flash of an eye he had sized us up, and I would swear he had decided on our business.

"Hullo, Bailiss!" he exclaimed. "What are you after?"

"We called to see Mr Skrimshaw, Mr Clayning," replied Bailiss. "Little matter to discuss with him. But it appears he's not come yet."

Clayning turned on the clerk. "Skrimshaw not come?" he said loudly. "Good God, and it's court day! He ought to have been up there with the papers! Here, give me the papers – it's nearly time now – I must go. Sharples, you come with me," he went on, beckoning to one of the lounging young gentlemen. "The letters must wait till I'm back. If Skrimshaw comes in tell him to follow me. Bailiss – come outside."

We followed him out into the street, where a smart chauffeur was awaiting him with a big car. He stopped at its open door, looking hard at the Superintendent.

"What do you want with Skrimshaw?" he asked.

"The business is private, Mr Clayning," replied Bailiss.

"Serious?"

"It may be."

Clayning motioned the articled clerk to get into the car; he himself turned again to Bailiss.

"I know of no reason that could make Skrimshaw late," he said. "He's a model of punctuality. Of course, he lives some way out of town–"

"We went to see him at his cottage last night," interrupted Bailiss. "We called there twice – he wasn't there. Mr Clayning, these gentlemen and I must see him, as quickly as possible! The matter is very serious."

"I'll tell you what I'll do," said Clayning. "When my chauffeur's run me up to the court I'll send him along to Skrimshaw's place to see if Skrimshaw's there; he may be ill, and of course he's no telephone there. Look in here at the office at one o'clock – I'll be back from court by then, and there may be some news – as I said before, I've no notion why he's not here. Now I must be off!"

He got into his car and drove away, and Bailiss turned to Chaney and me.

"We're not going to wait till one o'clock, doing nothing," he said. "We'll do something. Mr Camberwell, you know the Mitre, of course, and the old bar-parlour there? And you remember what I told you about Skrimshaw's habit of dropping in there every morning at eleven o'clock? Very well. You go up to the Mitre, get hold of the barmaid in the bar-parlour, and ask her – quietly, you know – if Skrimshaw was in there yesterday morning. Chaney, you come with me – Mr Camberwell will know where to find us when he's done his bit."

They went off together, and I turned on my heel and went slowly up the street towards the Mitre – slowly, because I knew that the old bar-parlour there wouldn't be open until eleven o'clock. And on the way I saw Aubrey Snowe in his car; he was evidently setting out on his round of professional visits. He saw me too, and pulled to the side.

"Any luck, Ronald?" he asked. "I expected you to drop in last night."

I told him how we had fared so far, and mentioned our interview with Skrimshaw's employer.

"What sort of chap is Clayning, Aubrey?" I asked. "Straight?"

"I don't know," he answered. "He's the reputation of being the sharpest practitioner in Wrenchester – the sort of man that all the people who get into trouble go to, in the hope that he'll get 'em off. But otherwise – can't say. I don't know him personally, only by sight. What next, then?"

"We must find Skrimshaw!" I replied. "That's imperative."

"Well, keep me posted up," he said. "Look here, you'll be stopping at the Mitre a night or two, anyway – remember, Ronald, you've absolute *carte blanche* from me as regards all and any expense in this matter – I will have it solved, whatever it costs me – I'm going to know who killed my uncle! Bring Chaney to dine tonight – eight o'clock. Then we can all talk."

"If we're free," I said. "If not, I'll phone you."

He went on, then, down the street, and I went up, and as the clocks struck eleven turned into the bar-parlour of the Mitre. I knew it well; during the fortnight I had spent at the Mitre on my recent cricket tour I had often been in it. It was the sort of place now rapidly becoming extinct in England : a big, old-fashioned room with a raftered ceiling and with panelled walls lined with old sporting prints and pictures. Except in the very height of summer, there was always a fine fire of logs in the ancient fireplace, and all over the room, and in its nooks and corners, the easy-chairs and lounges were so comfortable that when you were once in one of them you had no desire to get out of it. As to creature comforts, there was a bar at one end of the room, and this, at the time of which I am writing, was presided over by a pretty and well-mannered young woman who was so friendly to her customers that each and all addressed her as Dorothy – what her other name was I never knew.

Dorothy had just assumed the duties of her office when I entered, and her eyebrows arched themselves at sight of me, for though Chaney and I had stayed in the Mitre the previous night, it had been so late when we got there that we had gone straight to bed.

"Good morning, Mr Camberwell!" she exclaimed, in surprise. "Here again? More cricket?"

"Not this time, Dorothy," I replied. "Business! And that reminds me," I continued, thinking it best to make my inquiries while she and I had the place to ourselves, "can you help me a bit about my business?"

"I?" she said. "How?"

I leaned over the bar, in a fashion to suggest secrecy, and, perhaps, mystery.

"I know you're a good girl, Dorothy," I said. "You can keep a secret. And this is a secret that's got to do with something very serious. Do you know Mr Skrimshaw?"

"That very quiet man who comes in every morning about this time?" she asked. "Yes, I know him. But I never remember him talking to me, except to ask for his glass of bitter."

"Was he in here, as usual, yesterday morning?" I asked.

"Yes," she replied promptly. "Usual time. But he was here again after that, with Mr Clayning, the solicitor."

"What time was that?" I inquired.

"Just after one o'clock," she answered. "They sat over there in that corner for some time, talking – whispering to each other."

"And then?" I asked.

"They went out together, about a quarter to two. I think, but I'm not sure, that they turned into the coffee-room. The head waiter could tell you," she concluded.

"Has Skrimshaw been in this morning?" I asked.

"No, but then we're only just open," she said. "This is his time. He may be in any minute for his glass of bitter."

"Well, give me some, and I'll sit down and wait," I remarked. "And – you won't forget, Dorothy, it's a secret."

"I'll not forget," she said.

"Good girl!" said I. "You'll know all about it some day." I took the tankard of beer which she handed me, and went over to a corner of the room, to watch for a while. Men were beginning to come in for their morning drink; many of them I knew by sight; one or two I had met on the cricket-grounds. But no Skrimshaw came – nor had he come by noon, when I decided to seek Chaney and Bailiss.

I got in a word with Dorothy on my way to the door.

"He hasn't come in this morning," I said.

"Never knew him to miss before!" she responded. "First time ever since I came here, three years ago! Every morning at eleven o'clock – unfailing regularity. Shall you be coming in again?"

"I'm staying in the house for a few days," I replied. "I shall be in again."

She nodded her comprehension and I went off to join Chaney and Bailiss at the police-station, and, finding them together, made my report. They pricked up their ears on hearing that Clayning and Skrimshaw had been at the Mitre together on the previous day. And Chaney turned on the Superintendent with a direct question.

"This solicitor – Clayning. Is he a straight 'un?" he asked.

Bailiss answered that pretty much as Aubrey Snowe had answered the similar question I had put to him.

"He's a big practice – police-court practice," he said. "It's pretty nearly always on the defending side. The folk hereabouts," he went on, with a grin, "have the idea when they get into trouble that Mr Clayning can get them off. And, in a good many instances, he does."

"Well," said Chaney, "in my opinion, and until we know more, we'd best not tell Clayning anything. What we want is Skrimshaw. And all we want out of Clayning is – anything that'll help us to find Skrimshaw."

"You don't think it advisable to tell Clayning what you've discovered about Skrimshaw and the London bookshop affair?" asked Bailiss.

"No!" replied Chaney promptly. "Not even in confidence." Bailiss glanced at the clock and got up.

"Look here!" he said. "Don't you go round with me this time. I'll see Clayning and find out what his chauffeur said – if he got any news of Skrimshaw at Woodside Cottage. Then I'll ask Clayning, point-blank, when he himself last saw Skrimshaw, and if he can think of any reason – any reason whatever – why Skrimshaw has not turned up this morning. If he mentions his being with Skrimshaw at the Mitre yesterday we can conclude he's playing straight; if he doesn't it'll look as if he's keeping something back."

He went away on that, and Chaney and I settled down to wait.

"Bailiss," observed Chaney, "is improving. Ideas are coming into his head."

"It's a queer business, Chaney," I said. "Somehow, I don't trust that chap Clayning."

"Oh, well, we'll see," he answered. "Time will show. But queer? Of course it's queer; all these things are queer." Bailiss was away for half an hour. He came back as the clock struck one, dropped into his chair, and turned on us with a shake of the head.

"Learned – nothing!" he announced. "Clayning's chauffeur has been to Woodside Cottage. It's closed and locked, as it was last night, and there's no sign of life about it. The chauffeur spoke to two labourers working close by; neither of them had seen anything of Skrimshaw this morning. As to Clayning, he told me without any questioning that he last saw Skrimshaw early yesterday afternoon outside the Mitre Hotel where they'd lunched together – Clayning had taken him there so that they could discuss an important case which they have in hand. So – that's all."

"Skrimshaw must be found!" said Chaney.

Bailiss nodded his full agreement with that declamation.

"I mean to find him!" he replied. "And I suggest that we three go tonight to that cottage and get into it. There may be evidence inside – eh?"

We both agreed to that, and presently I went away and telephoned to Aubrey Snowe that we should not be able to dine with him that evening, but would call in later.

Chapter Nine

THE DEED-BOX

B AILISS WAS CERTAINLY WAKING up; he got to work on the matter of Skrimshaw's disappearance in a fashion which showed that he meant to do things. Inquiries were set on foot in the town and district without further delay; telephone communication was established with all the adjacent ports; a rapidly drafted handbill and poster were sent off to the printer; a police message was circulated to the broadcasting authorities, and the local Pressmen were bidden to write whatever they liked for the London Press agencies and to get their stuff in quick. Skrimshaw, said Bailiss, had got to be found!

The final result of all this dissemination of inquiry came at four o'clock that afternoon, when a young fellow who described himself as conductor of a motor-bus running on the Wrenchester-Kingsport route came into Bailiss's office while he, Chaney, and I were further discussing matters, and announced that he had something to tell.

"Tell it!" commanded Bailiss.

"Well, you're inquiring about this here Mr Skrimshaw, sir," said the visitor. "He got on my bus yesterday afternoon. Of course I know Mr Skrimshaw well – he's a regular passenger."

"Where did he get on your bus?" asked Bailiss.

"Just beyond the Mitre Hotel, sir."

"What time was that?"

"We were a bit late – it would be soon after half-past two, sir."

"Well, where did he go with you?"

"To his usual place, sir – corner of the lane leading down to Marbourne. That's where he always got off, and where he got on of a morning."

"You're sure this was yesterday afternoon – not some other day?"

"Dead certain, Mr Bailiss! It was yesterday afternoon. I can tell you something that could prove it, sir, if you like to make inquiries. As our bus passed the Mitre Hotel, on its way to the usual stopping-place, I saw Mr Skrimshaw come out of the Mitre with Mr Clayning the lawyer – I know him well too. I saw 'em part – and then Mr Skrimshaw came on to where we'd pulled up, and got in. Oh, yes, yesterday it was, sir!"

That settled one important point. We knew now that when Skrimshaw left Wrenchester after lunching with his employer at the Mitre he went home to Woodside Cottage. But – where then? Bailiss waited until twilight had passed and darkness fallen before taking us to Woodside Cottage that night; it was consequently very late in the evening when Chaney and I went to join him. There was a fourth passenger this time – one of Bailiss's most trusted plain-clothes men, who, Bailiss explained to us, was in charge of a bunch of keys specially borrowed from a locksmith in the town; very necessary implements, for we had noticed when examining the exterior of Woodside Cottage the previous night that the doors, back and front, were secured by what were evidently new locks. And, as Bailiss said with determination, into that cottage we were going! Everything was very silent and very lonely and very dark when we drew near to the cottage. There was not a gleam of light in any of its windows. We had not expected there would be;

we were all convinced, by that time, that Skrimshaw, for some reason or other, had fled. For form's sake, I suppose, Bailiss knocked at the door. When no reply came to his third knock he signed to his man to get busy with the keys. This, by the light of a bull's-eye lantern, he proceeded to do; within five minutes we were in the living-room, on which the door opened.

"Shut the door behind you, Thomson," said Bailiss. "Now, then, first thing we do is to see if there is anybody in this cottage. When we can say yes or no to that we'll go through everything in it."

Thomson lighted another bull's-eye and clumped heavily up the stairs. We heard him pounding about; then he came clumping down.

"Nobody up there," he said. "Two bedrooms – beds made in both." Bailiss turned his bull's-eye round the living-room. A big brass oil-lamp stood on an old oak sideboard that filled one side.

"Light that lamp, Thomson," he said. "Shake it! Is there oil in it?"

"Seems full," replied Thomson. He put a match to the wick, carefully adjusted the rising flame, and set the lamp on the centre table. Then, at a further order from Bailiss, he pulled down the window blind.

"Now let's see if there's anything –" he began.

Chaney was already handling something. Thrown carelessly away in the fender were some envelopes, large and small – tossed there, no doubt, by Skrimshaw when he opened his correspondence. A moment later, and Chaney had laid them out on the table beneath the full glare of the lamp. Two small envelopes he pushed aside, but on another, a full-sized foolscap, he put a finger.

"There!" he exclaimed. "See the blue lines and the postmark? This is the envelope – see the date! – in which Archer enclosed to Skrimshaw the sealed document he discovered at Harston's bookshop! And – here's the envelope of the document itself! Don't you remember,

Camberwell, Archer told us it was marked 'S. G.'? Well, there you are! But, of course, whatever was in this second envelope is gone – like Skrimshaw."

"Whatever was in there will be in Skrimshaw's pocket, Chaney," I said. "And I'd give a good deal to know what it is!"

"We'll take good care of these, anyway," remarked Bailiss. He pulled out a pocket-book and carefully put the envelopes away in an inner compartment. "These, of course, are full proof that Archer's registered packet was delivered to Skrimshaw here yesterday morning," he went on. "A most important thing to know. And now let's make a thorough search of this place, and see if there's anything at all that will help us. Chaney, you and Thomson take the upstairs rooms; Camberwell and I will take this and the kitchen."

We all set silently to work, examining drawers, cupboards, anything in which papers could be hidden. The stillness of that cottage and its surroundings began to impress me. I found myself picturing Skrimshaw sitting there, night after night, alone. Once an owl screamed in the wood close by – I am not a nervous man, but I dropped the thing I was handling.

It fell to my lot to make the next – and the really important – discovery. Bailiss and I were leaving nothing to chance – yet it was by an inspiration, I think, that it occurred to me to see if there was anything concealed beneath and behind the tattered flouncing of an old sofa that was shoved into a corner of the living-room. And when I lifted it and peered into the gloom I was at once aware of an old deed-box – one of those black japanned affairs you see in solicitors' offices, with names of clients painted on them. This had a name – I forget it – probably it was the name of a man long dead, for the box itself was destitute of half its paint, chipped, rusty, a derelict thing. But it was heavy when I pulled it into the light, and it was locked.

Bailiss turned from his job to see what I had got; both of us had keys in our pockets, and we tried several on the lock of the old box. Suddenly we were successful; the lock gave, and the lid went up. And there, lying open to our gaze upon a mass of papers and documents, confronted us an old book, calf-bound, and somewhat worn and frayed with constant usage, which bore on its spine in half-effaced gilt lettering the title "Flood's *History of Wrenchester*."

I stood staring at the book for a full minute; then I pulled it out of its hiding-place and flung it on the table.

"Bailiss," I exclaimed, "we know now who killed Mr Alfred Snowe! It was Skrimshaw!" He stared at me wonderingly; then pointed to the book.

"You think," he said slowly, you think that's the missing book?"

"Not a doubt of it!" said I. "Considering all the facts that are now in our possession – the instructions to Archer – the discovery, by Archer, at Harston's shop – the sending of the sought-for document to Skrimshaw – the finding of this book here – oh, of course it's the book! It was Skrimshaw who wanted that book, believing some document to be in it; Skrimshaw who broke into Mr Snowe's house; Skrimshaw whose hand choked the life out of the old man; Skrimshaw who found the book in its accustomed place and made off with it, only to find that what he expected to be inside it was not inside; Skrimshaw who instigated Archer's search! And – where is Skrimshaw?" Bailiss picked up the old volume and examined it curiously.

"If you're right –" he began.

"Right? Of course I'm right!" I said. "It isn't likely that Skrimshaw would have a copy of this very scarce book. Look round you! Skrimshaw wasn't a book man – I question, from what we see, if he was much of a reader. Are there half a dozen books in the place? No, that's old Mr Snowe's copy. But we can soon prove it."

"How?" he asked eagerly.

"Canon Revington will know," I replied. "He knew Mr Snowe's copy intimately; he'll be able to speak positively. Call the others down and let us hurry back to Wrenchester and call on Canon Revington."

Chaney, hurrying down with the plain-clothes man behind him, heard the story of my discovery in silence, nodding his head at the various points. At the end of it he picked up his hat and pointed to the book.

"That's the thing to do!" he said. "Have it identified at once. If this clergyman can positively swear to it – why, then, we know where we are. Let's get along to him, Bailiss – it's pretty late now."

"Did you find anything upstairs?" asked Bailiss.

Chaney dived into one of his capacious pockets and produced a handful of coloured circulars and folders.

"Nothing that I could attach any suspicion to but these," he said. "All this lot I found on a little table by his bed. You see what they are? Circulars about shipping, chiefly to South America, Royal Mail Line – Pacific Line – Blue Star – Nelson Line – dates of sailing, and so on. And one or two folders about other lines in other directions. Looks to me as if he'd been contemplating getting out of this country. But let's get on with the book affair."

Bailiss took advantage of the now almost deserted highway to rush us back to Wrenchester at forty miles an hour. It was just striking eleven o'clock as we pulled up at the front of Canon Revington's house. The house was almost wholly in darkness, but there was just a faint gleam of light in one downstairs window, and, as Bailiss said, we were bound to see Canon Revington at once, even if we had to knock him up. But at our first ring the Canon himself came to the door – already barred, bolted, locked for the night. When he had undone all these defences and thrown the door open and saw who it was that disturbed him he started with wonder – then, recovering himself as if he already realized what we were after, beckoned us to follow him into a large room just inside the hall – his study. He turned on more lights.

"Sorry to disturb you at this time, sir," said Bailiss. "But if you'd already retired we should have had to awaken you. The matter's serious." He turned to me, and I laid the book on the table before Canon Revington, who, at sight of it, gave a little gasp. "Now, sir," continued Bailiss, "can you tell us positively if that's the Flood's *History of Wrenchester* that belonged to the late Mr Snowe? Positively? Without the least doubt?"

Canon Revington picked up the book, opened it, put it down.

"Yes!" he said. "That is the copy that belonged to Mr Snowe."

"You could swear to that, sir?" asked Bailiss.

"Most certainly. And I could prove that it is," replied Canon Revington. "The proof is quite an easy matter. Yes, this is the copy that was stolen. Er – how have you come into possession of it, Superintendent?"

But Bailiss picked up the book and shook his head.

"You'll excuse me from giving particulars just now, Canon?" he said. "You'll know all in good time, sir. It'll come as a surprise – and again, it mayn't. But for the present – you understand, I'm sure?"

"I understand," assented Canon Revington.

He led us out to the door, and we thanked him for his help, and went away, Bailiss to his quarters at the police-station, Chaney to the Mitre, and I along to Little Straightway, in the hope of finding Aubrey Snowe.

Aubrey had not gone to bed – in fact, he was eating a very, very late dinner, or supper; he had been out on an urgent sick call all the evening. But he laid down his knife and fork when I began to tell my tale, and he didn't pick them up when I'd finished.

"Camberwell," he said, "there's some damned black work at the back of all this! Skrimshaw? There's something and somebody behind Skrimshaw! But, anyway, it's involved the murder – or, at any rate, the killing – of my poor old uncle, and by God, I'll spend every penny I have, if it's necessary, to get at the truth! What's going to be done next, now, Camberwell?"

"The first thing is to find Skrimshaw," I said.

"He's had a good start!" he remarked. "Several hours!"

"Yes," I replied. Then, having no more to say, I left him.

Chapter Ten

HEARD OF!

THERE WAS NOW NO doubt whatever in the minds of Chaney and myself – and I think there was none in Bailiss's – that Skrimshaw was the man who broke into Mr Alfred Snowe's house in Little Straightway in quest of the document which he believed to be concealed in its owner's copy of Flood's *History of Wrenchester*, nor that Skrimshaw's was the hand that had choked the life out of the unfortunate old gentleman who had had the ill-luck to detect his movements. But how had Skrimshaw come to hear of the existence of that document and to know its whereabouts in Mr Snowe's library? It was doubtless this document to which Mr Snowe had referred in his letter to Mr Heyman – the "most important discovery." But how should Skrimshaw know of it? He could only have got to know of it through some personal information from Mr Snowe himself, and there was nothing before us to show that Skrimshaw and Mr Snowe were even acquainted with each other. However, we were very soon to learn that they were.

On the morning following our visit to Woodside Cottage and the discovery of the Flood's *History* in Skrimshaw's old deed-box, Bailiss, Chaney, and I were discussing our future procedure when a caller was announced by the name of Mr John Martinson. Introduced to our presence, Mr Martinson proved to be an elderly, respectable-looking man whose blue reefer suit and somewhat rolling gait convinced me that he was a naval pensioner. And he was also – in aspect – a grave and serious man, and his tone was serious enough when he began to tell Bailiss why he had called on him.

"This hue and cry for Mr Skrimshaw, now, Mr Superintendent?" he said. "You want to find him?"

"We've got to find him!" replied Bailiss grimly.

Mr Martinson looked at Chaney, and then at me.

"I can speak before these gentlemen?" he asked.

"You can say anything you like before these gentlemen," said Bailiss. "Especially if it'll help to find Skrimshaw."

"Well, then, gentlemen, this is what I have to say," began the visitor. "I told your man my name, Mr Superintendent – John Martinson, late Royal Navy. I live at Number Three Pembroke Villas. Did you happen to know, Mr Superintendent, that those houses – Pembroke Villas – twelve separate houses – belonged to the late Mr Alfred Snowe?"

"No!" replied Bailiss.

"Nor would you know," continued Mr Martinson, "that the rents were collected for Mr Snowe by James Skrimshaw?"

"Certainly not!" said Bailiss. "Were they?"

"Had been ever since I came in as tenant, five years ago," said Mr Martinson. "Skrimshaw collected the rents once a month – first of the month, as a matter of fact. Of course, all the twelve tenants are aware of that. But they didn't know that at Clayning's, the solicitors."

"How do you know that?" demanded Bailiss sharply.

"Because I've just been to Clayning's, Mr Superintendent. I went there," continued Mr Martinson, "to find out if Skrimshaw collected the rents on behalf of Clayning's, or if he did it in his own spare time.

Mr Clayning tells me that he knew nothing, and never had known anything, about it, and advised me to call on you."

Bailiss looked at Chaney, and then at me. But neither of us responded; we were listening and thinking.

"When did Skrimshaw call for the rents, as a rule?" he asked.

"On the first of the month, in the evening," replied Mr Martinson. "So I suppose Mr Clayning was right in saying that Skrimshaw did this sort of thing in his spare time."

"What are the rents of those houses?" inquired Bailiss.

"Fifty pounds a year each," responded Mr Martinson. "Four pounds three and fourpence a month."

"Then he'd collect fifty pounds each time?" suggested Bailiss.

"Well, Mr Martinson, what do you suggest? What are you thinking?"

"That, sir," replied Mr Martinson, "is just what I don't know! I don't know what I'm thinking. But I thought – considering what I've heard said in the town – that I'd better tell you what I knew – and what, it seems, you didn't know."

"What's being said in the town?" asked Bailiss.

"Oh, well, Mr Superintendent, it's being truly said that Skrimshaw had something to do with the death of Mr Alfred Snowe!" said Mr Martinson. "And that that's the reason why he's disappeared."

Bailiss made no remark on this – beyond thanking his visitor for coming to see him. And Mr Martinson went away.

He had no sooner gone than another caller was announced – a ruddy-cheeked young fellow of twenty or so, obviously a country lad who had put on his Sunday clothes in order to visit the Superintendent.

"Now, my lad," said Bailiss, "what's your name and business?" Before the lad could reply I suddenly recognized him as one of the

Marbourne village cricket eleven, against whom I had played during my previous visit to Wrenchester. And I replied for him.

"Hall," I said. "Harry Hall. That's right, Hall, isn't it? You were in your flannels last time I saw you."

"That's right, sir," he replied, with a beaming smile. "I knew you, sir."

I explained matters to Bailiss, and he repeated his question as to our new visitor's business.

"Well, sir, about this Mr Skrimshaw," said Hall. "I met him, sir, night before last."

"Where?" demanded Bailiss.

"In Marbourne Park, sir. On the drive, leading to the house. He was about two hundred yards from the house, and walking sharply towards it."

"What were you doing in Marbourne Park?" asked Bailiss.

"Our village cricket-ground is in Marbourne Park, sir – we'd been having a bit of practice."

"What time was it when you saw Skrimshaw?"

"Just after it got fairly dusk. Some of us had stopped on the ground a bit late, rolling the pitch."

"Then you wouldn't be the only one who saw him?"

"Oh, no, sir! There were three others with me. We all saw him – said good-night to him. When we heard at Marbourne that you were looking for him it was settled that I should come in and tell you."

"You say he was walking up the carriage-drive towards the house – Mr Garsdale's?"

"Yes, sir."

"You didn't see him actually go to the house?"

"Oh, no, sir! Only walking quickly in that direction."

When Harry Hall had removed his full moon of a face out of the room Bailiss turned to me and Chaney.

"Very well!" he said. "Now we know what the next step is. We must run out to Marbourne Park. And at once!"

He was rising, to order his car, no doubt, but I stopped him.

"A moment or two, Bailiss," I said. "Let us just consider matters a little. We must go to Marbourne Park, of course – to inquire if Skrimshaw was seen there on the evening to which this lad Hall has just referred. But there's more than that in it. The owner of Marbourne Park is one Mr Henry – or Harry – Garsdale, I believe?"

"Yes, that's so," replied Bailiss. "Well?"

"I believe he inherited the place from an uncle, Samuel Garsdale, didn't he?" I continued. "Mr Snowe's copy of Flood's *Wrenchester* came out of this Samuel Garsdale's library."

"Yes, I've heard that he did," admitted Bailiss. "It was before I came to Wrenchester, but I've heard that. But what – ?"

"What am I driving at?" I said. "This! Do you remember that I told you that the closed foolscap envelope which Archer discovered in Harston's shop was marked on the outside with the letters S. G.?"

"Yes – yes!" he said. "So –"

"I think S. G. meant Samuel Garsdale," I continued. "What do you say, Chaney?"

"I think the same," responded Chaney. "And I think the document inside the envelope is one which has some reference to the Garsdale family. I also think that that document is the most serious and important discovery referred to in the late Mr Alfred Snowe's letter to his solicitor, Mr Heyman."

"I agree, Chaney," said I. "That's been my idea too, ever since we knew that the envelope fell the other day into Skrimshaw's hands. Now, then, shall I tell you my idea, my theory?"

"Tell me anything you like," said Bailiss. "Anything, as long as it helps."

"Very well," I went on. "Then my theory is that there's something in that document which, the document in his possession, puts the Garsdale family in Skrimshaw's power."

Bailiss slapped his hand on the desk at which he was sitting.

"Good, Camberwell!" he exclaimed. "Good – it's what I was trying to figure out for myself. But – there is no Garsdale family. This Harry Garsdale, I'm told, is the very last of his race."

"Very well," said I. "Then for Garsdale family substitute Harry Garsdale. And what sort of man is he? What's known of him? Although I played cricket a short time ago in his park I didn't see him there – he didn't come on the cricket-ground. What do you know of him?"

Bailiss made a grimace and spread his hands.

"No good!" he said. "Waster! Drinks heavily. I have seen him in the town – he's always half soaked. Unless he's thoroughly soaking. In short, it's said he's drinking himself to death."

"No one to look after him?" I asked.

"Well, of course, I don't know much about it," replied Bailiss. "Still, I do hear things – you know what gossips these country and country-town people are. There's a man there at Marbourne Park, man named Beecher, who's said to run things – whether he's butler, or steward, or majordomo, I don't know, but I've heard that he manages the place generally – he and his wife. I think she acts as housekeeper. I've seen this man Beecher now and then at the Mitre, and once he came here about some minor theft from the stables at Marbourne Park. Smart, clever fellow; wife a handsome, managing sort of woman too. Evidently, however, from all that's said, Harry Garsdale goes his own way."

"What's the estate worth?" I asked.

"I can only tell you what I've heard – more gossip," replied Bailiss. "Some few thousands a year."

"And Harry Garsdale is the last of his race, and is drinking himself to death, eh?" I said.

"So rumour says," assented Bailiss. "And from what little I know of the facts I should say rumour is right this time."

"Order your car," I said. "Let's go out there. And – with yours and Chaney's approval – let us, when we get there, and no matter whom we see, confine ourselves to a general inquiry, without particulars as to whether any of the inmates of Marbourne Park happened to see James Skrimshaw near the place on the evening of the day before yesterday."

They were both agreed as to the wisdom of this suggestion, and, Bailiss's car being brought round to the door, we once more set off on that Wrenchester-Kingsport road, which I was beginning to know so well, and within twenty minutes had reached one of the entrances to Marbourne Park. The gates were closed, but there was a neat stone-built lodge, covered with ivy and creepers, at the side, and an old man came out of its door to open them. Bailiss drove his car through, and then, pulling up, beckoned to the janitor.

"Do you know James Skrimshaw?" he asked. "Mr Skrimshaw, at Woodside Cottage, the other side of the Park? He's deaf," he muttered, as the old man put a hand to one of his ears. "Skrim-shaw!"

The old man's face lighted up.

"Yes – yes!" he answered. "Mr Skrimshaw – lives over there." Bailiss drove on.

"I'll bet that's about all we shall get anywhere," he said. "No-body'll have seen him. Now, if that lad was right, and he and his pals saw Skrimshaw near the cricket-ground, Skrimshaw must have come through that gate – unless he climbed the Park wall."

We made no comment on that – none was necessary. Presently we drove up to the house – a somewhat dull and depressing example of late eighteenth-century architecture – and got out at the front door. A footman appeared, and, in answer to Bailiss's inquiry, smiled a little mysteriously.

"I don't think you can see Mr Garsdale, sir," he said. "Better see Mr Beecher – Mr Garsdale isn't very well this morning. This way, sir."

He held the door wider, and the three of us trooped into an entrance-hall, the aspect of which seemed to me even more depressing than the drab walls outside.

Chapter Eleven

THE HOUSE-STEWARD

T HE ONE CHEERFUL THING in that gloomy, stone-walled entrance-hall was a great fire of logs piled up and burning brightly in the wide fireplace, and as that was a cold and chilly morning in what was bidding fair to be a wet and unseasonable summer we all instinctively made up to and crowded round it. But having once warmed myself, I turned and made an inspection of my surroundings. The entrance-hall, as I have just said, was walled with stone; there was no panelling and but little ornamentation of the blank surfaces; here and there, however, hung an old picture; over the fireplace a stag's antlers were flanked by a couple of foxes' masks. The furniture was old and worm-eaten: a chest or two; one or two old chairs; a tallboy in one corner; a press, with a date, 1676, carved on it, in another – these things were about all to be seen in what was a somewhat wide-spaced area. And in spite of the fire, roaring and crackling in the old iron-barred grate, there was a queer and sinister atmosphere in that hall – an atmosphere that chilled and repelled; somehow or other it suggested what I can call nothing else than a sense of – but I scarcely know what to call it. All I know is that if I had been asked what my first impression of that house was I should have replied promptly that some instinct told me that there was something wrong, perhaps something dreadful and even horrifying there.

The footman who had admitted us had vanished, and for some minutes we were left to ourselves. Then a door on the farther side of the hall opened quietly, and a woman appeared on its threshold. For a moment she stood as if surprised at our presence; then, not looking at us any more, and walking swiftly, she crossed the hall towards the foot of the staircase that led from one corner to a gallery above. And, Bailiss and Chaney turning from the fire at the sound of the opening door, we all three watched her as she climbed the stair, wondering who she was. For she was something to look at – a tall, handsome woman, probably of between twenty-five and thirty years of age, dark of hair and eye, and of a fine, perfectly shaped figure, and she moved with a curiously subtle grace that made me wonder if she had Spanish blood in her veins. For the rest, she was well and smartly dressed, and here again came in a suspicion of something not English, for there was colour and brightness in her clothes, and when she disappeared in the shadows of the gallery high above us it was as if whatever warmth and light there was in that dismal place had gone with her.

We all turned to the log fire again, and, wondering and silent, stretched our hands to the blaze. So we stood, saying nothing among ourselves, for another minute or two. Then a soft, smooth, essentially cultured voice spoke from behind us – two words.

"Well, gentlemen?"

None of us had heard anyone approach. We all three whipped round, startled. There in the centre of the hall stood a man who, I felt sure, was the person of whom Bailiss had spoken before we set out – Beecher. I looked at him in some surprise, not expecting to see what I did see. This was no butler in the conventional garb, no house-steward in sober black; rather, the man might have been, say, an officer of the Navy or Army, or – perhaps a better suggestion – an actor. Tall, dark, clean-shaven, with eyes and lips denoting intelligence and firmness, he was very smartly dressed in a perfectly cut suit of black-and-white check tweed. I noticed, being quick to take in such things, the glossiness of his linen, the carefully arranged cravat, the polish of his boots. Had somebody told me that this was the Squire of Marbourne I should have believed what I was told at once – but I should not have believed that the man belonged to even the higher rank of domestic servants.

Bailiss found his tongue.

"Oh, er – good morning, Mr Beecher!" he said hurriedly. "You know me, I think? Superintendent Bailiss, of Wrenchester. Can we have a word with you – in private?"

Beecher, who had quietly inspected all three of us while Bailiss was speaking, inclined his head with a polite gesture and turned on his heel.

"This way, gentlemen," he said, and, moving towards a door near the foot of the staircase, opened it and stood aside for us to enter. "My, room – business room," he continued. "We shall be quite private here. Be seated, gentlemen."

We sat down, and I looked round the room, a small apartment which was half parlour, half office. There was a modern roll-top desk in the centre, and at this Beecher seated himself and turned to Bailiss.

"Yes, Superintendent?" he asked, in quiet, businesslike fashion. "What is it?"

"Mr Beecher," began Bailiss, "you know, as I said just now, who I am. These gentlemen – Mr Chaney, Mr Camberwell – are two famous private –"

"Detectives!" interrupted Beecher, smiling, and accompanying the smile with a polite bow in our direction. "I am quite aware of Messrs Camberwell and Chaney's successes in crime detection, Superintendent. And – what is the present difficulty?"

"The present difficulty, Mr Beecher," replied Bailiss, a little surprised, in my opinion, in this proof of our celebrity, "is that we're trying to find a man called James Skrimshaw, and so far have failed in our efforts! Skrimshaw –"

"Oh, I know James Skrimshaw!" broke in Beecher. "He's one of Mr Garsdale's tenants. He rents Woodside Cottage, the other side of the Park. What do you want of Skrimshaw, Superintendent?"

"Haven't you heard that Skrimshaw has disappeared?" exclaimed Bailiss. "Utterly – vanished?"

"Frankly, I haven't," replied Beecher. "But I haven't been over to the town for some days, and we get little news here."

"Skrimshaw, however, has disappeared," said Bailiss. "And – we want him!"

"You want to – is it to arrest him?" asked Beecher. "That?"

"Call it that," assented Bailiss. "It comes to that." Beecher smiled; there was something enigmatic – or cynical – in his expression.

"Dear me!" he said. "Now, from what I know of Skrimshaw, I should have called him a very tame cat! What's he been up to?"

But Bailiss made no direct answer to that question.

"We came here," he went on, "to ask if Mr Garsdale, or you, or any of your people, know whether Skrimshaw came here during this last day or two? Because, as far as we can find out, Skrimshaw was last seen near this house."

"When?" inquired Beecher.

"Night before last," replied Bailiss.

"Where? And by whom?" demanded Beecher.

"By some young fellows – Marbourne young men – who'd been playing cricket in the Park," said Bailiss. "He was making – evidently – for your front door, and was within a short distance of it."

Beecher shook his head.

"I should have known if he'd come here," he answered. "He didn't."

There was a brief silence. Then Bailiss spoke, a little peremptorily.

"We've got to find Skrimshaw," he said. "I must see Mr Garsdale."

"That, Superintendent, is impossible," he replied quietly. "You can't see Mr Garsdale."

"Why?" demanded Bailiss.

"Because Mr Garsdale is not in a fit state to be seen. Mr Garsdale is at this moment in the hands of the doctor, who is in the house now. And," added Beecher, with a significant glance which included all of us, "of two male nurses."

Bailiss stared his surprise.

"What's the matter?" he asked.

"If you want the plain truth," said Beecher, "*delirium tremens.*"

There was something so exceedingly matter-of-fact in the tone in which the man made this not unstartling announcement that I looked – I think we all looked – at him in wonder; he could not have been calmer in tone if he had been telling us that he had just cut his finger, or that his master had a slight cold. And in the silence which followed he remained sitting easily at his desk, waiting our further pleasure.

"Sorry to hear that," said Bailiss. "No idea –"

"There is nothing surprising in it, Superintendent, to those who, like myself and his doctor and his servants, have known Mr Garsdale for the last few years," interrupted Beecher. "Any man of Mr Garsdale's habits – and they were formed very early in youth – is bound to end up as he is ending. My wife and I have done all we could for him – his doctor has done all he could for him – everybody near him has done all he or she could, and all is or has been of no avail. The truth is Mr Garsdale is an incurable dipsomaniac – and from the mere fact that he never knew any parental control, has no relations, and has always done precisely what he pleased he has been – ungovernable. However – the end will soon come!"

At that moment a shriek or scream from some quarter of the house closely above us rang out with such piercing vehemence that we all jumped. But Beecher remained statuesque.

"Sorry!" he said. "We are used to that – at times. The doctor, apparently, has not yet been able to quieten him down, though he has been with him an hour. The two male nurses, I believe, have had an awful night with him. Well, gentlemen," he went on, rising from the desk, "I can't help you! I know nothing whatever of Skrimshaw and his affairs or his whereabouts. It is quite true that Skrimshaw used to come here occasionally – he came twice a year, once at the New Year, once at midsummer, to pay his half-year's rent for Woodside Cottage. But he didn't come to this house the other night. I can, however, make a suggestion which may help you. Near the west side of the house, opening from the drive, there is a path over which the members of the general public have a right of way – a public footpath, in short. That footpath leads through the Park at the back of the house, across Marbourne Levels, to Marbourne Ferry, which is, as you, Superintendent, know, a village on this, the east, side of Marbourne Creek, which separates this promontory from that on which Kingsport stands. I suggest that if those cricketing boys saw Skrimshaw on our drive the other night, and near the house, he was on his way to Marbourne Ferry. There is a rather comfortable inn there, near the waterside, which, I happen to know, Skrimshaw occasionally – perhaps frequently – visited. But to assure you that he has not been here, or, rather, that he was not here the other night, just come with me."

He led us across the entrance-hall and down a corridor to the kitchen part of the house, and there, summoning the servants – three or four women, a footman, a pageboy – allowed us to question them. And none of these folk had seen Skrimshaw at the house – on the night referred to, anyway.

Beecher let us out into the courtyard at the side of the house; there were stables and garages there, and grooms and a chauffeur, and beyond the courtyard there were gardens and gardeners and their cottages; he made us free to go anywhere and ask any question of any of these people. We did so, and with no more result than in the case of the indoor servants. Nobody had seen the man we wanted.

Eventually we went back to Bailiss's car, which we had left at the front of the house. Beecher and his wife were at the front door; there was a grave-faced man with them, slowly drawing on his gloves; a car which we took to be his stood near ours – we had noticed it on our arrival. As we walked up this man went away and Mrs Beecher retired into the house; Beecher came across the drive to us.

"Well – any news, Superintendent?" he asked.

"None!" replied Bailiss.

"I didn't think you'd get any," said Beecher. "Skrimshaw, you may depend on it, was on his way to Marbourne Ferry; to be precise, to the Cod and Lobster Inn. You'll go there now, of course? Very well, continue down our drive till you come to the first turning to the left. Follow that, and you'll come to the west entrance to the Park. And there you'll turn along the highroad, left, to Marbourne Ferry. The Cod and Lobster –"

"I know it," said Bailiss. "Thank you – sorry to have troubled you, Mr Beecher. I hope there'll be better news of Mr Garsdale –"

Beecher gave him a queer, half-cynical, half-deprecating glance.

"There'll be no better news, Superintendent," he said. "The case is hopeless!"

He turned away, with bent head, and disappeared into the house, and Bailiss, without another word, drove off. Presently we were outside the Park and on the highroad. For two miles we wound in and out through wheat-fields and apple orchards over a dead, flat country; then, at a sudden turn, we emerged on Marbourne Creek, a mile-wide arm of the sea running far into the land. On its farther side, though some distance off, we could see the towers and spires of Kingsport and the dome of its City Hall; on our side lay a quaint, red-roofed little village, with boats drawn up on its beach, and red sails bobbing up and down in the water that lapped its one black-timbered quay. And there, at the landward end of that quay was the place we wanted – a ramblingly built old-world inn, on the signboard of which some rustic limner had painted a very blue cod and a bright red lobster.

Chapter Twelve

THE STOLEN BOAT

W E LEFT THE CAR on a bit of open ground, which stretched between the inn and the edge of the creek, and walked over to a door marked "Saloon Bar." But before we reached its threshold Bailiss stopped us.

"Look here!" he said. "I think it will be advisable, especially if there are others inside this place, if we say nothing about what we're after – at first, at any rate. The landlord knows me – if he's alone in this bar I may take him into our confidence; if there's company present – well, you're two friends of mine that I'm taking for a run round the district, eh?"

"Whatever you please," assented Chaney. "You're boss – at present."

Bailiss pushed open the swing-door, and we entered on a pleasant, bow-windowed room, the walls of which were ornamented with pictures of a nautical flavour, glass-fronted cases containing specimens of fish, and various exhibits of a more or less sporting nature. There was a small but well-equipped bar at one side and behind it a plump, rosy-cheeked, shirt-sleeved man, caught in the act of handing a glass of amber-tinted ale to a solitary customer, who leaned confidentially over the oak-topped counter. This man, a fat, podgy individual, turned sharply at our entrance, and revealed the face of a comedian, breaking into a delighted grin at sight of Bailiss. "Ha, ha!" exclaimed this person. "Enter Law, Justice, and what shall we call the other? And what does Superintendent Bailiss want at the Cod and Lobster – good entertainment for man and beast by John Ready – *vide* wording of sign outside – at this time o' day?"

"Just what Mr. Wattie Webster wants!" retorted Bailiss good-humouredly. "A glass of the Cod and Lobster's best bitter ale."

"Then have one with me!" cried Mr. Wattie Webster. "And your friends! What saith the good hymn? *'For your friend is my friend, And my friend is your friend'* – I haven't," continued Mr. Webster, "a bosom friend present, but we will call Mr. Ready by that sweet name, so, John! – your best for all of us, and welcome, gentlemen, to the Cod and Lobster, and –"

Here Mr. Webster suddenly ceased his flow of eloquence, and, assuming a very grave and serious expression, thrust a podgy forefinger into Bailiss's ribs.

"Ah!" he said, shaking his head. "I know what you're after! I know!"

"Well, what am I after?" asked Bailiss, affecting amusement. "You're a pretty cute specimen, of course. No concealing anything from you!"

"Well, no use the police attempting to do so," assented Mr. Webster. He turned and looked critically at my shoes and at Chaney's boots. "Just so!" he continued. "These gentlemen are not what I thought they might be at first – plain-clothes men. Oh, no! Those terminations to their extremities are fitted with London wear! Shows the matter is more serious than one would have thought. Scotland Yard gentlemen, no doubt. Thought you'd have to call them in, Bailiss! Pretty stiff job for mere country-town brains, what?"

"What's a stiff job?" demanded Bailiss.

"Catching Skrimshaw, my boy! Just that!" said Mr. Webster. "Well, to be sure, Skrimshaw did come to the Cod and Lobster, didn't he, John?"

The landlord, who by this time had furnished each of us with a glass of his certainly most excellent ale, folded his elbows on the counter and assumed a confidential and informing air.

"Skrimshaw," he said reflectively, "he came here regular – two, and sometimes three, times a week, and occasional on Sundays. Always of an evening. He'd drop in about 8.30 by that clock, and stop, having his drink and his pipe, till closing-time. And then, of course, he went. Regular and steady he done that ever since I came to this house, six and a half year ago come Martinmas, every week and never a miss. But this last week he ain't ever been near."

"Not at all?" asked Bailiss.

"Not once!" said the landlord.

"You're sure he wasn't in here night before last?" demanded Bailiss.

The landlord picked up his own glass and swigged off the contents.

"Certain!" he answered, setting the glass down with a confirmatory emphasis. "The man ain't been in this house since last Sunday night."

"He was seen, night before last, coming in this direction, anyway," remarked Bailiss.

"Who saw him?" asked the landlord. "Somebody as you can depend on?"

"Yes," replied Bailiss. "Some Marbourne village cricketers, who'd been practicing at their ground in Marbourne Park. They saw him on the carriage drive, near where the footpath turns off that leads straight here."

"What time might that be?" asked the landlord.

"About dusk," said Bailiss.

The landlord turned to Mr. Webster, who, glass in hand, was listening with rapt attention. A glance of significance passed between them.

"Well, now!" said the landlord. "I wonder if it would be him."

"Ah!" agreed Mr. Webster. "I wonder!"

Clearly there was a mystery here; these two knew something.

"Wonder what?" demanded Bailiss. "What do you mean? Wonder if what would be him?" The landlord seized a cloth and began to polish the counter vigorously.

"That night as you're a-talking about, Superintendent," he said, looking up for a moment, "my boat was stolen! Smart little craft, too – pleasure-boat; everybody on this here Marbourne Creek knows my boat – the *Eileen Norah* by name; called after my old woman. Well, the *Eileen Norah* was where I always keep her, safe tied up at a bit of a slip we have outside, at 8.30 that night, because I see her with my own eyes. And when I get up next morning – vanished!"

He folded up his cloth, flung it under the counter, and looked round from one to another of us.

"Clean departed!" he said. "As I say vanished. And now would that be – ?"

"Skrimshaw?" interjected Mr. Webster.

"Just so!" assented the landlord. "Skrimshaw is the name as was on the tip of my tongue. Skrimshaw James."

"Why should Skrimshaw steal your boat?" asked Bailiss.

The landlord looked at Mr. Webster; Mr. Webster looked at the landlord. Then they both looked at Bailiss pityingly. Mr. Webster took the floor again.

"Bailiss," he said, "I've no opinion of you as a sleuth, Bailiss! I don't consider you're an expert in the devious ways of criminals flying from justice: you're too innocent-minded, Bailiss. But I think you mean well, and you wish to learn, and I'll instruct you. Why should Skrimshaw steal John Ready's boat, the graceful *Eileen Norah*, christened – with a real bottle of champagne, Bailiss after the charming and beautiful Mrs. Ready? Well, I'll tell you, Bailiss! Because Skrimshaw wanted to get to Kingsport, and he wanted to get there in the quickest and most secret way possible. Not by bus, Bailiss, nor by train, Bailiss – too many people would have seen him, and Skrimshaw didn't want to be seen. So he sneaked across Marbourne Park and Marbourne Levels, and came to Marbourne Ferry and appropriated John Ready's boat, and rowed himself – but at this point, Bailiss, I pause! Because I don't know whether Skrimshaw rowed himself all the way to Kingsport, round Marbourne Point, or whether he just rowed himself across the creek and then took the by-lanes and footpaths to that maritime town. John! – another glass."

Chaney intervened here, to do the honours, and while the landlord was refilling the glasses there was a silence broken only by the plashing of the ale. And it was not Bailiss, but Chaney, who spoke next.

"How far is it from here to Kingsport by water?" he asked.

"Matter of seven sea-miles," replied the landlord.

"And across the creek?" inquired Chaney.

"Bit over a mile – here," said the landlord.

"And when you've crossed the creek?" continued Chaney.

"Then," said the landlord, "there's a footpath leads straight across country to Kingsport." "Have you made inquiries about the boat?" asked Chaney.

"Everywhere!" replied the landlord. "Kingsport and across the water. Up to now – ain't heard anything."

At this moment beauty descended on the saloon bar in the person of Mrs. Ready, a plump, pretty woman, who graciously acknowledged the salutes of friends and strangers alike, and, having caught her husband's last words, at once volunteered an opinion of her own.

"What I say to John, Mr. Bailiss, is this," she said, with an air of decision. "Whoever stole our boat stole it for a purpose, and that purpose was to get somewhere. It may have been Kingsport – and it mayn't. It may have been some spot on the other shore of the creek – and it may not. It may have been to reach some vessel waiting out at sea –"

"Ah!" exclaimed Mr. Webster. "Excellent suggestion! Mrs. Ready's brains are sharper than my own!"

"But wherever the thief's destination was," continued Mrs. Ready, giving Mr. Webster a glance which was intended to show that she quite agreed with him, "I say that when he'd achieved his object – I think that's the proper term, Mr. Bailiss – he sank the boat! And, of course, if he went out to sea in her the *Eileen Norah* is down among the dead men – and there you are!"

Nobody ventured to contradict Mrs. Ready's theory, and Bailiss turned to her husband with a matter-of-fact question.

"I suppose you haven't heard of anybody in the village who happened to see Skrimshaw that night?" he asked. "He'd have to pass through the village to get down here by the water, wouldn't he?"

"Not necessarily he wouldn't," replied the landlord. "He could turn off at this end of Marbourne Levels and come along the waterside. No! – I haven't heard a word of anybody seeing him, though there's been plenty of talk about him since you sent out those inquiries. May be something in what my wife here says – that he took the boat and put out to sea in her, to be picked up outside the bar. And in that case he may not have sunk the *Eileen Norah* – she may be outside yonder, on her own."

"No" said Mrs. Ready firmly. "No, John! It was a put-up job prepared beforehand, and he sank her when he'd done with her. And pray, Mr. Bailiss, what is it all about and what did Skrimshaw want to make himself scarce for? Has he been doing something? A very quiet, peaceable man Skrimshaw always seemed to me – quite the gentleman! Still, you never know –"

At this stage of these – to me and Chaney – very interesting proceedings Mrs. Ready was interrupted by the tramp of heavy feet outside the door of the saloon bar, and, this being thrust open, there walked in two men in blue jerseys and sea-boots, one of whom carried a black ebony walking-stick, ornamented by a heavy silver top. They advanced on the rest of us, smiling widely at the landlord, who, on seeing the ebony stick, gasped.

Then he suddenly threw up his hands in a gesture of amazement.

"That – that's Skrimshaw's stick!" he exclaimed. "Many's the time I've seen him with it in this here room! It was give him for a presentation at a Sunday school where he used to teach the kids. What're you doing with it, Jim Flint? And where did you come across it?"

Jim Flint laid the ebony stick on the counter and smiled knowingly.

"Foun' it aboard of your boat what you was a-missing of, Mr. Ready!" he said. "There it lay under the thwarts – leastways; it was a-washing about in a matter of water as had come aboard."

"My boat!" cried the landlord. "And where is my boat?" Jim Flint cocked a thumb in the direction of the creek. "Tied up outside," he answered. "I and Charlie here have just pulled her across. We found her the other side, way up the creek, fastened under some trees. And, as I say, this here stick in her." The landlord laid hands on two pint mugs, filled each to its brim, and pushed them across the counter.

"Well, that beats all!" he said. "Of course, he took my boat to get him across! But – what did he leave his stick in her for? That there stick – it was a presentation! And from a Sunday School!"

By that time Bailiss, Chaney, and I were examining the stick. It was the sort of thing that had cost money. There was a solid silver head to it, and beneath the head a broad silver band, on which was an engraved inscription: "To James Skrimshaw, from his class at Mount Sion Sunday School."

"He was proud of that stick," remarked Mrs. Ready.

"Mount Sion is some sort of a place of worship at Kingsport – Skrimshaw used to live at Kingsport."

"And apparently," said Mrs. Ready's husband, "it's to Kingsport he's gone back – a-using of my boat for transport."

We stayed a little longer at the Cod and Lobster, questioning Jim Flint and his friend Charlie. Then we went out to Bailiss's car. And Bailiss carried with him the silver-topped stick which Skrimshaw had received in recognition of his pious labours.

Chapter Thirteen

HISTORY OF A FAMILY

W E WERE BACK IN Wrenchester by soon after one o'clock, and when we came abreast of the Mitre Hotel Chaney asked Bailiss to come in and lunch with us. Once inside, Chaney got the head waiter to give us lunch in a private room – a circumstance which showed that my partner (who, up to now, had taken a very quiet and reserved share in our proceedings) had some notion in his mind. And I was not surprised when, lunch being over and the waiter gone, leaving us to coffee and cigars, Chaney, without preface, asked Bailiss to tell us, straight out, what he thought of this affair and what he proposed to do. Somewhat to my astonishment Bailiss replied to this invitation in the same candid spirit.

"To my mind," he said, "the whole thing's as plain as a pikestaff – as the saying is. Skrimshaw found something of value in that envelope, and he's off with it! That, in my opinion, is all there is to it."

"What do you mean by 'something of value'?" asked Chaney.

"Oh, well," replied Bailiss nonchalantly, "who can say? It might have been two or three banknotes for a considerable sum each – they issue them up to £1000, I understand. Or it might have been some easily convertible securities, or something of that sort. I don't know if you've heard of it, you two, but that old Mr. Alfred Snowe had the reputation of being a bit of a miser."

"How should Skrimshaw get to know that Mr. Alfred Snowe had anything of that sort hid away in an envelope which he kept in one of his old books?" asked Chaney.

"Oh, well, I see no difficulty in that," said Bailiss. "We've already ascertained that Skrimshaw collected rents for Mr. Snowe; Mr. Snowe may have taken him into his confidence. If Mr. Snowe trusted Skrimshaw sufficiently to trust him with the collection of his rents he'd trust him enough to tell him secrets of another sort."

"The envelope which Archer found and sent to Skrimshaw," remarked Chaney, "was marked S. G. on the outside. What do you make of that?"

"What do you make of it?" inquired Bailiss.

"We've heard of one Samuel Garsdale, former Squire of Marbourne," replied Chaney. "S. G. corresponds to his initials."

"Well, the envelope may have contained something that Samuel Garsdale put in it," said Bailiss. "There, again, was an old gentleman that was said to be a cheeseparer. Perhaps it was something that Samuel Garsdale had hidden in a book – something afterwards discovered by Mr. Alfred Snowe. Now I come to think of it, Mr. Snowe wrote to his London solicitor, Mr. Heyman, the day before his death, saying that he'd made a most important discovery and asking him to come down about it. That, of course, must have been it – that envelope and its contents!"

"Again I ask – how did Skrimshaw get to know of it?" inquired Chaney.

"Obvious!" replied Bailiss. "Mr. Snowe told him! And then Skrimshaw tried to secure the envelope. Broke in – was interrupted by the old gentleman – the old gentleman died – Skrimshaw handled him too roughly.

Then Skrimshaw didn't find the envelope, because Mr. Snowe had put it in a different book. Then the books were sold to Harston, up in London, and Skrimshaw employed Archer to search. And Archer searched and found, and Skrimshaw got what he wanted – and made himself scarce.

"That, gentlemen," concluded Bailiss, waving his cigar with an air of confident conclusion, "that is what I think!"

"You think Skrimshaw's gone – clean away?" asked Chaney.

"I think Skrimshaw's gone as far as it was possible to go in the time at his disposal," said Bailiss, with quiet confidence. "Whether by land or by water, he's put as much distance as he could between us and himself! He may be out of England – he could easily get across the Channel from Kingsport – or he may be in England. But wherever he is, I'll rouse the whole country for him before today is over – and the Continental police as well!"

Chaney threw away what was left of his cigar, and began to fill his pipe.

"That's your considered opinion, is it, Bailiss?" he asked. "Definite?"

"Definite!" replied Bailiss. "Fixed!"

"That Skrimshaw has – fled?" continued Chaney. "Hooked it?"

"Far, far away!" assented Bailiss, grinning. "Hoping to get – farther!"

"Very well. Now we know where we are," said Chancy. "Or, rather, we know where you are! For, you see, I don't agree with you."

Bailiss gave him a look of genuine surprise. "Eh?" he exclaimed. "What? You don't – ?"

"I don't!" said Chaney. "I believe that Skrimshaw is, at this moment, within five or six, or at most seven, miles of where we're sitting! Fact, Bailiss!"

Bailiss stared harder than before. "I can't see what grounds you've got for saying that," he muttered. "It's contrary to all the evidence."

"Not in my opinion," replied Chaney. "But all this leads to what I wanted to say. You, I take it, are going to raise the hue and cry for Skrimshaw, being convinced that he's run away?"

"I am – and at once!" replied Bailiss.

"Very well. Now, you see, I don't believe he's run away at all," continued Chaney. "So – at this stage Camberwell and I part company with you. We must work on our own lines from this point, Bailiss – you, of course, will go on working on yours. You see, young Dr. Snowe has given us a precise commission, and we are to spare no pains and no expense in executing it. So, as I say, here we part. We take up the chase from one angle; you from another. But I've a proposal to make, and I hope you'll see the reasonableness of it. We, on our side, promise to communicate to you any really important discovery that we make. Will you, on yours, keep us informed of anything that you find out?"

Bailiss was still puzzled by Chaney's declaration, and he seemed to be not over well pleased by it.

"Oh, well," he said, a little sulkily, "I suppose there's no harm in that. Of course, if you're going on your own lines I can't stop you. But you lick me, Chaney! Do you mean to say, in the face of what we've seen for ourselves and heard this morning, that you believe Skrimshaw to be about here – close at hand?"

"I do!" replied Chaney. "Absolutely!"

"Where is he, then?" demanded Bailiss, almost contemptuously. "Where?"

"That's precisely what Camberwell and I are now going to find out," said Chaney. "When we've found him you shall be the first to hear of it."

Bailiss rose and settled his uniform cap before the mirror. "Well, you surprise me!" he said. "However, I must go and do my bit in my way. Keep me posted – it's a bargain!"

He went off, and when the door had closed on his tall figure Chaney clapped a hand on my shoulder.

"Camberwell," he said, in a low voice, "perhaps even you don't see what I'm after?"

"Frankly, I don't, Chaney," I replied. "What is it?"

He pulled his chair closer to mine and spoke in a still lower tone.

"Camberwell," he answered, "Skrimshaw would not have left that stick in the *Eileen Norah*! Skrimshaw never went near the *Eileen Norah*! Skrimshaw, Camberwell, is *dead* – murdered!"

The effect of that last word was to make me jump literally – from my chair. I felt my heart leap. I daresay the blood left my cheeks. Erect, I turned, facing him.

"Good God, Chaney!" I said. "What do you mean?"

"Just what I say," he answered quietly. "Skrimshaw is dead – murdered!"

"By whom?" I exclaimed.

"Ah – that's what we're going to find out!" he answered, smiling. "Now, let's start at once. Put your hat on – we're going to see that parson, Canon Revington. But first I want to give them some orders at the hotel office."

I followed him round to the entrance-hall of the hotel. The manager happened to be in the office. Chaney drew his attention.

"I find," said Chaney, "that Mr. Camberwell and myself are likely to be here for some little time yet. We must have a private sitting-room, to be kept exclusively for our own use. What about the room we've just had lunch in?"

"Certainly, Mr. Chaney," replied the manager. "You can have that – or you can have a similar one, on the next floor, close to your bedrooms."

"That, perhaps, would be more convenient," said Chaney. "Have it reserved for our special use."

"I'll have a card marked *Private* put on it at once," said the manager. "Want your meals served there, Mr. Chaney?"

"No," replied Chaney. "We want the room for business purposes."

We went out then, and made straight for Canon Revington's house. Chaney had become very determined in tone and manner since cutting adrift from Bailiss I could see that he had schemes, ideas, notions, seething in his mind. But I asked no questions, and when we were admitted to Canon Revington's study I left him to do the talking – indeed, I had no conceptions as regards the object of our visit. Chaney, however, went straight to business.

"Canon Revington," he said, "I don't know if you're aware that Dr. Snowe has commissioned my partner, Mr. Camberwell, and me with the task of solving the mystery attaching to his uncle's death. He has, however, and we are to spare neither time, effort, nor expense. We are working independently of the police authorities, and perhaps on different lines, though we have promised help if and where these lines converge. Now we come to you, hoping for some information. In a previous conversation you gave us some information about Samuel Garsdale, to whom that copy of Flood's *History of Wrenchester* belonged before it passed into the hands of the late Alfred Snowe. Can you give us still more particulars about Samuel Garsdale and the Garsdale family of Marbourne? "

Canon Revington smiled an affirmative.

"Well, Mr. Chaney," he replied, "I can! In addition to my canonry here I happen to be Vicar of Marbourne as well – I have held the living of Marbourne for twelve years, but, as there is very little parochial work there, I have always resided here in Wrenchester. What is it you want to know?"

"Did you know Samuel Garsdale?" asked Chaney.

"Very well indeed!" replied Canon Revington.

"What sort of man was he?"

"A somewhat eccentric man. He lived a very hermit-like existence in a very gloomy house. Among his neighbours he had the reputation of a miser."

"Do you know if he left a will?"

"I know that he didn't! He died intestate. Anyway, no will was ever found. So the present owner of Marbourne Park, Harry Garsdale, who was the only son of a younger brother of Samuel's, then deceased, came in for everything. Harry Garsdale, in fact, was the only living relative that Samuel had. Harry, I repeat, got everything – and a sad use he has made of it, Mr. Chaney!"

"We know," said Chaney. "Drinking himself to death! Who is that man Beecher who seems to be in command there, Canon Revington?"

"I can't tell you, Mr. Chaney, for I don't know. All I know is that Mr. and Mrs. Beecher came there some little time ago, and that Beecher is, as you suggest, in command. He acts as steward, majordomo – everything!"

"And this Harry Garsdale has no relations?"

"None! He is the very last of his race – an old family too," said Canon Revington. "And from all I hear – and know – he will soon be gone. He has steadily drunk himself to death – nothing can be done for him now."

We went away soon after that. On our way back to the Mitre we had to pass through the Cathedral close; there were seats there under the trees, and Chaney, suddenly pausing by one of them, motioned me to sit down. He sat down too, and, though there was no one about, he dropped his voice to a whisper.

"Camberwell," he said, "you may as well know all that's in my mind! I've worked out a theory. Right it may be, and wrong it may be; but wrong or right, there it is! Go back to the envelope which Archer found in the book in Harston's shop, the envelope marked S. G. I think that that envelope contained a will, in which Samuel Garsdale left his money and property away from his nephew, Harry Garsdale. I think that Mr. Snowe found that will concealed in one of the books which had formerly belonged to Samuel. I think Mr. Snowe probably – no, certainly! – consulted Skrimshaw about it. When Skrimshaw eventually got the will from Archer he went to Marbourne Park with the idea of blackmailing Harry Garsdale. And Beecher saw Skrimshaw – and Beecher got rid of Skrimshaw! Beecher – that's the man we're after, Camberwell."

"You think Beecher murdered Skrimshaw in order to get possession of and to destroy the will?" I said. "Is that it?"

"That is it," he answered, with assurance. "Skrimshaw, Camberwell, is dead – murdered! And Beecher murdered him! That's my theory – now we've got to see if it's a correct one."

I said nothing just then. I was visualizing – all sorts of things. And I didn't see our next step. But there was one near. Next morning, as we were talking to Aubrey Snowe in our private sitting-room at the

Mitre, a note was brought to us. Chaney opened and read it, tore the paper in pieces, and threw it in the fire.

"From Bailiss," he said. "We're to meet him at the Wrenchester Old Bank at once."

Chapter Fourteen

THE BANK CLERK'S STORY

THE WRENCHESTER OLD BANK was only a few yards away from the Mitre Hotel, between it and Little Straightway. Hurrying there at once, we found Bailiss awaiting us at the door. He favoured us with a knowing grin.

"Keeping faith, you see!" he said. "I don't know what they want to tell us here, but I thought you might as well hear it at first hand. It's about Skrimshaw, anyhow."

"You don't know yourself, then?" asked Chaney.

"No more than you do," replied Bailiss. "Smart, the manager here phoned me to come over, as he'd some news for me in this Skrimshaw disappearance case. Come on – let's hear what it is."

He pushed open the swing-doors, and we walked into the bank's outer office. We – or Bailiss – had evidently been expected to respond at once to the manager's summons, for at sight of us a clerk came forward and led us to a room at the end of the counter. And there, a moment later, Mr. Smart, a sharp-eyed, scarcely middle-aged man, came to us. He gave Chaney and me a questioning look, and Bailiss hastened to introduce us.

"All working together, Mr. Smart," said Bailiss. "They in their way, on Dr. Snowe's behalf, and me on mine – in police interests. But any information we can secure is common to both, and I hope you've got some that will be valuable."

"Sit down, gentlemen," responded the manager. "Yes," he went on, seating himself at his desk, "I've certainly got something that I can tell you, though, of course, it's only because of the complexion that this Skrimshaw affair appears to be taking that I tell you anything at all. Now, to begin with, let me have an explicit answer to two explicit questions, Superintendent. First, do you believe that this man Skrimshaw was involved in the affair at the late Mr. Snowe's house in Little Straightway, and concerned in whatever it was that resulted in the old gentleman's death?"

"Undoubtedly, Mr. Smart!" replied Bailiss.

"And you think there's no doubt, either, that Skrimshaw has fled – absconded – or whatever you like to call it?"

"No doubt of that either, sir!" said Bailiss.

"Very well, then I'll tell you what we know here. Skrimshaw has been on our books as a client, or customer, for some years. He was evidently a saving man. As his little capital accumulated we used to invest it for him. He used to tell us what to instruct our brokers to buy for him. He always selected Government stocks – he was quite satisfied with four percent; everything he touched was in the nature of what one calls gilt-edged stuff. A cautious, wary man, Skrimshaw, which is why I think you'll have a stiff job before you in trying to find him.

"Yes, sir?" said Bailiss, disregarding the final expression of opinion. "And these securities?"

"About three weeks ago," continued the manager, "Skrimshaw came here one day bringing his securities. He handed them over to me personally, and gave me instructions to sell them, through our brokers, at once, and to credit his account with the proceeds. This, of course, was done and at the beginning of last week, a few days before the news of Skrimshaw's disappearance reached us, the balance showing in our books in his favour was" - here the manager consulted a slip of paper, "exactly £2053 12S 9d"

"Nice little sum, sir," said Bailiss. "Is – is it still there?" The manager laughed and touched a bell. A clerk looked in.

"Please ask Mr. Harborough to come here, he said. Then he turned again to us. "Harborough is our cashier. I want him to tell you himself what happened – I believe the very morning of the day on which Skrimshaw is believed to have left the neighbourhood."

"That," remarked Bailiss, "was last Thursday – half closing day."

"Exactly! Well –"

The door opened again. A man whom I recognized as having seen often in the Wrenchester streets came quietly in – a man of apparently thirty to thirty-five years of age – quiet-mannered, of an evident natural reserve and watchfulness; just the sort of man, one would have said, instinctively, to handle and take care of money. The days have gone by in which a bank clerk was expected to dress as if he were going to a funeral, and Mr. Harborough was attired in a tweed suit of a somewhat sporting pattern. Nevertheless, there was no mistaking his calling.

"Harborough," said the manager, "I want you to tell Superintendent Bailiss and his friends exactly what passed between you and Skrimshaw last – which day last week was it?"

"Thursday," replied the cashier. "Thursday morning."

"Thursday morning," repeated the manager. "Very good – tell."

The cashier turned to us, and before speaking looked Chaney and myself carefully over. Bailiss he evidently knew well.

"There is not a great deal to tell," he said, in a quiet, unemotional voice. "Mr. Skrimshaw came in a little before noon – we close at twelve o'clock on early-closing day. He asked me to tell him what his exact balance was. I looked it up, and told him it was £2053 odd. He then said that he was about to complete an important investment, wished to pay the money in cash, and wanted to draw two thousand pounds. He proceeded to write out the cheque for this. I asked him how he'd take the money. To my surprise he said he wanted it in one-pound notes –"

"What, the lot?" exclaimed Bailiss. "Two thousand pounds in one-pound notes! Why – what about carrying it?"

"I made some such remark to him myself, Mr. Bailiss," replied the cashier. "He held up a small brown leather suitcase, and said he'd carried more than that amount in it. I'd a bit of difficulty in finding two thousand one-pound notes; as a matter of fact, I had to send across to the Wrenchester and Kingsport Bank, over the way, to help me out. But I got what I wanted, and gave Mr. Skrimshaw twenty bundles of a hundred notes each. He packed them in his suitcase – and went away."

Bailiss glanced from cashier to manager.

"Queer business!" he said. "Carrying two thousand one-pound notes about! Is – isn't such a thing uncommon? I mean, for a man who wants to draw that entire amount to take it in notes of –"

"Of such small denomination?" said the manager. "Oh, well, that depends, Superintendent. It depends on what the money's wanted for. A big firm, for instance, employing several hundred workpeople would require a lot of pound notes and ten-shilling notes for pay-day. That's not the point – the point is that, considering the circumstances, we think that you ought to be acquainted with the fact that Skrimshaw, when he disappeared last Thursday, was carrying a small suitcase or attaché-case in which he had two thousand pounds in pound notes. And pound notes are not like five-pound or ten-pound Bank of England notes – nobody takes the numbers."

Then we all looked at one another. None of us seemed to possess any ideas arising out of what we had heard.

"I suppose," remarked Chaney, after a moment's silence, and addressing himself to the cashier, "I suppose Skrimshaw didn't tell you what the investment was that he spoke of?"

"Oh, no!" replied Harborough. "He told me nothing about that."

"What time do you say it was when he was in here?" continued Chaney.

"Just before noon, our closing-time. We closed immediately he left."

Chaney turned to Bailiss.

"He went with Clayning to the Mitre about one o'clock," he remarked. "We'd better see Clayning."

We left the bank and went round to Clayning's office. Clayning was in the outer room, talking to a clerk. He gave us an enquiring glance.

"Hullo!" he said. "News?"

"Not of the sort we want," replied Bailiss. "We want some from you, Mr. Clayning. You took Skrimshaw to the Mitre last Thursday, didn't you? You'd lunch with him there?"

"Well," asked Clayning, "and what of it?"

"Can you remember if he carried with him a small leather suitcase or attaché-case?" asked Bailiss. "Brown leather."

Clayning's face assumed a thinking or recollecting expression. But the clerk at his side spoke up with readiness and assurance.

"Yes, sir, he had," he said. "Mr. Skrimshaw was carrying that case when he went out with you. It was the case he brought in every day, sir – used to bring his lunch and his papers in it."

"Aye, well, I think I do recollect he'd something in his hand," said Clayning. "Yes – yes--a small case. Aye! – I remember now – he put it under the table between his feet, or put his feet on it, when we were lunching. What about it?"

But Bailiss did not say. Outside Clayning's office he spoke to us, however.

"Of course, he took that case home with him," he said. "You remember, he got on the Kingsport bus when he parted with Clayning outside the Mitre? I can see what he drew that two thousand pounds in one-pound notes for – fivers and tenners would have been traced. Well, he's made a very good clearance of himself! I have had Kingsport fairly combed out, and there isn't a trace of him. And yet he must have gone to Kingsport!"

We left Bailiss clinging to that conviction, and went back to our room at the Mitre. But not to stay in it; we had had our own car sent down from London by that time, and within a few minutes we had it round to the front of the hotel, and were off to Marbourne, to see Harry Hall and such of his mates as had been with him when he saw Skrimshaw near the cricket-ground in Marbourne Park. For we had a question to put to these lads – had they noticed if Skrimshaw, when they saw him on the evening round which so much centered, was carrying a small suitcase?

We left our car at the inn at Marbourne, and went off on foot to find Harry Hall at the farm on which he worked; eventually we ran him to earth in a field which lay between Marbourne Park and the wild stretch of country known as Marbourne Levels. He had with him another youngster in whom I recognized still one more active member of the Marbourne cricket eleven. Both grinned delightedly at sight of us. And after talking to them a bit about cricket I went straight to the question.

"Now, boys," I said. "I want to get a bit of information from you. You both remember seeing Skrimshaw on the carriage drive, going in the direction of the house, in Marbourne Park? Very well, now tell me this – was Skrimshaw carrying anything?"

They both replied so quickly that I had no hesitation in concluding that they were telling me of a fact.

"Yes!" they said, in the same breath. "He'd a stick in one hand and a small portmanteau in the other."

"You're sure of that?" I asked. "You saw both these things?"

They nodded silently. It was evident that they wondered a little why I should repeat my question after their first assurance.

"You didn't see Skrimshaw actually go to the house?" I continued. "No, I thought not. Now, it's been suggested to us that he went off across Marbourne Levels. How would he get into the Levels from the Park?"

They motioned me and Chaney to step over to the hedgerow near which we were talking; then, at a gap in the hawthorn, they pointed across the corner of the Park.

"See that clump of holly?" asked Hall. "That's where the path across the Park cuts into the Levels. Then it's two miles and a half across to Marbourne Ferry. And about here they're saying that that's where Skrimshaw made for that night."

"Can we get into the path by following this hedgerow?" asked Chaney.

"Can if you go through this gap and keep to the right," replied Hall. "Bit of a low fence to climb, farther on."

We left the two lads, still curious and wondering, and made our way to the path that ran across the Levels. For we had decided on our way to Marbourne that it was now time we made a personal inspection of the piece of country which Skrimshaw was supposed to have gone over on his journey from his own cottage to Marbourne Ferry; even if he never had gone over it (which was Chaney's opinion) it would never do to neglect the possibilities that an examination of it might yield some clue. So we at once set out on our walk, and presently we found ourselves in the heart of a wild, desolate expanse, half marsh, half moor, destitute of human habitation, and apparently given up to sea-birds and shy creatures of wood and stream. Yet before we had gone a mile over the springy turf we came on signs of human life where we had fancied there was none. This was – obviously – a gipsy encampment in a sudden, sheltered declivity. There was a gay fire burning in a brazier that stood near the tent, and a black pot hanging from the tripod set above it, and as a light wind was blowing towards us from that direction our nostrils were presently titillated with an odour which convinced us that the pot contained some exceedingly appetizing fare.

Chapter Fifteen

THE GIPSY TINKER

A NOTHER STEP OR TWO brought us round a curtain of gorse-bushes, and we came into full view of the lord and lady of this habitation in the wilderness. At a little distance from the crackling fire and its babbling and steaming pot a man sat busied with some work of tinkering – soldering, I think, some kettle or other adjunct of kitchen life. He was sideways to us, and his features, accordingly, were half concealed, but we could catch the swarthy hue of his cheek, the blackness of his hair, and the gleam of the gold ring in his ear. He was a gay fellow too, for his waistcoat was fashioned out of some plush or velvet-like material of a bright crimson, and about his bent neck was knotted a yellow handkerchief. And mingled with the crackling of the fire beneath the swinging pot came the low notes of some song with which he beguiled his labour.

But there was another piece of humanity at hand – a woman. If there was any doubt in our minds as to the man's claim to gipsy blood, there could be none about hers. She was the gipsy woman all over –

the dense black, snake-like hair, the dark skin, flushed with lively red on the high cheek-bones, the muscular and sinewy build, the garments of warm tints, from the crimson skirt and yellow bodice to the bright blue silk about her neck and throat. And she too sported earrings of a somewhat red gold, but while the man's were just rings, plain rings, hers were of a size and weight that tinged on the barbaric.

Suddenly aware of our approach, these two turned sharply and simultaneously, the man from his tinkering, the woman from some job of food preparation with which she was busy at the tail-board of a tilt-covered cart that stood drawn up beneath the shelter of the overhanging trees. Their eyes rested on us for a moment; then they turned to each other and a whispered word passed between them. The next instant the man was busy at his kettle again, and the woman was calmly pursuing her preparations for the midday meal.

"Gipsies!" muttered Chaney. "And evidently been here some time, judging from the evidences – fires in half a dozen spots. Come on, we'll see if we can get anything out of them. Good morning!" he continued, as we drew near to the man. "A fine morning for your job!"

The tinker lifted a weather-beaten face and looked Chaney over knowingly before giving me a look which was not quite so searching.

"The top of the morning to you, master," he responded, with a good-humoured smile. "And a very fine morning for your job too!"

"Why, what do you think is our job?" demanded Chaney. "You aren't a thought-reader, are you?"

"No need to be – though I can do a bit that way too," replied the tinker. "But when you know that there's a man missing from these parts, and that he's badly wanted, and you see two gentlemen coming along the path by which he is supposed to have fled from – shall we say justice? – well, master, one draws one's own conclusions. And my conclusion is that I have the distinguished honour of looking upon two gentlemen connected with the very well conducted and admirable police force of this country!"

"You're a sharp chap – and a talker!" said Chaney, admiringly. "Well, I suppose you're not far off it. But I say, how long have you and the misses – my best respects to you, ma'am! – how long have you been here?"

"Matter of two weeks," answered the tinker.

"Three, Zeph, three!" said the woman, who had left the cart and come over to us. "Three, master. He," she continued, nodding at her husband, "never takes no proper account of time."

"Well, two or three," said the tinker. "If Nance says it's three it is three. And what then, master?"

"If you've been here three weeks, or even two," replied Chaney, "you must know this bit of country pretty well, and the path that runs across it too."

"We do, master," assented the tinker, "and we know the man you're looking for as well as we know these Levels – Skrimshaw."

"You know him?" exclaimed Chaney.

"Many are the time he'd come and have a jaw, master, as he went or came 'twixt here and the Ferry. And not only this time, but in years past – we come here, me and the misses there, about this time every year, for a while. Oh, yes, we know Skrimshaw!"

"A very quiet gentleman," observed the woman. "Not a great one to talk."

"But a great one to listen," said her husband. "Fond of hearing old tales and old songs."

"Such as you could tell him or sing to him, I'll be bound," said Chaney. "Well, we're looking for Skrimshaw! Can you tell us anything about him?"

"Nothing more than I have told you, master," replied the tinker. "We've heard about his disappearance, and when he disappeared, but we saw nothing of him that night, though if he passed this way to the Ferry, where, we understand, his stick was found in a boat, he must have gone close by us."

"You're a sharp-witted chap, you know," remarked Chaney. "Have you got any ideas, any theories of your own, about the man's disappearance?"

The tinker put aside his work and looked his questioner squarely in the face.

"Would Skrimshaw be likely to have money on him? Or anything of value? Anything that would be of value to other people?" he asked. "Would it be worth the while of – somebody – to get rid of him?"

"He had money on him," said Chaney, with emphasis, "and it would have been to the advantage of – somebody – to rid themselves of, perhaps not him, but something that he carried about him."

The tinker nodded once or twice, as if to show his understanding, and he rose to his feet.

"Well, master," he said, "there's a spot near here where a man could be got rid of and nobody know of it – the very spot for a murder! And if you and your friend will tarry a bit and take pot-luck with us I'll walk on with you and show you the place I mean."

"That's very kind of you, I'm sure!" exclaimed Chaney. "And the smell of that pot of yours is – but what does the lady of the house say?"

"She says bide and welcome, master," said the woman heartily. "There's enough in that pot for six hungry men. For you never know who mayn't turn up, and it must never be said that Zephany and Nance Shepperoe let anybody go by wanting a bite!"

"Nor a sup either," said the tinker, casting a sidelong glance at a big bucket full of water, in which stood a promising-looking stone jar.

"The ale's cooling, gentlemen! Some people, I understand, put their champagne in a pail of ice, and some pop their French claret down to the fire, but I put my beer in the native element – and we'll try a glass before dinner!"

"You're a true hand at hospitality," said Chaney. "The genuine article!"

"Well, there's naught like it, master," replied the tinker. "What's better than to see friendly faces round you while you eat and drink? And here's to you and to all of us; and, as they say up North, may we never want anything, none of us!"

"Hear, hear to that!" agreed Chaney. "Good health and luck to both of you."

The tinker had poured his cool ale into four horn drinking-cups and handed them round. His wife, with a muttered expression of good wishes, drank her ale off at a draught, tossed the horn cup on the turf, and shot into activity. From the depths of the tilt-cart she produced a tablecloth, plates, knives and forks, spoons, and even napkins. Within five minutes the table laid spread on the level turf, and we settled down to eat as Roman patricians did in their days – reclining.

I do not know what was in the stew which presently smoked on our plates, but I do know that I had never before tasted anything so good, and that Chaney, who prided himself on being an epicure, grew almost lyrical in his enthusiasm and his praises. But our host and hostess only laughed when he tried to extract the secret recipe.

"Trick, master, trick!" said the tinker. "Trick of cooking. Us as lives in the open gets to know a great deal that isn't known to people who lives in houses. Herbs, now – if Nance there told you what she knows of the herb creation – ah, it would astonish you! Knowledge, master, as has come down is familiar from one old wife to another through as many generations as I have years. Another helping, master?"

There was a fine cherry tart to follow the stew, and Chaney had cigars in his pocket to follow the cherry tart (Mrs. Shepperoe, I am bound to say, filled and lighted a well-blackened clay pipe), and we had a pleasant hour of rest after our dinner, talking, mostly of the tinker's wanderings. But then came business; Mrs. Shepperoe began to wash up the crockery, and Shepperoe bade us follow him across the Levels. We left the hollow, and once more began to thread the path that wound in and out among the gorse and the coarse vegetation. Now and then, crossing some bit of rise, we caught glimpses of the sea; always we had about us the crying of sea-birds and the sharper note of the peewit's circling overhead.

All of a sudden the land dipped into a hollow, deeper, darker, more closely confined than that in which we had enjoyed the Shepperoes' unexpected hospitality. It was ringed about on all sides with a thick growth of old trees, chiefly oak, and was altogether an eerie and gloomy spot. Yet once upon a time it had been a scene of some human activity, for on one side of it stood the ruins of what had evidently been a small farmstead. There was a house and outbuildings, an enclosed garden, a well, the remains of a surrounding wall, the wreckage of a gateway or two. But everything was in a tumbledown state; the garden was a mass of weeds, thistles, nettles; the top-hamper of the well lay in a tangle of wood and iron about its mouth; the gable of the outbuilding had fallen before some forceful wind, and the roof of the house had gone, and laid, no doubt, a mass of beams and tiles within the four tottering walls. Not for a long time had anyone lived in that place.

"This is the place you mean?" asked Chaney, as we paused on the edge of the hollow.

"This it is, master," replied the tinker. "Piperscombe they call it. Been like this, all in mess and ruin, ever since me and the wife started coming into these parts, and that's a good many years ago."

"Who's it belong to?" inquired Chaney.

"It's on this Marbourne Park estate," answered the tinker. "Garsdale's. I reckon there came a time when nobody would take it – what is there for either sheep or cattle to eat on these Levels but bad, coarse stuff? And then it was just let go to wrack and ruin, as you see it. But now look here, masters – I said it was the proper place for a murder, didn't I? Well, now, you say this Skrimshaw had money on him. Supposing somebody knew that – somebody who was acquainted with his habit of walking across here to the Cod and Lobster at Marbourne Ferry? What better place than this to waylay, murder, and rob him?"

Chaney made no answer. He was looking about him. Suddenly he lifted a hand and pointed to something on the opposite rises of the hollow. Following his pointing finger, I became aware of two small bell-tents, set up on the edge of an overhanging coppice.

"Not so lonely as you think, Shepperoe," he said. "At present, at any rate. Those tents mean there's somebody camping out there. And they overlook this entire place."

"Quite right, master," agreed the tinker. "They do when there's anybody in them! But I know all about those two tents. They belong to two young fellows from Wrenchester – they've come here, camping out, for this last year or two. But they only come here weekends – Saturday afternoon to Monday morning. At all other times this dingle is as solitary as any place can be."

"Still," said Chaney, "this path, from Marbourne village to Marbourne Ferry, runs right through it."

"Yes, master, but there's precious few people come by this path," said the tinker. "You could follow it, the whole course, twenty times a day, in either direction, and never encounter a soul! And, as I say if a man wanted to waylay another man – here's the spot!"

"Well, let's have a look round," replied Chaney. He was obviously sceptical – but I knew why: he still clung to the opinion that Skrimshaw's journey had ended at Marbourne Park. "Let's see that well – perhaps the man's at the bottom of it!" I think he meant that as a joke, but one glance at the rusty iron and mouldering woodwork heaped over the mouth of the well showed us that nothing had disturbed either for many a long year. Nor was there anything to be seen anywhere about the ruined walls, inside or out, which suggested a basis for the tinker's ideas. And bidding him to keep his eyes and ears open, and to communicate with us if he ever heard or saw anything, we turned back by the way we had come, to get our car and return to Wrenchester.

As we entered the village street at Marbourne we were aware of the steady, solemn tolling of a bell in the tower of the church – a dismal, mournful tolling.

"Somebody dead?" asked Chaney of the first man we met.

The man turned a lifted thumb in the direction of Marbourne Park.

"Squire!" he answered. "Mr. Garsdale. Died just after two o'clock."

Chapter Sixteen

THE SQUIRE'S WILL

G OING INTO THE INN to settle with the landlord for garaging our car, we found the bar-parlour full of villagers; it still wanted half an hour to closing-time, and at Chaney's suggestion (he was always a keen hand at picking up anything he could chance on in the way of gossip) we ordered a drink and sat down to listen to what was being said – the topic of conversation, as we knew from the first overheard remark, being, of course, the death of the young Squire. Within a minute or two of our sitting down we became aware that the chief anxiety of the company was as to the disposition of the Garsdale property – who would come in for it?

"Because Squire, according to all accounts," one man was saying, "he hadn't no relations – not a single relative in this here entire wide world! Seems a strange-like thing to say of a man, but so I have heard. Neither wife nor child, nephew or niece, uncle, aunt, cousin – nobody! A lone man, that's what he was."

"That's true," said another reflectively. "I have been assured, time and again, he hadn't neither kith nor kin, as the saying is. Just himself. What they term last of his race. Which is a sad thing to think on, when you does come to think of it at all."

A third man set down his mug of beer with a thump, and turned a sceptical eye on the company.

"Ah!" he said, shaking his head. "I don't believe any of them tales! Ain't anybody in this here world as ain't got somebody in the way of relatives? If it ain't brothers and sisters it's cousins. I know what'll happen in this here case, like it does in all such. There will be relatives turning up from what they calls the uttermost part of the earth – foreign parts, like America and Africa, and then places where the missionaries goes. Where there is money to share out, as in this present circumstance, there will be them to claim it. Always – don't you make a mistake?"

"Makes bold for to say, mister, as how it's you as is making a mistake," remarked a fourth speaker. "'Tis well known as this here young Mr. Harry was the very last of his family – ain't another Garsdale, of his family at any rate, not nowheres, anywhere, in this created world, from one end to the other. That is known to all and sundry, and set up by the lawyers, so I've heard."

"Aye, it be right enough, that!" chorused several voices. "Been known to all us in Marbourne ever since young Harry comes into the property. Heard him say so himself, too, many a time," asserted a voice which emerged from the chorus. "And he'd know."

"Oh, aye, there ain't any doubt about it," said the first speaker. "Very last as ever was of them Garsdales he was. And so I says again what I did say to begin with – who will come in for the property and the money and all that mortal man is obliged to leave behind him in this here vale of tears, so to speak? Who'll get it?"

A dead silence followed this pertinent question, broken only by the lifting up and setting down again of mugs, tankards, and glasses. Then an old man, who sat in a corner, sucking at a short clay pipe, his face inscrutable, his eyes fixed on the floor, looked up. His expression was withering and sarcastic as he glanced round the ring of faces.

"If so be as any of you knew anything about the law," he said scornfully, "you would never ask such fool questions! But I can tell you where that property will all go – and no question about it!"

There was a murmur of appreciation from all but the man who had scouted the no-relations idea.

"Ah, you'll know, I'm sure, Master Appleyard," said one man. "I forgot you were present, sir – you were that quiet. And where will it all go, Master Appleyard?"

Mr. Appleyard took his pipe out of his mouth and spat into the sawdust.

"It will go," he answered irascibly, "where all suchlike property goes. To the King's Majesty!" An awestruck silence fell upon the bar-parlour; the landlord, polishing his glasses and pewter behind the bar, moved more softly.

"Ah!" said somebody. "So it goes to the King, Master Appleyard?"

"To the King!" asserted Mr. Appleyard. "His Majesty, which is law!"

In the midst of another silence, full of deep reflection, a new voice made itself heard.

"Seems a strange-like thing that, too!" said this voice. "What does the King want with another man's bit of property? He ain't a relative of Mr. Garsdale's as I ever heard of. What's the reason of it, Master Appleyard?"

"It is the law," replied Mr. Appleyard. "The law of this land."

"It ain't nawthen of the sort!" exclaimed the sceptical man in the other corner. "Master Appleyard, he doesn't know what he's talking about. It ain't the law, no how. What Master Appleyard says is right if a man dies what they call intestate. If he dies intestate – "

"What might that there word signify?" interrupted somebody.

"It does signify if you die without making a will," replied Mr. Appleyard's opponent. "If you don't make any last will and testament, and you ain't got any relations of a sort whatsoever, then your estate does go to the King. But if you do make a will and testament, then the King he doesn't come in anywhere – you leave your money and property to whoever you like."

"Yes," said somebody. "I always did understand as how those as has money could leave it to whosoever they please. And so that's the proper law, is it, Mr. Chipwood?"

"It is!" answered Mr. Chipwood. "The pure and unadulterated! And what do you say to that, Mr. Appleyard?"

"I say you be a litigious fool," retorted Mr. Appleyard. "You don't know nawthen at all about the law!"

Mr. Chipwood began to smile – unpleasantly.

"No, I am not a litigious fool, Mr. Appleyard," he said. "An 'tis you as don't know nawthen about the law, nawthen!"

"I know all about the law!" exclaimed Mr. Appleyard indignantly. "I bin' at 'Sizes afore ever you was born!"

"Dessay you have, Mr. Appleyard," said Mr. Chipwood teasingly, "Dessay you have, sir. But excuse me asking a little question. Were you on the Bench, Mr. Appleyard, or were you in the dock? Because –"

Here the landlord thought it well to intervene.

"Order, order, gentlemen!" he said. "No personalities, gentlemen. Five minutes to three, gentlemen – any further orders before closing time?"

Chaney paid our garage fee, and we went out into the village street. And there, a few yards away from the front of the inn, we saw Beecher, who was talking to the carpenter at the door of the latter's shop. Beecher caught sight of us and came forward.

"I suppose you have heard of Mr. Garsdale's death?" he said quietly.

"We have," replied Chaney.

"It was only what we had been expecting for some days," remarked Beecher. "It was – inevitable!"

"An unhappy career!" said Chaney. He hesitated a moment, watching Beecher narrowly. "Last of his family, wasn't he?" he added. "The very last?"

"Not a blood-relation in the world," assented Beecher. Chaney nodded at the inn.

"In there," he said, "there's a gathering of village wiseacres exercising their wits on the question of whether Mr. Garsdale made a will, and what'll happen to the property."

"He did make a will, some little time ago," replied Beecher. "To what effect I, of course, don't know. But I hope he's remembered his servants in it – we've had enough to do for him, I can assure you! My wife and I are about worn out. Good morning, gentlemen – I'm arranging about the funeral."

He made us a polite bow and turned back to the carpenter, and Chaney and I got our car out of the innyard and set off to Wrenchester.

Nothing happened for the next three or four days. We were at work every day endeavouring to trace Skrimshaw, and all our efforts were unavailing – Skrimshaw, for all we heard of him, might have been dissolved into vapour. Then, on the fifth day after our visit to Marbourne Levels and the traveling tinker, Bailiss sent for us one afternoon. We found him in his office, and he looked at us with a queer expression.

"Heard anything?" he asked.

"We?" I answered. "No!"

"Um!" he said. "Well, I don't know – seems a bit – however, I have! Harry Garsdale was buried this morning. Canon Revington buried him, at Marbourne; it's he who's given me this information. When the funeral was over Clayning, who was present, asked Canon Revington and two or three other gentlemen to go back with him to Marbourne Park – Clayning, I should tell you, was the family solicitor to the Garsdales. Well, when they got there Clayning informed them that he had Harry Garsdale's will in his pocket, and as there were no relations he invited them to hear it read. He then read it, after – just mark this! – telling them that not a soul in the world except him and the two witnesses to the will knew its contents. It was a very short will, according to Canon Revington – practically no more than a sentence. Harry Garsdale left everything he had – land, money, stocks and everything – to Mr. and Mrs. Beecher!"

"Good God!" muttered Chaney. "Everything?"

"Everything!" said Bailiss.

We were all three silent for a minute or two. Then a thought occurred to me.

"Did Canon Revington see the will?" I asked.

"Yes," replied Bailiss. "Clayning showed it round."

"Who were the witnesses?" I inquired. "Did he tell you that?"

"Yes," answered Bailiss. "Clayning's two clerks. Skrimshaw was one; Sharpies the other."

"I wonder if they knew the contents." I said.

"I'll bet Skrimshaw did!" exclaimed Bailiss. "Trust him! The will's been in Clayning's custody ever since it was made, and Skrimshaw was Clayning's confidential clerk."

"Did Canon Revington tell you what happened after Clayning had read the will?" asked Chaney.

"Yes," replied Bailiss. "Clayning fetched in Mr. and Mrs. Beecher and read it to them. Mrs. Beecher nearly fainted, and then began to cry. Beecher looked as if he couldn't believe his ears. Canon Revington assured me that he watched them both narrowly – and the Canon's no fool, I can tell you! – and he's convinced that the news came to them as an absolute surprise."

"I suppose – if anyone attempted it – the will couldn't be upset?" suggested Chaney. "Even if relations turned up?"

"I raised that point with the Canon," replied Bailiss. "He says that Clayning assured him that you could no more upset that will than you could melt the Arctic regions with a bucket of boiling water! So there you are. Marbourne Park belongs to Mr. and Mrs. Beecher."

Chaney and I were so much surprised by this news that we forgot to tell Bailiss (whom we had not seen in the interval) about our encounter with Shepperoe and our investigations near his encampment; we went away from his office in silence, and in silence had walked nearly to the Mitre before Chaney spoke.

"Camberwell," he said, "I don't like this at all. It strengthens my suspicion about Beecher. I don't place any reliance on Canon Revington's impression of Beecher and his wife: I think they're both clever enough to do a bit of real good acting."

"You don't believe the terms of the will came as a surprise to them?" I said.

"Frankly I don't!" replied Chaney. "I think Beecher knew. And I think Skrimshaw knew. Now, then, figure this out – Skrimshaw found, in that S. G. envelope, a will made by Samuel Garsdale, in which Samuel devised his property otherwise than to his nephew Harry. Knowing that Harry was rapidly drinking himself to death – knowing, also, the terms of Harry's will – what more likely than that Skrimshaw approached Beecher and told him what he'd discovered –

that Harry had no right to the property, and therefore couldn't leave it to Beecher? What more probable than that Beecher made an end of Skrimshaw and possessed himself of Skrimshaw's weapon – the contents of the S. G. envelope? Yet – how to get any evidence against Beecher licks me!"

It was at this point that we came to a sort of standstill. Some little time went by. Nothing was heard of Skrimshaw. Bailiss made no progress. Neither did we. Once or twice we relinquished the job and were busy in London on other cases. But we kept going back to Wrenchester, at Aubrey Snowe's request. We were down there about six weeks after Harry Garsdale's death, and heard news of the Marbourne Park estate. Beecher was selling it; he and his wife were going to live at Brighton. Indeed, they had already left Marbourne Park. The house was closed; all the servants had been dismissed.

It was one of the dismissed servants, a young, smart-looking woman, who called on Chaney and me one afternoon at the Mitre, saying she had been sent to us by Canon Revington.

Chapter Seventeen

WHERE WAS HE?

I THINK CHANEY AND I both had a pretty good notion of our visitor's object in coming to see us; all the same, we looked at her with a good deal of curiosity. As I have already said, she was a smart-looking young woman, pretty, demure, intelligent, and, as far as my limited experience of femininity went, dependable. And as she was evidently somewhat nervous and shy I left my more experienced partner to do the talking.

"Come from Canon Revington, eh?" began Chaney. "And – your name?"

"Matilda Ayres, sir."

"Any message from Canon Revington?" asked Chaney.

"No, sir. Canon Revington said that I was to come and see you, and mention his name and tell you what I'd told him. He said it would be better to see you than to go to the Superintendent – as I didn't want things talking about."

"I see!" said Chaney. "Yes? And what is it you don't want talking about?"

Our visitor – whom I had accommodated with our easiest chair – fidgeted a bit with her umbrella.

"Well, you see, sir, what I told Canon Revington was about something that I saw at Marbourne Park, the late Mr. Garsdale's place –"

"Stop a bit," interrupted Chaney. "Were you living at Marbourne Park in Mr. Garsdale's time?"

"I was parlourmaid there, sir. I didn't leave until Mr. and Mrs. Beecher left the place. I – I didn't like to tell you what I've told to Canon Revington until I'd left. Perhaps I ought to have told before. But I was frightened."

"Of whom? Of what?" asked Chaney?

"Mr. and Mrs. Beecher, sir. I daren't speak while – while I was in the same house with them."

"I see," said Chaney. "Well, you needn't be afraid here, Matilda. You can tell us anything you like, in strict confidence."

"So Canon Revington said, sir – else I wouldn't have come. Of course, sir, I went to him because he's a clergyman, and he's Vicar of Marbourne too."

"Exactly!" agreed Chaney. "Well, now, what was it you told him, Matilda? Let's have it – all of it."

Matilda trifled a little more with the umbrella; then she faced up to her job.

"Well, sir, of course, there's been a lot of talk all round the place about the disappearance of that Mr. Skrimshaw," she began. "It's been said that the very last people to see him were Harry Hall and some other of those fellows that play cricket in Marbourne Park, hasn't it, sir?"

"That's so, Matilda," agreed Chaney. "Quite right!"

"Well, it's all wrong, sir. I saw him after that – I mean, after they had seen him."

"When – and where?" asked Chaney.

"Same night, sir, and close by where they saw him. But some minutes later. Do you know Marbourne Park, sir – house and gardens?"

"We've been in the house, and we have had a look into the gardens, and we have crossed the Park several times," replied Chaney.

"Well, sir, perhaps you haven't noticed a summer-house that stands at the end of the gardens, close to where you get off the Park on to what they call the Levels? It's right at the end of the Yew Walk, in a corner. You can see out of it on to the Park in one direction, and on to the Levels in another. An old, ramshackle place, with a thatched roof, sir."

"I've seen it," said I, intervening for the first time. "It's near the wicket-gate by which you get from the Park to the Levels."

Matilda's face brightened.

"That's it, sir! Well, I was in that summer-house the night that Harry Hall saw Mr. Skrimshaw in the Park, and –"

"A moment!" interrupted Chaney. "Were you alone?" Matilda's already brightly coloured cheeks reddened a little.

"No, sir, I wasn't!" she said.

"Sweetheart there too, eh?" suggested Chaney.

"Yes, sir. I would slip out to meet him there – of course, I oughtn't to have been out at all. But I knew he would be there, and – well, I did slip out. And it was while we were there that I saw Mr. Skrimshaw. He was coming along the path that leads from the cricket-ground to the wicket-gate."

"By himself?" asked Chaney.

"Yes, sir. He was carrying a little case in one hand and a stick in the other. Of course, I wasn't surprised to see him. My – my young man and I, sir, we've often met in that summer-house, because nobody ever goes there from the house, and we'd seen Mr. Skrimshaw more than once. My young man, sir, says that Mr. Skrimshaw used to go that way to the Cod and Lobster at Marbourne Ferry."

"Quite right – he did," said Chaney. "Well, what next?"

"Well, sir," continued Matilda, "just after we'd seen Mr. Skrimshaw coming along we heard footsteps on one of the garden walks close by the summer-house. And all of a sudden Mr. Beecher walked past the summer-house. He never turned his head to look inside as he passed, or he would have seen us but he went straight on. And as he turned the corner of the Yew Walk he and Mr. Skrimshaw met – just near the wicket-gate. Of course, we saw them meet, plainly."

"Did you hear them talk?" asked Chaney.

"We heard them talking, sir, but not to catch a word – they were too far off. Besides, they didn't stop when they met."

"What did they do?" inquired Chaney.

"They went through the wicket-gate, sir, and away by the path across Marbourne Levels."

"Together?"

"Yes, sir – side by side, talking. And in a minute they were out of sight among the bushes."

"And that was the last you saw of them together?"

"Yes, sir."

Chaney considered matters during a moment's silence.

"Is that all, then?" he asked, giving the girl a sharp look. "Is there more?"

"There is more, sir! That's why I went to Canon Revington. You see, sir – Mr. Beecher never came home that night."

Chaney screwed up his lips. I thought he was going to let out a whistle of astonishment. Suddenly his lips relaxed again, and he looked at me. I understood that look; Chaney was signaling to me that at last we were getting at something of real importance.

"Ah!" he said, again giving his attention to our visitor. "So Mr. Beecher didn't come home that night?"

"No, sir!"

"Were you in a position to know that?"

Matilda Ayres seemed to be puzzled by this question, and Chaney supplemented it by another.

"I mean, couldn't Mr. Beecher have come in without your knowing it? He might have come in very late, for instance."

But Matilda shook her head.

"Well, sir, all I can say is that I'm sure he didn't!" she answered. "You see, sir, it was my duty to wait on Mr. and Mrs. Beecher – I always waited on them, instead of the menservants attending to them. And when I was laying the table for their supper that night, in their private sitting-room, the telephone bell rang – the telephone is in Mr. Beecher's office, close by. Mrs. Beecher answered the ring. I heard her talking for a minute or two, and then she came back and said that I needn't lay for Mr. Beecher, for he was going to stay the night with a friend that he'd gone to see."

"Did she mention the friend's name?" inquired Chaney.

"No, sir."

"Have you any idea who the friend would be?"

"No, sir. Mr. Beecher did go out for the night sometimes."

"Well, what about his return. When did he come home?"

"Next morning, sir. He walked in while Mrs. Beecher was having breakfast."

"You didn't hear him say where he'd been?"

"No, sir, I didn't."

"Were you one of the servants – there were several of you – that I questioned when I came to inquire about Skrimshaw at Marbourne Park?" asked Chaney. "I don't remember you, Matilda."

"I was there, sir. You spoke to the women servants in the servants' hall."

"Why didn't you tell me then what you're telling now?" said Chaney.

"Well, sir, for one thing, you didn't ask if any one of us had seen Mr. Skrimshaw! You asked if any of us knew whether Mr. Skrimshaw had called at the house that Thursday evening. Of course, he hadn't – at least, not to my knowledge. And I didn't dare to tell you I'd seen him."

"Why not?"

"Because I was afraid of Mr. Beecher, sir. I didn't know what he might say. Mr. Beecher, sir, was a regular tyrant in that house. We were all mortal afraid of him, and of Mrs. Beecher too."

Chaney gave Matilda Ayres another thoughtful inspection.

"I dare say you could tell some tales about Marbourne Park?" he said.

"I could, sir!"

"Queer tales, perhaps?" suggested Chaney.

"Queer enough, sir!"

"Well, Matilda, we may ask you to tell them to us – presently," said Chaney. "But not just now. And as regards what you've just told us, don't tell it to anybody else. Leave me your address, and when I want you I'll write. Don't forget, now, my girl – keep all this to yourself!"

Matilda gave us her address and her faithful promise, and went away; and when she had gone Chaney got up and put on his hat.

"Come on, Camberwell," he said, "we've got to tell all that to Bailiss. I see no reason to doubt that girl's story, and it only confirms my suspicion about Beecher. Beecher, Camberwell, has got to explain his movements that night!"

We found Bailiss in his office, and Chaney told him what we had heard. Bailiss began to be doubtful about his own theories.

"Then – then you think Beecher has something to do with Skrimshaw's disappearance?" he asked. "That – if he'd liked – he could have told us something when we called on him that morning at Marbourne Park?"

Chaney did not reply to this question immediately. Instead, he motioned to me to walk with him to the farthest side of the room.

"Shall I tell Bailiss what my theory is?" he whispered. "Seems to me we've got to a stage when it's useless – and might be foolish – to keep anything back."

"I agree," said I. "Tell him, Chaney."

We went back to Bailiss's desk, from which he had been regarding us with looks of astonishment.

"Look here, Bailiss," said Chaney, "I'm going to be frank with you. You think that Skrimshaw took his hook that night, and has managed to get clear away. I told you I didn't – I said I believed Skrimshaw was to be found within a few miles of Wrenchester. But I didn't say whether alive or dead, did I?"

Bailiss started. "Alive or dead?" he exclaimed. "You don't mean?"

"My belief, Bailiss, is that Skrimshaw's dead, and that he was murdered!" continued Chaney. "Listen! I think that envelope marked S. G. contained something which, brought to light, would have made some tremendous difference in the ownership or ultimate disposition of the Garsdale property – a will made by Samuel Garsdale, perhaps, and discovered by Mr. Alfred Snowe, who confided the secret to Skrimshaw. I think that Skrimshaw imparted his knowledge to Beecher, and that Beecher got rid of Skrimshaw in order to secure the document, or whatever it was, and to destroy it. That's my idea, anyway, Bailiss."

"In a few words, you think Beecher killed Skrimshaw that night?" asked Bailiss. "Is that it?"

"It is! It looks like it, anyhow," said Chaney. "I think he got rid of Skrimshaw somewhere on the Levels, and then, to give people the impression that Skrimshaw had absconded, went along to Marbourne Ferry, taking Skrimshaw's silver-topped stick with him, stole Ready's boat, and went across the creek. He left the stick in the boat as a blind, walked into Kingsport, stayed the night there, and returned home next morning. That, Bailiss, is how I figure things."

"I know where Beecher is," said Bailiss. "He and Mrs. Beecher are at the United Empire Hotel at Brighton – they're living there till they can find a house to suit them. We'd better get into my car and go there at once – it's only an hour's run. We oughtn't to let this thing slide –"

Just then the telephone bell rang, and Bailiss went over to where the instrument was fixed and picked up the receiver. For a minute or so we heard nothing but exclamations of surprise from him; then suddenly came a more decisive note.

"All right – coming at once!" he said. Then he turned to us. "Well," he exclaimed, "you're right, Chaney! They've found Skrimshaw's dead body – on Marbourne Levels!"

Chapter Eighteen

FOUND

B AILISS HURRIED US OFF to Marbourne Levels at once, stopping a moment in the town to leave a message for Dr. Wellsted; a second car, with three plain-clothes men, followed us. As there
was no road across that part of the Levels, we had to leave the cars
at a point near Marbourne Ferry and cross the marshland on foot.
Before we reached Piperscombe we became aware that the news had
spread; near the ruins of the old farmstead quite a number of people
moved about against the skyline, and as we drew close we noticed one
person in particular – the reporter of the Wrenchester paper whom I
remembered as having tackled Aubrey Snowe when he left his uncle's
house in Little Straightway on the morning after the old gentleman's
death. And tapping Bailiss's elbow, I pointed out this busily engaged
individual.

"There's a man there who's got to be silenced, Bailiss!" I said. "That
reporter chap!"

"Why?" asked Bailiss, a little puzzled. "Can't muzzle him, I'm
afraid."

"We've just got to," I said. "There mustn't be a word of this in the
papers before we've found and interviewed Beecher. If Beecher saw

that Skrimshaw's body had been found he'd be off. Leave this reporter to me."

"Camberwell's right," said Chaney. "We mustn't let any news out till Beecher's been seen."

Bailiss nodded his assent, and while he and Chaney went on to the main group of bystanders I made up to the reporter, who, notebook in hand, was busily questioning Shepperoe. Motioning the tinker away, and giving him what I meant to be an understanding look, I drew the representative of the Press aside. His face fell when I had explained my mission. I knew, of course, what he was after – he was keen on a big scoop.

"But the reason, the reason, Mr. Camberwell?" he exclaimed. "To suppress news, sir, news of this sort –"

"Look here!" I said. "If the news of this discovery is in tonight's papers – and I suppose it could be –"

"Plenty of time for tonight's late edition, Mr. Camberwell," he said. "That's what I'm after. There's a telegraph office close at hand – two, in fact: one in the village, another at the Ferry. I wanted –"

"If the news of this is in tonight's papers," I repeated, "the ends of justice will be – you understand? You'll spoil everything."

"But why – why, Mr. Camberwell?" he persisted. "Spoil? My scoop will be spoiled!"

"This is why," I said, as gravely as possible. "Before midnight we hope to lay hands on the man whom we believe to be the murderer."

He jumped at that – visibly.

"Murder?" he exclaimed. "You think it's murder, then? But there isn't a mark on the body! Murder? Nobody's said it's murder!"

That fairly nonplussed me; I stood looking at the reporter in perplexity. He waved his pencil towards the group of men which Shepperoe had now rejoined.

"Go look for yourself," he said. "Not a pleasant sight, but there's nothing to show that the man was shot, or stabbed, or beaten to death. Murder? Well, now, nobody's said it was murder, so far."

At that moment Dr. Wellsted, who had followed us in his car, came hurrying up, and I joined him and went forward to where Bailiss, Chaney, and the policemen were gathered about the dead man. What remained of Skrimshaw was not good to look upon; that part of the Levels was infested with small animals that would readily prey on anything, and after a glance I turned away. The doctor was thicker-skinned; besides, it was his job. And in a minute or two he confirmed what the reporter had said – there were no marks to show that Skrimshaw had succumbed to any murderer's assault.

"Who found him, and where?" asked Dr. Wellsted. Shepperoe stepped forward.

"I found him, master," he replied. "Leastways, my dog did. He was nosing about in that coppice and – well, he come across him, lying in the undergrowth, and in course he made such a fuss, that dog did, that I went in to see what he was after. Wonder nobody thought of looking in there – he was scarce covered up, though whoever would put him there had done a bit that way."

"Not much," remarked the local constable. "He was easy to see."

"You shouldn't have moved him till I came," said Bailiss, a little testily. "You shouldn't have touched him."

The village constable muttered something about it being mainly dark in that coppice, and his opinion that it would be better to bring it into the light.

"Did you find anything lying near him?" asked Bailiss. "He's known to have had a small case with him, and a stick."

"There was nothing, master," said Shepperoe. "Nothing! I made a careful search myself. There was just him. But," he added, with a meaning look, "He'd been taken there! Dragged there – or carried there."

"I wonder!" said the doctor reflectively. "I was thinking – as there's no outward sign of violence that I can see, at present – and I'm sure there isn't – that he may have had a seizure, and laid down, and so died. But he'd scarcely have gone into that coppice to lie down if a seizure had come on suddenly. Of course, there'll have to be an inquest – and an autopsy – and –"

"What parish is this in?" asked Bailiss suddenly.

"Marbourne," replied the local policeman. "All this part's in Marbourne, Superintendent."

"He'll have to be removed there for the inquest," said Bailiss. "Some of you must see to that at once. But before you do that I want to know if there's anything on him. Robinson, go through his clothing."

Robinson, a young plain-clothes man, showed no special inclination to perform this gruesome task, but on the principle that duty is duty he proceeded to undertake it at once. And from Skrimshaw's soaked and tattered garments he brought out a lot of things – a gold watch and chain; money in pulpy notes and tarnished silver; an old pocket-book, stuffed with papers, and various small articles of the sort that most men carry about them. Bailiss took charge of these, and while he was making a note of them Dr. Wellsted, Chaney, and I drew aside and talked.

"Got any theory, doctor?" asked Chaney.

The doctor shook his head.

"I don't see any marks of violence," he answered.

"I'm wondering – it's mere speculation, of course – if he's been poisoned?"

"Poisoned!" exclaimed Chaney. "What, by somebody? Or by himself?"

"Either," replied Dr. Wellsted. "But we shall find that out at the autopsy. He hasn't been shot or stabbed, or anything of that sort – that's quite certain. Of course, as I said before, he may have had what people call a seizure. I didn't know him, so I can't say if he was a likely subject. He may have had a weak heart. But if it's a case of murder I should say – poison. We shall see."

Bailiss came up. And after him came the reporter.

"I've done everything that's immediately necessary," said Bailiss, nodding at the doctor. "You'll make your own arrangements, of course, about that *post-mortem*; I'll have the coroner notified." Then he turned to Chaney and me.

"Come on!" he said, in an undertone. "Let's be off! You know where – Brighton!"

The reporter seized my sleeve. His look was almost imploring.

"Can't I get to work, Mr. Camberwell?" he asked plaintively. "If it's murder, sir –"

"It's just because it may be murder," I answered. "But look here – go back to your office and get your stuff written up. Wait for a telephone message from me. As soon as possible I'll send you a mere word – proceed! When you get that go ahead as hard as you like."

"But when, Mr. Camberwell, when?" he asked eagerly.

I made a hurried calculation. We should be in Brighton in an hour. If we found Beecher there – "Within three hours," I said. "Perhaps within two. Anyway, as quickly as possible. And look here – when you get back to Wrenchester don't spread the news. How did you get to know of it at all?"

"Village policeman telephoned us," he answered. "We give those chaps a little bonus now and then, do you see, Mr. Camberwell. Much obliged to you, sir."

Bailiss was waving me impatiently to come away: he was all eagerness to get to Brighton and Beecher. But I went after Shepperoe, who, with his wife, was going towards their encampment.

"Shepperoe," I said as I joined them, "what's become of the tents that were up there? I see they're gone."

"Man came from Wrenchester this morning, took them down, and carried them off in a cart, master," he answered. "I reckon the two young fellows have had enough of it – they weren't here last weekend, neither."

"You still don't know who they were?" I asked.

"Never heard their names, master," he said. "We'd no truck with them. Know nothing of them beyond seeing them about now and then."

I left him and Mrs. Shepperoe and hurried with Bailiss and Chaney across to the car. Bailiss was evidently bent on business.

"Thirty miles to Brighton!" he remarked, as he laid hands on the wheel. "I'll do it in an hour, for all we've two or three towns to go through. We must see Beecher before he gets to know of this afternoon's work!"

He slewed his car round and set off at a fine pace; there was scarcely any traffic on those by-roads, and he made the most of his opportunities till we struck the Kingsport-Wrenchester highway at the Marbourne signpost. And in the back seat Chaney and I, bumping against each other, made some effort to discuss what we had just seen and heard.

"Strange business this, Camberwell," said Chaney. "Not a mark on the body I wonder if there's anything in that idea of the doctor's? Poison? And if it is poison – there's no reason known to us why Skrimshaw should have poisoned himself. And if Beecher saw him alive that night, and if he died that night – as he must have done, considering what we know about the theft of Ready's boat and the finding of Skrimshaw's stick in it later – who could have poisoned him in the interval between his meeting with Beecher and his arriving at the spot at which his body was found?"

"One must do a little more supposing, Chaney," I said. "Supposing Beecher knew what it was that Skrimshaw had on him – the S. G. papers, whatever they were – that Skrimshaw had taken him into his confidence? Supposing that Beecher was bent on getting them – that he accompanied Skrimshaw on his walk – that he contrived to give him poison – say, a drink out of a pocket-flask? There was nothing, then, to prevent Beecher from possessing himself of whatever it was that Skrimshaw carried, hiding the body, and going on to Marbourne Ferry to appropriate the landlord's boat, cross the creek, and leave Skrimshaw's stick in the boat as a blind. We know, at any rate, that Beecher never went home that night."

"Maybe," agreed Chaney, "but it's all supposition, and the devil of it is that nobody but Beecher really knows! And you may bet your life that Beecher won't tell!"

Bailiss heard the last remark. He flung one of his own over his shoulder.

"We'll see about that!" he exclaimed. "If Beecher can't give me a satisfactory explanation of that girl's story, and account for himself that night, back he comes to Wrenchester! Even if it's with bracelets on! He's lied to us once, but he won't do it again."

"Um!" muttered Chaney. "Bit optimistic, aren't you, Bailiss? My experience is that men who lie once go on lying!"

"Not to me!" declared Bailiss, with a grim face. "Once is enough! Mr. Beecher will see that I mean business – when we meet."

But it was not ordained that Bailiss and Beecher should meet – that night, at any rate. We pulled up in front of the hotel at which

Beecher and his wife were staying in Brighton within seventy minutes of leaving Marbourne Levels – good time and we lost none in entering the palatial reception-hall and stating our business at the office. The clerk in charge shook his head.

"Mr. and Mrs. Beecher left for Paris yesterday," he replied to Bailiss's question. "But," he added, seeing his questioner's disappointment, "they'll be back here in about ten days – they've rebooked their rooms here."

"That's unfortunate," said Bailiss. "Most important business with Mr. Beecher, and we fully expected to find him here. You can give me his Paris address, perhaps?"

The clerk consulted a book.

"Letters," he said, "are to be forwarded to the Grand Hotel – for a week from now."

We sat down in the lounge, ordered some tea, and consulted on our next move. We had to decide quickly – with the help of a Bradshaw's railway guide. And eventually we decided that Bailiss should return to Wrenchester, and that Chaney and I should catch the night boat across-Channel at Newhaven – that would get us to Paris early next morning, before the newspapers were out.

Bailiss could wire or telephone us at an address we would give him on arrival if anything important turned up. So Bailiss returned home, and Chaney and I went round from Brighton to Newhaven and had a night's journey by boat and rail, and at an early hour next day presented ourselves at the Grand Hotel and asked for the man we wanted. And here again came a stoppage – Mr. and Mrs. Beecher had gone the day before to Fontainebleau, where they were staying the night. But, added the clerk, they would be back at the hotel early that evening.

Chapter Nineteen

ALIBI!

C HANEY AND I LOAFED about Paris all that day, chafing at our enforced idleness, and made all the more anxious because the Paris edition of the *Daily Mail* contained the news of the discovery of Skrimshaw's dead body – a bare announcement of the fact, without any details. And by five o'clock in the evening we had posted ourselves in the hall of the Grand Hotel, on the look-out for the return of Mr. and Mrs. Beecher. Just before six they came in, and immediately caught sight of us: Beecher, calm and collected as if he were in the habit of meeting us every day, at once came forward.

"So Skrimshaw has been found?" he said carelessly.

"That's just why we're here, Mr. Beecher," replied Chaney. "As you may already have guessed."

"I thought your presence might be explained by what I read in the *Daily Mail* this morning," answered Beecher, nonchalant as ever. "You want to have some talk with me? Yes? Then come up to my rooms."

He led us to a lift, up which Mrs. Beecher had already ascended. In silence we went up to the third floor; in silence he conducted us along a corridor and to an open door, and into an elegantly fitted sitting-room; as we entered it Mrs. Beecher was disappearing into the bedroom beyond. She closed the door; we were alone with Beecher. He motioned us to chairs; then pointed to a sideboard, on which stood a spirit-case and mineral waters.

"Have a drink?" he asked. "Whisky and soda?"

"Not at present, thank you," replied Chaney. "Business first. Mr. Beecher, we've come especially to Paris to see you – on behalf of Superintendent Bailiss, and, of course, on our own."

"Long way to come!" remarked Beecher, somewhat sarcastically. "But since you have come – why?"

"You will remember that Bailiss, my partner Mr. Camberwell, and I called on you at Marbourne Park a little while ago," said Chaney. "We wanted to get some information from you as regards Skrimshaw."

"You wanted to know if Skrimshaw had been to Marbourne Park – that is, to the house – on the evening on which he was seen by some village lads near the cricket-ground," said Beecher. "You got your information. Skrimshaw had not been to the house."

"We asked you if you'd seen him that night," began Chaney.

Beecher lifted a warning finger.

"Pardon me!" he said. "You never did anything of the sort! You asked me if Skrimshaw had come to the house during the evening of his disappearance. I said not to my knowledge. I let you question the servants – your question and their answer –"

"All that," interrupted Chaney, "sounds like quibbling. Did you see him?"

Beecher, who had lighted a cigarette and was calmly smoking, nodded.

"I did!" he said.

"Why didn't you tell us?" asked Chaney.

"Why should I tell you?" retorted Beecher. "It was no part of my business to assist Bailiss, and as for you, Mr. Chaney, and your partner Mr. Camberwell, I didn't know why I should assist you either. Had you or Bailiss asked me, categorically, if I had seen Skrimshaw that evening I should have replied that I had seen him."

"We know now that you did!" remarked Chaney. "We've evidence of that." Beecher smiled.

"Oh!" he said, cynical as ever. "You'll have got that from one of the servants. Am I right?"

"I don't mind saying that you are," replied Chaney. "We know that you were seen to meet Skrimshaw near the gate which leads from the Park into the Levels, and to walk on with him across the Levels."

"For – how far?" asked Beecher, smiling. "Do you know that, Mr. Chaney?"

"For how far? No!" replied Chaney.

"Then I'll tell you," said Beecher. "Perhaps forty, perhaps fifty, yards. And then we parted, having exchanged no more speech than was necessary to discuss the weather prospects of the next few days."

"Where did Skrimshaw go then?" asked Chaney.

"Straight before his nose, Mr. Chaney – on the path that leads across Marbourne Levels to Marbourne Ferry, by way of Piper-scombe," replied Beecher.

"And – you?" inquired Chaney.

Beecher laughed, and, throwing away his cigarette, got up and went over to the sideboard.

"Come!" he said. "I see I shall have to tell you the whole story. It would be too bad to let you come to Paris for nothing. But have a drink first; then I'll tell you all about it."

We let him give us a drink; Beecher was one of those men who seem able to get their own way in their dealings with other men. He filled a glass for himself and sat down with it in his hand.

"Don't go through the farce of wishing me good luck, Chaney!" he said, with one of his sarcastic smiles. "You're probably hoping to take me back to England and get me hanged. You won't, of course! However, that's neither here nor there at present. You want to know about that night – that very important night? Now, first, what do you already know?"

Chaney was becoming a little surly; he had a tiring night and a tiring day; also, he thought Beecher was pulling his leg.

"We know that you met Skrimshaw," he replied, in his grumpiest accents, "and that you never came home – you were out all night."

"Ah, servants again!" assented Beecher calmly. "But quite true – I did not go home that night. Now for the plain truth. Have you, or either of you, ever heard of Sandside Farm, on Marbourne Levels? No? Well, it's there, on the east side, close to the sea. Sandside Farm is the most important holding on the Garsdale – I mean on my – estate. Recently it was let to a friend of mine, John Merrick – make a note of his name, Mr. Camberwell. Now, on the night we're talking about I decided to go over to see Merrick, just to hear if he'd settled in all right; I telephoned him that I was coming, and at what time. I set off about dusk. As I reached the gate between the Park and the Levels I encountered Skrimshaw. He was carrying his usual little case and his silver-topped stick. We walked on a few yards in company; he said he was going to Marbourne Ferry. Forty or fifty yards from the gate our paths diverged; he went right, I went left. We parted – and I never saw him again."

Chaney was sitting twiddling his thumbs; up to now he had left his whisky and soda untouched. He was watching Beecher intently.

"Could you prove that?" he asked suddenly. "If you could –"

"Very fortunately I can!" said Beecher quietly. "John Merrick, knowing what time I was setting off, had walked across the Levels to meet me. He came up just as I and Skrimshaw parted. I went away with him, and he can prove to you that from that moment until ten o'clock next morning, when he set me down at my own door, having driven me over from Sandside Farm on his way to Wrenchester, I was never out of his sight; I stayed the night at his house. That's the plain truth, and the whole story. So, you see, Mr. Chaney, I didn't murder Skrimshaw – if he was murdered, as the newspapers seem to suggest." Chaney picked up his glass, drank off the contents, and rose.

"I never said you did, Mr. Beecher," he answered. "And I don't know that Skrimshaw was murdered, though the doctor thinks he was poisoned. But I think you might have told us all this when we called at Marbourne Park. However, may I ask if you're staying long in Paris?"

"Between a week and ten days," replied Beecher. "Not quite so long, if my wife's finished her shopping."

"And then?" asked Chaney.

"Back to Brighton," said Beecher. "We shall be at the Grand Hotel there until we've found a house to suit us. I'm selling the Marbourne Park estate. I couldn't live there for anything."

"Your evidence will be wanted, you know," said Chaney. "At the inquest, I mean – the adjourned inquest. Bailiss will let you know when."

"I'm at Bailiss's service," said Beecher. "When I get back."

We went away then. Outside, Chaney took me by the elbow.

"Camberwell," he said, "I want to think all that over. We'll have to stay in Paris for the night. But not there. We'll leave Beecher alone for a bit. I know a likely spot where I stopped last time I was here – the

Petersburg, Rue Caumartin. Come round there – only a street or two away. We'll have a comfortable dinner and a good night's rest."

We went round to the St Petersburg and booked a couple of rooms. Chaney was grumpy; a good dinner, eaten leisurely, and a good cigar after it did little to restore his equanimity. I knew what was the matter with him; he had gradually come to believe firmly in his theory about Beecher, and now it was being upset.

"After all, Camberwell," he said, breaking into speech after a long fit of silence, "we've only Beecher's word for it! I mean, as regards his explanation about his movements and whereabouts that night. And we don't know this man Merrick that he speaks of. Merrick might be – well, another Beecher. The two of them might have got rid of Skrimshaw for purposes of their own. If only we knew what it was that Skrimshaw had on him – what was in the S. G. envelope originally! I still cling to the idea that it was a will – a will in which old Samuel left his estates and property elsewhere, in which case it wasn't in Harry Garsdale's power to leave Beecher anything. But it may have been something other than a will."

"Such as what, Chaney?" I asked.

"Oh, I don't know, Camberwell! Money in some form or other," he replied. "Haven't we heard that old Samuel was a miser? Well, misers are up to all manner of tricks. For anything we know there might be a mere scrap of paper in that envelope which would be worth no end to a finder. No! – I'm not satisfied. Beecher's such a plausible chap. And damned clever!"

"What do you propose to do, Chaney?" I asked.

"I've been thinking," he answered. "I think a watch ought to be kept on Beecher until we're certain that he's been telling the straight tale about that night. If he has – well, I shall be prepared to say I've been wrong. But I want to know! So I suggest that I go back by the early train tomorrow morning, and get along to Wrenchester at once and see Merrick, leaving you here to keep an eye on Beecher. As soon as I've seen Merrick I'll 'phone or wire you. If the message is 'All right,' then it will be all right. And if it isn't – well, then we'll have to consult with Bailiss."

"How am I to keep an eye on Beecher?" I asked. "I can't go sitting in the lounge or entrance-hall or on the steps of the Grand Hotel all day long!"

"Ah!" he retorted. "Now I'll tell you what I'm going to do. I propose to tell Beecher!"

"Tell him what?" I asked.

"That you're being left here to watch him," he answered, with a grim chuckle. "Seems a queer thing to do, Camberwell, that I – to tell a man that he's going to be under observation but I'm going to do it. And tomorrow, after I've gone, just try to cultivate Beecher's acquaintance a bit, and draw him out, and –"

"Chaney," I said, interrupting him, "you're forgetting that we've no hold on Beecher! I can't stop Beecher from going anywhere he likes. Besides that –"

Chaney interrupted me there, chuckling again.

"No hold?" he said. "Ah, stop a bit, my boy! When we see Beecher tonight, and I tell him that you're being left behind to keep an eye on him, do you know what I shall say supposing he objects? No? Well, I shall just say that in that case I walk round to the police headquarters. Oh, no, Camberwell," he continued, "Beecher won't object! Come on – we'll go round to see him again."

We went round to the Grand Hotel; at its very entrance we ran up against Mr. and Mrs. Beecher, in gala dress; they were going to the Opera. Chaney drew Beecher aside and bluntly told him what he proposed to do. And Beecher laughed, openly and without affectation.

"Good idea, Chaney!" he said. "Camberwell, you come and lunch with us tomorrow at one o'clock, and we'll have a talk. Good-bye, Chaney – you and Bailiss will find John Merrick a dependable fellow. Now you'll excuse us."

Chaney made no remark on this episode. We returned to our hotel, and he went to bed early. And next morning I saw him off to England by the 8.25 train from the Gare du Nord.

"I'll be in Wrenchester by tea-time, Camberwell," he said, "and before seven o'clock you shall hear from me about Merrick. Bye-bye, my lad, and keep your eyes and ears open."

So there I was left alone in Paris, with little to do that I considered of any consequence. It was a fine morning, and I walked back towards the hotel from the station, idling lazily through one crowded street after another. And suddenly I got a surprise. Turning the corner from the Rue de Lafayette into the Boulevard Haussmann, I caught sight of a face that I knew – a face turned full on me for a second from the window of a taxi-cab – the face of the Wrenchester bank clerk Harborough.

Chapter Twenty

THE THREE HEADLINES

I WAS SO MUCH astonished to see Harborough there in Paris that for the moment I could do nothing but stand transfixed on the kerb, staring open-mouthed after the rapidly retreating taxi-cab. But within a few seconds it had disappeared among the masses of traffic, and I recovered my senses and asked myself what there was of the wonderful or surprising in what I had seen. What was there remarkable, or out of the way, in Harborough's presence in Paris? Paris is so easily accessible from the south-east corner of England, so readily reached from London, that one need never be astonished at meeting anybody there. Actually, Harborough in Paris was nearer Wrenchester than he would have been at Exeter, or York, or Liverpool. No, there was nothing to be astonished at; he might have come to Paris on banking business, or he might be there for a holiday. A holiday most likely – I had had time to notice that he was wearing a grey tweed suit, such as Englishmen affect when assuming the *rôle* of tourist or traveler. No – nothing in it!

But something excited my suspicion. Was it no more than coincidence that Harborough and Beecher should be in Paris at the same time? True, I had no means of knowing if Harborough and Beecher even knew each other. But I thought it likely: I had an idea, gained I could not at the moment remember how or where, that the Garsdale account was kept at the bank of which Harborough was cashier. Anyhow, Wrenchester was so small a place that it was very probable that Harborough knew Beecher, and Beecher Harborough, if only as nodding acquaintances. Well and here they both were, in Paris. Was there any connexion?... That was a beautiful summer morning, and the air was full of joyousness and gaiety and the scent of flowers. I suddenly remembered that I had over-slept myself a little, and had not had time to break my fast before rushing off with Chaney to the Gare du Nord. Now I was hungry; but the day was too enchanting to think of exchanging for the interior of the hotel. I walked along till I came to the Cafe de Paris; taking a chair on the *terrasse*, I bade a waiter bring me coffee and rolls. And sitting there, eating and drinking, and while my eyes watched abstractly the panorama around me, I began to think, hard and deep, going back over all that had happened since that morning on which Aubrey Snowe had fetched me to see his uncle's dead body.

Suddenly a thought flashed into my mind – and the next instant I felt like punching my own head because that thought had never come there before! Why, oh, why, had Chaney and I never thought of it?

What? Nothing – but just this: when James Skrimshaw left the Wrenchester Old Bank on the morning of that Thursday on which he disappeared for ever he had two thousand pounds in one-pound notes in his possession, and *Harborough knew it!* Now, supposing...

Of course, it was all supposing – all except the fact that Harborough did know it. Harborough cashed Skrimshaw's cheque. Skrimshaw particularly asked for one-pound notes; he had brought an attache-case in which to carry them away. That wasn't supposition – that was fact. Harborough knew that Skrimshaw took two thousand pounds away with him.

But to get back to a little reasonable supposition. We had been supposing all along that Skrimshaw, when he finally got possession of the S. G. envelope, found inside it something of a very valuable nature. We had given up the notion that this might be a will made by old Samuel Garsdale and hidden away out of sheer mischief or malicious design; we had come to the conclusion that it was much more likely to be negotiable securities of some sort. Now, supposing it were – what more probable than that Skrimshaw, when he cashed his own cheque that morning, asked Harborough – without going into particulars – how such securities could most easily be realized? Bankers are always being consulted on such questions. Anyway, Harborough certainly knew that Skrimshaw was carrying two thousand pounds about him in notes – pound notes, not readily, if in any way, traceable.

But was Harborough the sort of man to murder another man for the possession of two thousand pounds – plus whatever else it was that Skrimshaw had found in the S. G. envelope? How did I know? He might be. How did I know Harborough's character or his financial needs?

Then I began to consider Harborough as the murderer and thief. According to the doctor's suspicions, Skrimshaw had been poisoned. But how had Harborough contrived to poison him? Had he – ?

All of a sudden I got another illuminating idea. Was Harborough one of the two men who, at the time of Skrimshaw's disappearance, were camping out near Piperscombe? He might be. If he was, probably he lured Skrimshaw into his tent, gave him a drink, and poisoned him.

That seemed a good theory. But it presupposed certain things. First, that Harborough was at the tent that Thursday night when Skrimshaw went by on his way to Marbourne Ferry. But we had been assured by Shepperoe that the occupants of the tents were never there except for weekends. And this had been the affair of a particular Thursday evening. At least, so we believed. Perhaps – now I came to think of it – it hadn't.

As to my sitting there, on the terrasse of the Café de Paris, doing just nothing but staring at the folk who passed and re-passed, I had just then no chance of doing anything else. True, Beecher had asked me to lunch. But I wasn't going; I hadn't said I would go. I had made no reply to his invitation. As a matter of fact, I thought he'd a damned cheek to give it! No, I wasn't going to see Beecher until I got Chaney's message. And if that message was satisfactory I saw no reason why I should communicate it to Beecher. For one moment I half thought of going to Beecher and asking him if he'd seen Harborough in Paris; but I threw the idea away at once. No – better keep all that. I loafed about Paris all that day. I wandered down to the quays and spent the morning in turning over the stocks of the *bouquinistes*, and bought two or three books small enough to go into my pockets. I lunched at an amusing restaurant and idled an hour or two afterwards in sitting outside it, always watching the tide of life. Finally I drifted back to the hotel and tried to kill time there by reading the newspapers. But I had dined there before they called me to the telephone. There Chaney's voice came through.

"That you, Camberwell? The message is quite satisfactory – Merrick corroborates. So you'll come back first thing tomorrow?"

"All right," I replied. "But, Chaney, listen! Find out at once who the two men were who had those tents at Piperscombe. Important!"

"Why?" asked Chaney from far-off.

"Never mind – do what I ask. Set Bailiss on to it, somebody there will know. Tell you reason tomorrow."

I rang off. Now, was I going to see or ring up Beecher and tell him his friend corroborated his story? I did neither. Instead, I went out, spent the evening lounging about, and, coming back, turned into bed.

I caught the 10.36 at Saint-Lazare next morning, bound for Dieppe and Newhaven. I had slept a bit late, and had not seen a newspaper until I got into the train. When we were fairly off I opened the Paris edition of the *Daily Mail*. The next instant I found myself staring at three headlines set in big black letters:

TRAGIC ACCIDENT NEAR ROUEN

FATAL FALL OF AN ENGLISH TOURIST

Has he friends in France?

Chapter Twenty-one

THE FATAL SLIP

T HERE WAS A FULL column, perhaps more, of print following these sensational headlines, and, running my eye down it, I suddenly caught the name 'Harborough.' And at that I folded the paper to a convenient angle, and read:

From Our Special Correspondent ROUEN, *Thursday evening*

A fatal accident occurred this afternoon at Saint-Martin-de-Boscherville, a few miles from Rouen, the victim being an Englishman, believed to be a tourist. The circumstance is all the more tragic and unfortunate in that the dead man was unaccompanied and that his exact address in England is not known.

According to the information I have so far been able to obtain the victim of what can only be considered a most unusual accident arrived in Rouen shortly before noon this morning. He registered a room at the

Hotel de la Poste, in the Rue Jeanne d'Arc, under
the name Charles Harborough, giving as address the
mere name 'London.' He was shown up to his room
and his luggage – a large suitcase – was taken there;
a short time afterwards he came down and lunched
in the restaurant attached to the hotel. After lunch
he remained in the lounge for some little time, smoking a cigar and drinking coffee. About two o'clock he
approached the *concierge* and asked him if he could
recommend a nice route for a motor ride? Having ascertained how far Mr. Harborough wished to go, and
how long he wanted to be out, the *concierge* advised
a ride by way of Canteleu, the Foret de Roumare,
round to Saint-Martin-de-Boscherville, with a stay at
the last-named place to inspect the famous Abbey
Church of Saint-Georges-de Boscherville. Thence,
continued the *concierge*, the journey might be pursued
by the road along the banks of the Seine beneath the
Fork de Roumare, through Hantot and Sahurs, to
Croisset, where, the *concierge* suggested, Mr. Harborough might inspect the Pavillon Flaubert and its museum of relics of the world-famous novelist. Mr. Harborough expressed himself as pleased by this itinerary,
which he had followed on his map of the district, and
the *concierge* accordingly called a car for him and gave
its driver full instructions. Mr. Harborough, it may be
mentioned, did not speak French fluently, though he
appeared to have some fair knowledge of the language.
The car left the Hotel de la Poste at just after two
o'clock.

Little more than an hour later the car-driver, much concerned, returned to the hotel and informed the *concierge* that his fare had met with a fatal accident, and was lying dead at Saint-Martin-de-Boscherville. He said that after inspecting the church of Canteleu Mr. Harborough bade him drive on to the village just named. There Mr. Harborough got out seeing the Abbey Church of Saint-Georges. He had not been inside the church many minutes when the sacristan rushed out to the car, motioning the driver to come to him. The driver went in and found Mr. Harborough lying dead on the floor of the nave. It appeared that he had gone up to the clerestory. This is unprotected by any railing or balustrade, and it is conjectured that the unfortunate gentleman had slipped on the stone paving, been unable to recover himself, and had fallen over the edge to the floor below, a distance of some sixty or seventy feet. Death, of course, had been instantaneous.

Leaving the body in charge of the village authorities, the driver immediately sped back to Rouen, and informed the management of the Hotel de la Poste of what had happened. They at once placed themselves in communication with the police and with the British Consul. By the courtesy of the latter I was permitted to accompany him to the scene of the accident and to acquire details of what happened at first hand.

Here followed the correspondent's account of what he saw and found at the Abbey Church of Saint-Georges-de-Boscherville, which

I omit, as I almost immediately afterwards went over the same ground myself.

> The personal effects of the deceased gentleman have
> been taken charge of by the British Consul, and the
> suitcase left in his room at the Hotel de la Poste, after
> being examined by the police authorities, has been
> placed in the same hands for safe custody. No papers
> giving any definite address have been found, and, as
> I have already stated, Mr. Harborough wrote merely
> 'London' after his name in the hotel register; in the
> customary police-notice he had described himself as
> 'gentleman.' There is some indication that he had re-
> cently stayed in Paris; it is, of course, known that he
> traveled from Paris to Rouen on the morning of his
> death. I have already communicated the news of the
> fatal accident, with the particulars given here, to the
> London Press, in the hope that Mr. Harborough's
> friends may come forward, and I am asked by the
> British Consul to request any person now in France
> who may know Mr. Harborough to communicate
> with him at the British Consulate in Rouen without
> delay. At the further request of the police authorities
> and the British Consul I append a description of the
> deceased gentleman.

Here followed – concluding the article – a full description of Har-borough's personal appearance and of the clothes he was wearing.

I laid down the paper wondering what this sudden death meant. Was it a pure accident? Or was it suicide? That the man was the Harborough I knew there seemed to be no doubt – he must have been on his way to the Saint-Lazare station, *en route* for Rouen, when I caught sight of him in the taxi-cab only the previous morning. And of course there was only one thing for me to do – I must break my journey at Rouen and go at once to the British Consul.

I was in Rouen soon after midday, and, leaving my suitcase (a new one, bought and stocked in Paris the day before, Chaney and I having, of course, come away without as much as a comb or a toothbrush) at the station, I drove straight off to the British Consulate. I was fortunate enough to find the Consul in; I think he knew what I had come for before ever I spoke.

"You know this dead man, Mr. Camberwell?" he asked, after he had glanced at my professional card.

"I can't say that I am a friend, or that I am even an acquaintance of his," I replied. "If he is the man I take him to be from the newspaper description, I know who he is, however, and I have talked to him once, in my professional capacity. I believe him to be the Harborough who is – or was – cashier at the Wrenchester Old Bank – Wrenchester, in Sussex."

"I know Wrenchester well enough," said the Consul. "I'm a Sussex man myself." He glanced at my card again. "I've heard of your firm," he went on, eyeing me with what I thought to be interested curiosity. "So you won't mind if I ask you a question. Are you after this Har-borough?"

"That's a question which is difficult to answer," I replied. "I think things were developing in such a fashion that we – and the police – would have been after him very soon. But I had better explain – you will have read in the English newspapers the various accounts of the – what is being called the Wrenchester mysteries –"

"Murder of old Mr. Snowe and later, in all probability, of the lawyer's clerk, Skrimshaw," he said, nodding his affirmation. "Yes – as a matter of fact, I hail from near Wrenchester, so it interests me. But you were saying –"

"I was going to say that we are beginning to believe that Harborough has some knowledge, if not of Mr. Snowe's murder, at any rate of Skrimshaw's," I continued. "There is a man now in Paris of whom we had some suspicion – we went over to see him. I saw Harborough in Paris yesterday morning; he was in a taxi-cab, probably on his way to Saint-Lazare to begin the journey which has ended fatally here. Now I am more suspicious than ever – it seems to be rather more than a coincidence that Harborough and the other man should be in Paris together. And – I want information."

The Consul nodded, and, picking up a telegram from his desk, handed it over. I read it.

Believe man described in newspapers as having had fatal accident near Rouen is our cashier. Manager coming over at once. Wrenchester Old Bank.

"The manager," I said, "is Mr. Smart. He will be able to identify him positively."

"But you can do that," remarked the Consul. "This wire, you see, wasn't handed in at Wrenchester until eleven o'clock, so Mr. Smart couldn't possibly catch the morning boat at Newhaven. You had better see the body at once, and –"

"The effects – belongings?" I asked. "They are in your possession?"

"I have them here – sealed," he answered. "But I can't break the seals nor show anything to you except in the presence and with the permission of the French authorities. What we had better do is this – we will go to the Hotel de la Poste for lunch; you may like to ask a question or two there. Then we will go out to Saint-Martin-de-Boscherville where the body is lying, and you shall identify it. If you positively identify it, then on our return I will get a police official here, and you shall examine the dead man's belongings. Mr. Smart, of course, cannot get here before early tomorrow morning – by the direct route, anyhow."

We went to the Hotel de la Poste, and after we had had lunch I made a few inquiries. No one had noticed anything unusual in Mr. Harborough's behaviour – that is, no one had seen any indication of nervousness or worry or excitement; it was evident that to everybody who had had anything to do with him, from reception clerk to *concierge*, he had seemed the conversational, phlegmatic Englishman, out for a quiet holiday.

We went out to Saint-Martin-de-Boscherville in the Consul's car. It was a lovely summer afternoon, and when we had cleared the crowded riverside of Rouen, climbed the hill to Canteleu, perched high above the Seine, and had entered the Forest of Roumare I wished that we were on an excursion of pleasure together instead of an errand of unpleasant duty. But we had scarcely entered on the woodland beauties of the forest before the road ran out on a shelving hillside, at the foot of which, still far off, but rising high above the landscape and the red roofs of its village, I saw the tower, turrets, and roof of a great church. I am afraid I listened apathetically and absentmindedly to the Consul as he told me that there before me stood one of the finest specimens of Romanesque architecture in France; that it had been founded by Raoul de Tancarville, sometime tutor and afterwards Chamberlain to William the Conqueror; that it had been cleverly restored in keeping with its original design, and that its Gothic chapter-house was entered by a still beautiful triple Romanesque archway.

I heard all this, and subconsciously registered it – but I was thinking of the man who lay dead somewhere in the village, and wondering if at last I was nearing a solution of the mysteries which had baffled us for so many weeks.

The car pulled up in front of the great church, and the Consul and I entered. He led me a little way into the nave and pointed upward.

"You see the clerestory?" he said. "It runs clean round, from the west end here to the transepts. You gain it by the winding stair there; through that door. Harborough went up by himself. Now, you see that the clerestory is unprotected – there is neither balustrade nor railing. And the floor of the clerestory, of stone, of course, slopes inward a little. I noticed that Harborough was wearing boots studded with nails worn very smooth: probably he slipped almost as soon as he reached the clerestory – there is where he fell. And – you can imagine the rest!"

I could imagine the rest so well that after one glance at the clerestory, some sixty or seventy feet above our heads, I made rapidly for the door and the open air, and for a minute or two felt as if I were going to be violently sick. Imagine, indeed...! It needed little imagination!

We went then to see the dead man; he lay in some place close by, the village policeman in charge of him. One glance was sufficient.

"Yes," I said, "that's Harborough"

We went swiftly back to Rouen and to the Consulate. The Consul had already arranged for the presence of a police official, and after due explanation the seals of the suitcase and of a small parcel of personal effects were broken and I was allowed to make an inspection. There was nothing whatever in the suitcase that was of any help to me; indeed, it contained nothing but clothing and toilet articles. Nor at first did I find anything in the various things which had been taken from the dead man's pockets. There was a fair amount of money,

English and French, some £50 or £60; there was a gold watch and its chain and the pocket articles that most men carry. In a pocket-book there were a few papers – at first I found nothing of any note. Then all of a sudden I found a letter and a receipt. The letter, addressed to Harborough at the Hotel du Louvre, Paris, was from Beecher; the receipt bore the name and address of a Wrenchester tradesman. And with a word of apology to my companions I sat down to read both.

Chapter Twenty-two

GONE!

IT needed but one glance at the letter to see that I had hit upon a link between Beecher and Harborough. Written on a sheet of Grand Hotel notepaper and undated, it was nothing but a mere line or two, but quite enough for my purposes. Knowing that the French police authorities would not allow me to take it out of the Consul's keeping, I copied it in my notebook:

Dear Harborough [it ran], *you had better meet me at the Café Frontignac at 11 o'clock tomorrow morning. B.*

This was important; it convinced me of the truth of my suspicion that Harborough and Beecher had mutual business in Paris. But it was, perhaps, not as important as the Wrenchester tradesman's receipt, which I also copied:

51 MARKET STREET
WRENCHESTER
July 19

– HARBOROUGH, ESQ.
   Dr. to Thomas Shoreham

To conveyance of 2 bell-tents from Wrenchester to Piperscombe and setting up of same:	£1 8s. 6d.
To taking same down and conveyance from Piperscombe to Wrenchester:	£1 8s. 6d.
Storage of same:	15s. 0d.
	£3 12s. 0d.

This was duly receipted. And now I knew that the two tents which I had seen at Piperscombe belonged to the man who lay dead at Saint-Martin-de-Boscherville, and that it would now be necessary to discover the identity of his companion. But there was work to do in Paris before I could return to Wrenchester.

Restoring the two documents to the Consul, I began to busy myself about practical things. It was still little more than the middle of the afternoon when I got on to Chaney by telephone. I went straight to the point.

"Chaney, you have seen about the fatal accident to a man named Harborough at a village near here – Rouen, from which I'm speaking?"

"Heard of it – yes. They know it here. Smart, the bank-manager, has left for Rouen."

"Chaney, I've made two discoveries. Harborough and Beecher are mixed up in something! That's one. It was Harborough who lived in those tents at Piperscombe! That's another."

"Good! Well?"

"You must come across here at once, by the night boat from Newhaven. You've plenty of time. I'll meet you on your arrival at

Dieppe, and we'll go back to Paris together – we must see Beecher at once."

"Real grounds, Camberwell?"

"Certain of it – certain there's something, anyhow. You'll come?"

"I'll come. Dieppe Harbour Station, then, 2 A.M. I believe Smart will be on the same boat – he's left for Newhaven already. Camberwell, I'd better bring Bailiss."

"Think so? As you like, of course."

"Better. I'll find him at once. Expect both of us. Bye-bye."

I could do no more at Rouen; nothing could be done about the dead man until Mr. Smart arrived. And after arranging with the Consul that Smart should be met in the early hours of the morning I left for Dieppe.

I thought that evening and the early part of the night that followed upon it would never pass. I turned in to the Hotel Metropole when I arrived at Dieppe, spent as much time as ever I could over my dinner, and idled a long time afterwards in the lounge. Then I went along to the Casino and tried to kill time there; eventually I wandered back to the hotel, wondering why time seemed to go with doubly weighted feet round about midnight.

The fact was that I was fretful and nervous about Beecher.

Beecher, of course, would have seen the Paris *Daily Mail* that morning, and Beecher might have judged it desirable to remove him and Mrs. Beecher to other regions. If he had he'd have twenty-four hours' start – and twenty-four hours' start in the case of a clever man with plenty of money at his disposal is a serious handicap to those who are after him.

The time of waiting slipped by at last, and at two o'clock I was on the quayside at the harbour station, shivering in the wind that blew off the Channel. The boat came in to time, and in the glare of the yellow lamps I soon spotted Chaney's big form. And behind him came Bailiss, and another man, in whom I recognized Mr. Smart, the bank manager. I had already ascertained that the train for Paris, which stood drawn up on the other side of the quay, would stop at Rouen, so we all four got into a first-class compartment and shut ourselves in; until Rouen, when Smart was to alight, we could discuss matters with him.

But Smart knew little. He was not even sure that Harborough had any near relation; he had never heard him mention any. Harborough, he said, was a hermit-like sort of fellow, who kept himself to himself. He had been in the employ of the Wrenchester Old Bank some eleven years, but though Smart himself had been manager nearly all that time he knew little of him outside his duties. And he hadn't the ghost of a notion as to who it was that kept Harborough company in those weekend visits to the two tents at Piperscombe.

"All I can do at present," he said, concluding his account of his late cashier, "is to arrange about having him buried and so on. When I get back I suppose we shall have to examine his belongings at Wrenchester at his lodgings. He'd lodged at the same house for years – there may be something there. You're suspecting, of course, that Harborough, knowing that Skrimshaw had two thousand pounds on him, murdered Skrimshaw by poison, and, with the assistance of his companion, hid the body where it has recently been found?"

Neither Chaney nor Bailiss answered this question; each glanced at me.

"What I'm most concerned about, Mr. Smart," I said, "is to find out what was in a certain packet which I believe to have been in Skrimshaw's possession when he was murdered, and what has become of it."

"You mean the contents – whatever they may have been – of what Superintendent Bailiss and Mr. Chaney call the S. G. envelope?" he replied.

"Originally in the S. G. envelope," I said. "We have the actual S. G. envelope – I found it in Skrimshaw's cottage. I'm referring to what was in it. Because I think Harborough got hold of those contents – and I'm beginning to think it was his possession of them that brought him to Paris. By the by, as you'll be leaving us in a few minutes, can you tell me if your bank has agents in Paris, and, if so, who they are?"

"Certainly," he replied. "The Credit Lyonnais – head office."

"Do you know if they knew Harborough there – personally?" I asked.

"Yes," he answered. "Harborough has been over two or three times there to transact business which couldn't easily be transacted except in person."

"Do they know you too?" I inquired.

"Oh, yes – that is, certain of the officials do," he said.

"Harborough was not over here on business, though, was he, Mr. Smart?" inquired Bailiss. "I heard he'd gone for his holiday."

"That is so," agreed the bank-manager. "He was having a fortnight's holiday. I had no idea that he was going to Paris. He told me he was going into Normandy and Brittany."

We were just running into Rouen then, and Mr. Smart, after I had given him the address of the British Consulate and advised him to go to the Hotel de la Poste for the remainder of the summer night, left us. The train moved on again for the run to Paris, and Bailiss, Chaney, and I began to discuss our plans.

Chaney – it may have been because of his hurried movements, necessitating loss of sleep, interruptions of his regular routine for meals, and so on during the last few days – was doleful and pessimistic. What, he asked, had we to go on? There was nothing in the note from Beecher to Harborough. All Beecher said was "Meet me at the Café So-and-so." What was there in that? And Merrick had proved to him and Bailiss that on the night on which Skrimshaw met his death Beecher had never been out of his, Merrick's, sight – so to speak. Anyway, when he was out of his sight he was fast asleep in Merrick's best bedroom at Sandside. And so on and so forth – Chaney didn't see what good we were doing. Still –

"Listen here, Chaney," I said at last. "You say that on the night on which Skrimshaw was murdered Beecher was in safe-keeping at Merrick's. Which night do you mean?"

Chaney stared – first at Bailiss, then at me.

"Why," he exclaimed, "that night we've always talked about – that Thursday night. Night of the day he was last seen in Wrenchester!"

"How do we know Skrimshaw was murdered – if he was murdered – that night?" I asked.

They both stared at me then.

"Um!" muttered Bailiss. "What's in your mind, Mr. Camberwell?"

"Just what I've said, Bailiss," I replied. "How do we know it was that night?"

"You're forgetting, Camberwell," said Chaney suddenly. "That was the night that Ready's boat was stolen! And Skrimshaw's stick was in it."

"That's no proof, Chaney!" I retorted. "The boat-and-stick business may be explained in all sorts of ways – may be explained yet, I mean. The fact of the case is we don't know *when* Skrimshaw was murdered, or died. But I'm beginning to get more and more certain that Harborough knew, and that Beecher *knows!*"

They appeared to be impressed by my convictions, but Chaney was still dubious as to what we were going to do. Eventually I begged him to leave matters to me on our re-arrival in Paris – in the initial stages, anyway. For during that tiresome period of waiting at Dieppe I had been thinking and thinking, and had evolved various plans – anyway, I was going to find Beecher."

We reached Paris in the very early morning – half-past five, or some such unholy moment – and, going to the hotel I had left not twenty hours before, whiled away our time miserably until between eight and nine o'clock. Then we went round to the Grand Hotel. We were all very sleepy and very silent; Chaney and Bailiss, leaving me to make the inquiries, looked as if they hoped and expected nothing.

And there was nothing to cheer or encourage them. We were too late. Mr. and Mrs. Beecher had left the hotel early the previous day – which was exactly what I had half expected.

Chapter
Twenty-three

BEARER BONDS

I T LOOKED AT FIRST as if we were not going to get much information about Mr. and Mrs. Beecher and their departure in haste. But the production of our professional cards won the deep interest of an inquisitive under-manager, and his speedy examination of various clerks, servants, and porters quickly placed certain facts at our disposal. During Mr. and Mrs. Beecher's stay at the hotel it had been the custom to send up their coffee, or their tea, at eight o'clock every morning, and to accompany the rolls and butter with a copy of the Paris *Daily Mail*. Yesterday morning, before half-past eight, Mr. Beecher had come down to the office and had announced that he and his wife must leave at once for England; they must catch the noon train. Henceforth all appeared to have been hurry and bustle: Mr. Beecher was in and out of the hotel all the morning; Mrs. Beecher, who had brought a great deal of luggage with her, was frantically packing, aided by chambermaids and floor-waiters. Eventually they were got off, but only just in time. And the last recorded saying of Mr. Beecher was that if they missed the train at the Gare du Nord they must be taken to Le Bourget, for he must be in London that evening, and if he couldn't do it by train and steamer he must charter a special aeroplane and fly.

I think we all three understood what had happened. Beecher had read the account of the fatal accident to Harborough as he drank his morning coffee, and had straightway resolved to return to England; probably there was some reason, arising out of Harborough's death, for such a return. Still, as Chaney pointed out, we wanted to know more than we had learned at the Grand Hotel. Why not try the Hotel du Louvre, where, presumably, Harborough had stayed? Beecher's note to him, anyway, had been addressed there. So to the Hotel du Louvre we repaired, and there by some persistent and patient investigation we found out a good deal more than I had expected to find. First of all we discovered that Harborough was well known at that hotel; he always stayed there, we heard, when he visited Paris. Second, there was a waiter in the restaurant, who spoke perfect English, who knew Harborough very well as a customer who turned up once or twice a year, and there was a door porter, a smart fellow, whose peculiar gift it seemed to be to remember names and faces. And eventually we knew this: the day before Chaney and I arrived in Paris (we checked the dates carefully) a gentleman who from a double description was without doubt Beecher came to the hotel and lunched with Harborough, and at a due interval after lunch went off with him in a taxi-cab. And the smart young door porter remembered where.

"To the Credit Lyonnais, m'sieur," he said in answer to my explicit question. "Monsieur Harborough told me himself where he wished to be taken."

"And the other gentleman was with him?" I asked.

"In the cab with him, m'sieur. To the Credit Lyonnais, as I have said."

This necessitated another consultation between Chaney, Bailiss, and myself. We now knew that Beecher and Harborough had had some mutual interest, probably of a financial nature. We knew that the Credit Lyonnais was the agent in Paris of the Wrenchester Old Bank, and that Harborough was known to its officials. And we knew that he and Beecher had gone to the Credit Lyonnais. Well, we should have to go to it too, as things turned out. But – would its officials tell us anything?

"You must go, Camberwell," said Chaney. "You've the readiest tongue and the best gift of explanation. Get hold of some high-placed official who speaks English, and tell him what we're after, and persuade him to tell you, if he will, what business it was that took Harborough and Beecher to his bank the other afternoon. And – anything else that he likes to tell."

"He won't like to tell anything, Chaney," I said. "My belief is that I shall draw that covert blank! Why should he tell me?"

"Police business," muttered Bailiss.

"Not quite that, Bailiss," said I. "Chaney and I are amateurs. You go – you're a professional!"

"Can't speak or understand a word of their lingo," replied Bailiss. "You can! And even if this monsieur spoke English – no, no, I'm no good at banking matters. You'll do far better, Mr. Camberwell."

"Far better, far better!" said Chaney sympathetically. "We'll wait."

I left them at a comfortable *café*, each with a cigar, and went to the head office of the famous bank. And after a long, long wait, and having answered no end of questions put to me by intermediaries, I was at last ushered into the presence of a very great figure who wore a bit of crimson ribbon in the silk-fronted lapel of his irreproachable frock-coat, but spoke English far better than I myself did. Already, through the intermediaries I have mentioned, he knew something of what I was after.

"You are inquiring into the death of Mr. Harborough, killed accidentally near Rouen, Mr. Camberwell?" he said politely, glancing once more at my professional card.

"Not so much into the circumstances of his death, monsieur," I replied, "as into certain matters that preceded it. I am aware of all the circumstances of his death: I went into all that at Rouen yesterday, in company with the British Consul."

"It was really – an accident?" he asked, regarding me closely.

"From what I saw, monsieur, and from what I learned, I should say unhesitatingly that it was an accident," I answered.

"No suspicion of foul play?" he suggested.

"I heard of none, monsieur."

He remained silent a moment, watching me. Then "What is it you want of us, Mr. Camberwell?" he asked.

"Certain information which I believe you can give, monsieur," I said. "I am here in Paris with my colleague and partner, ex-Detective-Inspector Chaney, once of our Criminal Investigation Department, and with us is Superintendent Bailiss, of the Wrenchester police. We wished to get some information of, and from, Harborough himself, and a man named Beecher, who has been stopping at the Grand Hotel, but Harborough is dead, and Beecher has left –"

He stopped me with a gesture.

"Pardon!" he said. "You mentioned the name Wrenchester. I read the English papers. Is all this relative to the – what is called Wrenchester Mystery?"

"Precisely, monsieur!" I replied. "It is very much relative! We have ascertained, here in Paris today, that a few days ago Harborough, in company with Beecher, visited your bank –"

Again he stopped me.

"Harborough," he said, "was cashier of a bank, the Wrenchester Old Bank, for which we are agents in Paris. An old, very old connexion. We knew Harborough, of course. He has been here on business several times."

"And he was here the other day, monsieur, as I have suggested?" I asked eagerly.

"Certainly he was here the other day," he answered.

"What, monsieur, was his business?" I went on, still more eagerly. "For we have strong grounds for believing –"

He stopped me very definitely that time – with lifted hand.

"That, Mr. Camberwell, I cannot tell you," he said. "It is impossible to reveal our clients' secrets to – shall I say, anyone? If you came authorized by the Wrenchester Old Bank, now –"

I jumped at that opening – literally, for I sprang to my feet and seized my hat.

"Monsieur," I exclaimed, "do you know Mr. Smart?"

"We know Mr. Smart well," he answered.

"Would you tell Mr. Smart?" I demanded.

"In the way of business – yes," he said, waving his hand. "Oh, yes!"

"Mr. Smart is now at Rouen, monsieur," I replied. "I will telephone to him – at once. He shall call on you tomorrow morning."

He rose and made me a polite bow.

"We shall be pleased to see Mr. Smart," he said. "I would have helped you if I could, Mr. Camberwell, but – you comprehend? Business rules – eh?"

I assured him that I had infinite powers of comprehension, paid him my compliments, and went away. And before seeking Bailiss and Chaney, who, being in Paris, were inclined to be sybaritic in their doings, and to leave the hard work to me, I got on to the phone, and, ringing up the British Consulate at Rouen, came into touch with Mr. Smart. Mr. Smart promised to leave for Paris at once. He joined us that night at our hotel, and next morning I walked with him to the Credit Lyonnais, and at its doors left him and returned to Chaney and Bailiss – to await his return and his news.

We had to wait a long time; it was well past noon when he returned. Our first glances at his face showed us that he carried serious news. In silence we all four grouped ourselves in a corner. For what seemed a long time – in reality, perhaps, no more than a few seconds – Mr. Smart preserved the silence; when he broke it his tone was that of a man who has serious news to tell.

"Well, gentlemen," he said, "I have solved, if not the whole mystery, at any rate the question of why Harborough came to Paris. I had better tell you the plain truth at once. Harborough the other day called at the Credit Lyonnais, where, of course, he was well known as cashier and under-manager of our bank, and presented certain French bearer bonds for collection. Of course, there was no difficulty about that; the amount was paid to him at once. And," added Mr. Smart, "it was a large amount. In English money fifty thousand pounds."

We were all too much astonished to say anything. All we could do was to wait for more information.

"I have already said – Harborough was well known at the Credit Lyonnais. As a matter of fact," continued Mr. Smart, "Harborough, of recent years, has often been over here on business, not merely from us, but from another bank in whose service he had been before he came to us; he was a man of considerable experience in banking affairs.

Consequently the Credit Lyonnais – I am referring to the officials who saw him the other day – had full reliance on his word. He told them that these bearer bonds were the joint property of himself and a friend, and that they had recently come into possession of them through the death of a relation. And of course they were bearer bonds. Fifty thousand pounds! Well, gentlemen, there is no doubt in my mind that we now know what was in the envelope marked S. G., which eventually came into the hands of Skrimshaw. Old Samuel Garsdale always had the reputation of being a miser, and it was matter of much speculation when he died as to what he had done with his money. Here is the answer – he had bought French securities. And Harborough got hold of them!"

Chaney broke the silence, which had up to now hung heavy over the three of us who were listening.

"You say the amount – fifty thousand – was paid at once, Mr. Smart?" he said. "How was it paid? Camberwell says there was nothing much on Harborough's dead body – just a fair amount, such as a traveler would want."

"The amount was paid, at Harborough's request, by two drafts or cheques on sight to the London branch of the Credit Lyonnais, in Lombard Street," replied Mr. Smart. "One was in favour of Harborough himself; the other was a bearer cheque, uncrossed. Each was for twenty-five thousand pounds. Probably Harborough sent his draft or cheque to his bank in London – he kept a private account at a London bank, unconnected with ours. As to the other–"

"Beecher, of course!" muttered Chaney. "Beecher! "

"Probably," agreed Mr. Smart. "However, I haven't told you all. I got the Credit Lyonnais to phone their branch in London to see if the bearer cheque had been presented. And – it had! It had been presented and paid out this morning, just before we phoned across."

"Beecher again!" said Chaney. "That's why he went off in such a hurry. He'd get there last night, and he'd no doubt present his bit of paper first thing this morning. Bailiss," he went on, turning to the Superintendent, who was evidently mystified by the bank-manager's story, "we'd better be getting back. Never mind the money part of it – we're not after swindlers, but murderers!"

Mr. Smart shook his head. "You think Harborough and Beecher were responsible for Skrimshaw's death?" he asked. "You think?"

"I think they'd something to do with it," said Chaney. "This is certain – those French bearer bonds you tell us of formed, without doubt, the contents of the S. G. envelope, which, through Archer, came into Skrimshaw's possession. Well, Skrimshaw is found dead – poisoned, we suspect – and the bonds come to Paris in Harborough's hands, and he and Beecher share the proceeds. Faugh! – the thing's too obvious! Camberwell, what's the next train for England?"

"Four o'clock," I answered promptly. "Victoria 10.45."

"Then for God's sake let's get some lunch, or *dejuny*, or whatever they call it here, and get off!" exclaimed Chaney. "We're wasting time here, and I want to get to work on that chap Beecher! Beecher – Beecher! I told you it was Beecher from the beginning!"

That night on the boat I pulled Chaney aside.

"Chaney," I said, "who was it interviewed that man Merrick the other day? You or Bailiss?"

"Bailiss!" He answered. "Not me – I never saw him. Bailiss. But why?"

"Never mind," I replied. "But first thing tomorrow morning you and I are going to Sandside Farm."

Chapter Twenty-four

SANDSIDE FARM

T HE BOAT WAS LATE and the train was late that night, and it was past eleven o'clock when we got into London. Rather than go to our respective homes at such a late hour we turned into the Grosvenor Hotel at Victoria, and so did Bailiss; Smart had returned from Paris to Rouen, where he expected to meet certain of Harborough's relatives. Chaney and I sat up late that night, talking things out, but we were up early next morning, and on our way to Wrenchester by the first fast train, leaving Bailiss, who went to consult the Scotland Yard people, to follow by a later one. And by eleven o'clock we had garaged our car at the little inn at Marbourne and were crossing the Levels in quest of Sandside Farm and its tenant, Mr. Merrick.

We had not previously explored that side of Marbourne Levels, and as we followed the path which – according to our information – Beecher had taken on the night of Skrimshaw's disappearance I looked about me with curiosity and interest. And the first thought that came into my mind was one of wonder that such a name as the Levels should have been given to what, in reality, was a stretch of undulating and diversified country. The ground rose and fell in irregular waves – now topping some rise, you could see the sea glistening ahead beyond wide stretches of silvery sand, on which the morning tide was curling and breaking in white foam; now sinking into deep depression, you saw nothing beyond the finger of young fir and pine which had been planted of recent years. All this part of the Levels was clothed with a coarse, rank vegetation; the grass, I should say, was inedible, and consequently neither sheep nor cattle were to be seen.

Here and there were stretches of heather and broom; here and there great clumps of gorse. For a long way there was no sign of any human habitation; the place was a solitude. For nearly two miles we walked by a narrow path which in any other country than that I should have taken for a sheep-walk – yet here there were no sheep. Then we chanced on a side-track, broad enough to give room for horses and carts – but Chaney was quick to point out that no recent marks of hoof or wheel could be traced on it. The nearer we approached to the sea the more solitary and deserted became our surroundings; still, there were evidences of life, for here and there rabbits scuttled into their burrows, and over our heads sea-birds wheeled and broke the silence with melancholy crying. And suddenly, crossing a range of sand hills, we came into final and uninterrupted view of the sea, flashing mackerel-blue in the morning sun, and of Sandside Farm, lying between us and the creaming sweep of the incoming tide.

My first impression of this place was that it conveyed an even deeper sense of solitude than the solitary waste on the edge of which it stood. A sort of ravine ran down to the sea there; a deep cut in the land, shaded by stunted trees on each side; we could see where a stream, evidently flowing through this depression, ran out and spread itself over the sands. The farmstead stood at the foot of this, on the side opposite to us, an old, time-worn pile of grey stone; while we were still half a mile from it we could see that it looked – I was going to say ruinous, but at any rate in a poor state of repair. It formed a square. The house, looking out on the beach and the sea, made one side; the outbuildings and a high, tumbledown wall the other three. There was a courtyard before the house, and in one corner stood a flagstaff from which dangled the tatters of what had once been some gaily coloured flag.

We walked along the ridge of sand-hill until we came to a point wherefrom we could look down and into this lonely habitation, and the next impression I had was akin to, but much deeper than, the one that had preceded it. Desolate! It was impossible to imagine anything more desolate. There was not a sign of life about the place. No human form moved about the buildings; no cattle stood in the fold, which seemed to be empty of straw; there was not a sign of sheep, or pig, or fowl, nor was there a dog to bark the news of our approach. And – surest sign of desolation – not a wisp of smoke curled from the queer-shaped chimneys.

"Looks to me as if there was nobody there," remarked Chaney.

I made no reply to that. I was thinking the same thing. And after a moment's silence, during which we continued to gaze at the apparently deserted farmstead, Chancy spoke again, thoughtfully.

"Can't understand this, Camberwell," he said. "We've been given to understand that this place, Sandside Farm, is – well, do you remember what Beecher said about it that morning we found him in Paris? 'Sandside Farm,' he said, 'is the most important holding on my estate.' Well, if that's so, Camberwell, whatever are the rest like? We've come two miles across these Levels, and hang me if I've seen enough grass to feed a rabbit on, let alone sheep or cattle! And we've seen no sheep or cattle – and this spot at our feet looks, from here, anyway, as if there

wasn't a scrap of litter in the fold or a grain of corn in the stackyard –
and I'll bet there's nothing in either barn or granary, or stable either."

"Beecher said that it had only recently been let to his friend John
Merrick," I remarked. "Merrick may not have stocked it yet."

Chaney shook his head.

"No, no!" he muttered. "That won't do, my lad. There's something
queer about this place – some mystery. Come on! Let's go down and
have a squint at it at close quarters."

We descended the sandhills to the level above the ravine on which
farmstead and outbuildings stood baking in the midday sun. And at
once I saw that, as Chaney had said, there was nothing in either fold
or stackyard; each was bare to the stone and soil which formed their
flooring. We passed through the fold on our way to the house; stables,
byres, piggeries, were all empty.

"And you can bet the house will be too," said Chaney, suddenly
voicing what I also was thinking. "We're going to draw the covert blank
this time!"

It looked like it – for as we passed the first window of the house and
glanced through its neglected panes I saw that the room within was
destitute of even a chair. And when we knocked at the front door the
sound of our knocking came back to us from a hollow.

There was no response. Chaney had knocked mightily on the panels, and when the echo inside had died away we were in the midst of a
deep silence, broken only by the wash of the tide on the beach below
the house. I turned from the door to look at the garden which lay
in front. It was a mass of tangled weeds, and looked as if it had been
neglected for months. Altogether, it was difficult to believe that the
place was tenanted at all.

Chaney made three vigorous assaults on the door – all without
effect. So we began a tour of the house, going round its outer walls

and peering in at every window. And each room into which we looked was empty – until, turning a corner, we came across what appeared to be a modern addition to the structure, a square tower built on at an angle of the walls, having three storeys, and apparently a room in each; the lower room in this contained certain furnishings. But they were elementary in their simplicity – a table, a few chairs, an old sofa, and on the fire-range some pots and pans, as if the occupant or occupants had done his or their cooking and eating all in this one room. There were plates, glasses, and crockery on the table, with some evidence of food, and in the grate were the ashes of a dead fire.

"Chaney," I said, as we stared into this desolate scene, "you said that Bailiss interviewed Merrick. Where did he see him? Here?"

"No," he replied. "He saw him – met him, in fact – in Wrenchester."

"And Merrick assured him – what did Merrick assure him of?"

"Merrick – respectable sort of man, according to Bailiss – said that Beecher was with him the whole of the evening and night of Skrimshaw's disappearance."

"Here – at Sandside Farm?"

"So he gave Bailiss to understand."

"Poor accommodation, I think, for a night's entertainment!" I said. "Well, there seems to be nobody here now. What's to be done?"

Chaney took another, and a longer and more searching, glance into the empty room.

"I will lay anything there's been somebody here not long since, Camberwell," he said. "And I would bet, too, that this spot is mixed up with the Skrimshaw affair more than we've guessed at. Do? Well, it seems to me that we might do worse than keep an eye on Sandside Farm. I wish we'd got Chippendale here."

Chippendale – as those who have followed my recollections so far will remember – was our clerk, ubiquitous Cockney, sharp-witted and resourceful, who had been of immense use to us on several occasions.

"We can get Chippendale here in a few hours," I said. "No difficulty about that."

"Then we'll have him," replied Chaney. "I suppose Marbourne will be the nearest telegraph office?"

"I should say," I answered, after considering our exact geographical situation, "that Marbourne Ferry is nearest. Here we are on the east side of this promontory; Marbourne Ferry is straight across here, on the west side. If we make a beeline across the point–"

"Come on!" he said, turning to the sandhills. "Let's get there. And now I come to think of it, I noticed a telephone in the bar of the Cod and Lobster – we'll get the landlord to let us phone Chippendale – it will save an hour or two. And Chip shall come down at once and meet us at Marbourne."

I was right in my surmise as to our situation. Forty minutes' sharp walking across the point of the promontory brought us to the Cod and Lobster. And there I phoned to Chippendale in London, bidding him catch the very next train to Wrenchester, take a taxi at the station there, and meet us at the inn at Marbourne. And this done, and it being past noon and a long time since breakfast, Chaney and I refreshed ourselves with bread, cheese, and beer, and between mouthfuls answered or parried such questions as the host and hostess, who by that time knew pretty nearly as much as we did about recent developments, put to us out of their inquisitiveness.

"You don't seem to be getting no farther, then, gentlemen?" suggested the landlord.

"That's not for them to say," remarked the landlady. "These gentlemen know better than to tell us."

"That's an observation that does your judgment great credit, madam," said Chaney. "It wouldn't do to tell everything one knows."

The landlord, busy polishing glasses, gave one of his tumblers a final rub, and set it down with a thump.

"Aye, well, what I say is that I could put my tongue to a name!" he exclaimed. "To a name, you understand?"

"Just so," said Chaney. "And what name, now?"

"Ah!" replied the landlord. "To be sure! What name? Exactly." Thereat he wagged his head, as if to imply that if we would keep our tongues quiet so could he, and continued to polish the glassware, shutting his lips tight.

"Names," observed the landlady, "is things that one shouldn't mention."

We went away from the Cod and Lobster presently, and set out across the Levels for Marbourne. Passing the ruined farmstead at Piperscombe, we came across Shepperoe and his wife. They had shift-ed their quarters somewhat – on account of their horse, they said; he had eaten up all the available herbage on the old camping-ground. And Shepperoe wanted to know what luck we had had, and were having and likely to have. We had no objection to telling Shepperoe anything; we had set him and his wife down as straight folk from the first, and Shepperoe himself had an acute sense which made his remarks and suggestions useful. Being in no immediate hurry, we sat down and talked to them.

"Never, or very rarely, having occasion to darken the doors of a bank," said Shepperoe, "I shouldn't have recognized Harborough as one of the two young fellows that came camping hereabouts if I would ever been at close quarters with him. But, as a matter of fact, we never were at close quarters with those two. Weekends only it was they came, and when they came they kept themselves very close. If we happened to go near their tents, for instance, the younger one would pop into cover and keep there, shy as a squirrel –"

"And good reason – in my way of thinking!" muttered Mrs. Shepperoe.

Shepperoe turned a whimsical smile on his better half. Then he smiled and winked at us.

"The wife," he said, "has got a theory, a notion of her own, about that younger one. Whether there be anything in it or not, I can't say. Tell them, missis!"

"Tell them yourself, Zeph," replied Mrs. Shepperoe. "I ain't no hand at the gab – you are."

Shepperoe smiled at the invitation, and again gave us a wink.

"Aye, well," he said. "Just this it is – and Nance has as sharp eyes as another, to be sure. You see, masters, Nance here was coming home one evening from a round with her basket – she goes a-selling our wares in the neighbouring villages – and she saw the younger of these two campers coming across the Levels on a bicycle. And, as I said, Nance has sharp eyes – and is a woman, which adds point, master, to what I'm going to tell you. For they were at close quarters, these two, the rider on the bicycle and Nance with her basket. And nothing will convince Nance but what the rider was no young fellow at all, but a girl in riding-breeches!"

Chaney jumped from his seat. It was as if a sudden illumination had flashed upon him. He turned sharply on the tinker's wife.

"A girl?" he exclaimed. "A – you felt sure of that, Mrs. Shepperoe?"

Mrs. Shepperoe gave him a glance of mingled shrewdness and modesty.

"I'm a woman myself, master," she said. "I know a woman when I see her – howsoever she be dressed. And that was a woman – a young 'un."

Chapter Twenty-five

IN STORAGE

T HIS EMPHATIC PRONOUNCEMENT FROM Mrs. Shepperoe produced a sudden start of astonishment from Chaney. He pursed up his lips as if to whistle – a trick of his when some unexpected illumination flooded his mind – and he turned to Shepperoe. And Shepperoe gave him a sly look and a wink of his left eye.

"Such," said Shepperoe, "is Nance's opinion. And Nance is a pretty cute observer, master – and nobody knows it better than yours truly!"

"A woman?" remarked Chaney musingly. "And a young'un, Mrs. Shepperoe?"

"Gel!" replied Mrs. Shepperoe. "Maybe nineteen or so. Young gel."

"Sure it was, she always saw you with Harborough about those tents?" asked Chaney.

"We never knew it was Harborough," answered Shepperoe. "All we knew was that at weekends two of them used to come and occupy those tents – Saturday afternoons to Monday mornings. They kept to themselves, and we never saw them at what you might call close quarters. If I happened to go that way – our horse would sometimes stray near them – I did notice that the younger one, the one that was always in these khaki riding-breeches, like those land-girls used to wear, used to pop into one of the tents, as if shy of being seen. Which, masters, inclines me to the belief that Nance here is right. A girl!"

"Course it was a gel!" muttered Mrs. Shepperoe. "Ain't I got two eyes in my head?"

We went away then, and Chaney was very thoughtful.

"I've no doubt Mrs. Shepperoe is right in her surmise, Camberwell," he said, after we had gone some distance along the Levels in the direction of Marbourne. "Harborough was a sort of secret chap, and this is just the thing you'd expect. But – who's the young lady? We shall have to search into Harborough's past – there must be somebody in Wrenchester who can tell us something about him. However, the first thing is Merrick. We have got to find him."

We went on to the little inn at Marbourne, where we had left our car. And we had not been long there when Chippendale arrived. Chippendale, with characteristic promptitude, had caught a fast express to Wrenchester, chartered a taxi-cab as soon as he got there, and stepped out of it at Marbourne, exactly two and a half hours after leaving London. Knowing our Cockney clerk's capacity for seeing into the heart of things, we put him in possession – over an early cup of tea and its suitable accompaniments, to which he did full and silent justice – of everything we knew and had discovered up to that moment, including Mrs. Shepperoe's considered opinion as to the sex of Harborough's weekend companion. And having stored his mind with all this matter, we awaited Chippendale's judgment.

Chippendale slowly considered matters over swilling of tea and mouthfuls of plum-cake. Eventually he vouchsafed some questions.

"Didn't you say, Mr. Camberwell, that in examining Harborough's effects and papers at Rouen you came across a receipt from some Wrenchester tradesman for work done in connexion with those tents?" he said.

"I did, Chippendale," I replied. "A bill for putting up and taking down the tents."

"Well," continued Chippendale, "I should say that man might know something as to the identity of Harborough's companion. Try him."

"That's a good idea," said Chaney. "He might. Who is the man?" I consulted my memoranda.

"The man is one Shoreham," I replied. "I know his shop. He's an athletic outfitter, in Market Street. The bill was for setting up and taking down the tents and for storage."

"Storage?" said Chaney. "There may be something other than the mere tents stored there! Effects, perhaps – luggage."

"We can soon find that out," said I. "But, now that Chippendale's come, what about this Sandside Farm business? For anything that we know, Merrick may return there at any moment – and we must get in touch with him. Merrick probably knows where Beecher is. It's not yet four o'clock – let's decide upon what Chippendale is to do, and then you and I will run into Wrenchester and see this man Shoreham and find out if he knows anything."

Eventually we worked out a plan for Chippendale. Although he had never been in that neighbourhood before, he quickly picked up his bearings from my instructions, aided by a map of the district which I had in my pocket, and in a few minutes knew exactly where to go and what to do when he got there. Chippendale was to make his way across the Levels to the point from which we ourselves had looked down on Sandside Farm, and was to hide himself there in some convenient cover, keep an eye on the farmstead, its surroundings, and the stretch of beach and sea immediately in front of it, until we joined him. And as we had no notion as to the length of time he would be thus engaged, he took with him a parcel of food, which I procured from the landlady of the inn, and Chaney's pocket-flask – carefully filled by Chaney himself with what he considered the right proportion of whisky and water for one of Chippendale's tender years.

While Chaney got out our car from the innyard I set Chippendale on his way to Sandside Farm, and gave him his final instructions.

"It may be after dark when we join you," I said. "We shall come by the path that you're going to follow now. When we get within easy distance of the farmstead whistle – like this – once. If you've seen nothing, heard nothing, give one whistle in reply. But if you have seen or heard anything whistle twice. You understand?"

"That's all right, Mr. Camberwell," he answered. "I will remember. But have you any idea as to what time you'll be there?"

"It will – purposely – be after dusk, Chippendale," I said. "Why?" He took something from an inner pocket, which turned out to be a calendar.

"Nearly full moon tonight," he said. "As a matter of strict fact, Mr. Camberwell, the moon becomes full at twelve seconds twenty-three minutes after ten, and as she rises a good bit before she will be pretty high in the sky. Now, as I suppose we are not to be seen, what do I do when we have exchanged these whistle signals? Do I come to you, or do you come to me?"

"We to you," I said. "You'll find a lot of cover on top of the sandhills above the house; keep in its shelter – we'll join you there. And now you've nothing to do but keep along this path until you come in sight of the sea and the farmstead."

He nodded silently, and went on without as much as a backward glance, and I returned to Chaney and the car. We drove off to Wren-chester, and within half an hour of my leaving Chippendale on his way to the Levels were interviewing the man whose bill I had found in Harborough's pocket over at Rouen.

Shoreham, a man of evident shrewdness and intelligence, gave us a somewhat slyly amused look when I told him what we wanted.

"I'm a bit surprised – been a bit surprised, I should say, that you haven't been here before," he remarked. "Either you – or Bailiss."

"Oh?" I said, in surprise. "Why?"

"I've got things of Harborough's here that are probably worth examining – for your purposes," he replied. "I have thought once or twice that I would step across to Bailiss and speak to him, but one thing or another's prevented that. However, come this way, and I'll show you what I've got. You see," he went on, leading us through his shop to a warehouse at the back, "when Harborough gave me instructions to take down and bring away those tents he also told me to bring away with them some trunks that were left there. And here they are – I haven't examined them, but I do know that they aren't locked, so you can go through them now, if you like."

The articles which Shoreham pointed out and referred to as trunks proved to be two moderately sized suitcases. One, considerably worn, bore Harborough's initials on its front; the other, almost brand-new, had neither name, initials, nor labels. We opened the old one first, and began a systematic examination of its contents. A suit of well-worn tweed, linen, pyjamas, toilet articles, a book or two, a case of stationery, a camera and photographic apparatus and material – that was all that came to light. We had hoped there might be letters and papers – of that sort of thing there was nothing.

But there were some illuminating things in the other suitcase. We had no sooner opened it than we saw at once that it was filled with what Chaney called woman's gear. There is no need to particularize: there were all sorts of things that a woman makes herself attractive in, and they were all of good quality and taste – too good for knocking about in a tent existence. But there was also something else – a complete suit of khaki stuff, of the cut and style that the land-girls used to wear during the War days. It bore evidence of having seen a good deal of rough wear.

"This is what Nance Shepperoe saw the girl in," muttered Chaney. "She probably kept it at Harborough's tents to wear when they went there."

He began to examine the pockets. Presently from a hip-pocket of the breeches he pulled out a crumpled envelope, and after a glance at it turned excitedly to me. "Camberwell," he exclaimed, "look at this! Here's a find! See the postmarks – Wrenchester on one side, Kingsport the other. And the date! The day before Skrimshaw disappeared!"

"There's a letter inside, Chaney," I said. He pulled out a half-sheet of notepaper, and let out a sharp exclamation. "Bank notepaper!" he said. "Wrenchester Old Bank! Camberwell, this note is from Harborough! Who's it to?" he went on, turning to the envelope again. "'Miss Celia Morris, 39 Lavender Tree Terrace, Kingsport.' Now, then, what's the note about?"

There was not much in the note – a line or two scribbled hastily across the half-sheet of bank notepaper:

Am going to camp tomorrow afternoon – meet me there as near five o'clock as possible.

There was no signature, but we had no doubt that the handwriting was Harborough's. And Chaney immediately put letter and envelope into his pocket and began to bustle the things we had been examining into the suitcase.

"Now we're on the track, Camberwell!" he said. "I'm beginning to see things. The companion Harborough had at those tents was, as Nance Shepperoe said, a girl. On the Wednesday before Skrimshaw disappeared Harborough decided to go to the tents next day, and wrote to the girl to meet him there. That she did so is proved by the fact that the note is found in this suitcase. Well, the next job is to find the girl. For you may bet your last shilling, Camberwell, that this girl knows what happened at Harborough's tent that Thursday evening!"

"Regarding Skrimshaw?" I asked. "Is that what you mean?"

"Exactly what I mean! Skrimshaw called at, or was inveigled into, Harborough's tent – and never left it alive. Remember, Camberwell," he went on, "Harborough knew what Skrimshaw had on him! He knew that Skrimshaw was carrying two thousand pounds' worth of one-pound notes – he may also have known that Skrimshaw also had those French bearer bonds. Come on – we must see Bailiss and get to Kingsport."

Shoreham had left us alone while we examined the suitcase; we stayed a moment in his front shop to ask him to lock them up until they were wanted; then we hurried away to the police-station. And he chafed and fidgeted while I, making the story as brief as possible, told Bailiss of what we had discovered. When I had made an end, and before Bailiss could open his lips, Chaney cut in with a sharp question.

"How far is it from here to Kingsport?"

"Exactly eighteen miles," replied Bailiss.

"Then come on! Our car's at the door, and it's faster than yours," said Chaney. "Hurry up! We must see this girl at once."

"Shall we find her?" asked Bailiss. "I should say – not! Harborough probably took care of that." I was very much of Bailiss's opinion, but it was useless to put any opinion before Chaney just then, and we followed him out to the car.

"Now, Camberwell," he said, "get us to Kingsport as quick as you can. You attend to your driving; I'll talk to Bailiss about my view of things."

I knew the way to Kingsport as far as Marbourne crossroads; beyond that I had not gone. And coming at last to the outskirts of the town, a big, overgrown shipping-place, I found such a press of traffic that Chaney began to fume in the back seat. Then we had difficulty in finding Lavender Tree Terrace. That proved to be a drab and shabby little row of houses in a quarter of the town through which we had already passed; altogether it was approaching the end of the afternoon when we finally – through the offices of a policeman – found what we wanted. A word of explanation from Bailiss, and the policeman assumed guard over the car; on foot we all three proceeded to Number 39. A mean house; dirty curtains in the front windows; a general air of shabbiness – and when the door opened a shabbily dressed, elderly woman whose face at once became anxious and perhaps frightened.

"Is Miss Morris in?" demanded Chaney peremptorily. "Miss Celia Morris?" The woman's face grew still more frightened. She looked from one to the other of us, and she caught her breath in a gasp.

"What – what might you be wanting?" she asked falteringly. "I don't know –"

"My good woman, we want to see Miss Celia Morris," replied Chaney. "And our business is important. If she's in you'd better call her at once."

The woman half turned in the narrow doorway. A door had opened in the passage behind her, and a girl appeared. She waved the woman aside, and came forward.

"I'm Celia Morris," she said. "I expect you're the police. I knew you'd come – some time."

Chapter Twenty-six

HALF-WAY TO SOLUTION

A S WE STOOD THERE, hesitating, all three of us a little taken aback by the sudden appearance of the girl, I had a curious feeling that at last we were on the very verge of a solution of the problems we had so long been trying to solve. And I looked keenly at the face and figure before us, wondering if this girl really held the key to the situation. She was quite young, apparently not more than nineteen or twenty years of age; pretty, slight of figure, simply and neatly dressed. She faced us bravely and quietly, and if there was no lack of resolute assurance in her manner, there was certainly also nothing of boldness. It struck me, indeed, that here was the demeanor of one who has been steadily expecting something to happen and at last finds that the moment has come. And just as suddenly as she had appeared she suddenly turned, paying no attention to the elder woman, and beckoned us to follow her into the room from which she had entered the little passage. Once within, and the landlady, or whatever the other woman was, shut out, she looked us over carefully, one by one, and spoke again, in a dull, submissive voice.

"You are police, aren't you?" she asked.

"Superintendent Bailiss – Wrenchester," replied Bailiss. "These gentlemen are – with me."

"I knew you'd come – some time," the girl said, still in the same lifeless voice. "I knew you'd find me out somehow. Will you sit down, and tell me what – what you want?"

We sat down, and I looked round. A shabby, drab, comfortless little room, ill-furnished; the sort of place which, let as a lodging, would bring in a few shillings a week. I formed the impression that it was usually let to the more poorly paid members of the theatrical profession, for there were a few signed photographs on the mantelpiece, chiefly of young ladies who exhibited wide smiles and gleaming teeth, and were sometimes in tights and sometimes in ballet skirts. And the idea came to me that the girl before us had, or had had, some connexion with the stage, and had probably been left here – stranded.

My two companions, I think, were somewhat taken aback by our sudden discovery, and looked at each other as if doubtful which should speak first. But Bailiss was clearly anxious that we should begin whatever interrogation was imperative, and as Chaney nodded at me I took the matter in hand without further delay.

"We are right in supposing you to be Miss Celia Morris?" I asked.

The girl nodded. She had sat down facing us, and now that the light fell full on her face I saw that she was not as young as I had first thought, and that there were lines about the corners of her mouth and eyes, which showed that she had known trouble, if not actual pain.

"My stage name," she said. "It doesn't matter about the other." Bailiss made a sort of murmur, but I motioned him to silence. At that moment the real name did not matter.

I went straight on to what I wanted to be sure of at once.

"You knew the late Mr. Harborough, I think?" I asked her.

She looked from one to the other of us for a second, and for another second she hesitated.

"He and I were going to be married," she replied. "We were going to live abroad – in France. He went to France to find a place – a cottage, he said he'd get, in Normandy or Brittany, somewhere quiet. I was to join him over there when he'd found what he wanted. But – he was killed."

"I don't want to ask any unnecessary questions," I continued, "but how long had you known Mr. Harborough?"

"How long? Sometime – a few months," she replied. "I – well, I was stranded here----something went wrong with the company I was in, and I got left here. And I got to know Harborough, and – and then I used to go and spend weekends with him at the camp he had out Marbourne Levels way. You'll have found out about that, of course?"

"To come to the point," I said, "at any time that you stayed with Harborough at that camp did you ever see a man named Skrimshaw there?"

I knew from the look she gave me that she knew everything – things, at any rate, that we did not know. But I wasn't prepared for her answer.

"Skrimshaw died there!" she replied.

Before I could speak Bailiss intervened.

"Mr. Camberwell," he said, "I think this young lady ought to be warned that anything she says –"

"I think we'll leave that over a bit, Superintendent," I replied, with a glance that was meant to warn him. "Time enough for that. Yes," I continued, "you say that Skrimshaw died there? At the camp?"

"In Harborough's tent," she answered. "We'd two tents there. It was on a Thursday night. You see, Harborough only used to go to the camp for weekends, as a rule. But Thursday's the weekly closing day at Wrenchester, and now and then we'd go to the camp on Thursday afternoons, and when he did he'd let me know, and I'd join him there. It was one of those Thursdays that Skrimshaw came there, and died."

"Just tell us all about it," I said. "Tell it in your own way."

"There's not much to tell," she answered listlessly. "I got a note from Harborough that morning –"

I held up a finger to stop her, and after searching my pocket-book held out for her inspection the note which we had found during our search at Shoreham's.

"Is this it?" I asked.

She showed no surprise, and after a mere quick glance nodded her head.

"Yes," she said. "Where did you find it? Of course, I left a lot of things there."

"Go on with your story," I said.

"Well, I went there," she continued. "I got there towards the end of the afternoon. Harborough was already there. After we'd had tea we went photographing down Marbourne Ferry way. When we came back we started developing what he'd taken. He used to turn one of the tents into a dark-room for that. But he mixed the stuff he used in the other tent. I don't know what it was – he called it hypo. Perhaps you know?"

"Well?" I said, affecting to disregard the question. "Go on."

"Well, in the evening – I can't say exactly what time Skrimshaw came along. He was walking towards Marbourne Ferry, carrying a little suitcase. Harborough –"

"Wait a moment, young lady," interrupted Chaney. "Had you ever seen Skrimshaw before?"

"Yes. He'd sometimes called in at the tents of a Saturday or a Sunday evening, to have a talk with Harborough. They seemed to know each other very well."

"Yes?" said Chaney. "Well – and so Skrimshaw dropped in this Thursday evening that you're talking of? What happened?"

"Nothing at first, but that they talked. We were in the tent in which Harborough had been doing his developing. He'd finished then, but the tent was rather dark; that's perhaps why Skrimshaw made the mistake."

"What mistake?" I asked.

"Well, after they'd talked a bit Harborough asked me to go to the other tent and mix them two whiskies and soda. I went and did that, and carried the two glasses back. I knew exactly how they both liked it, because I'd mixed drinks for them before. I set the two glasses down on a little table we had in that tent. And close by where I put them there was the glass – a glass just like those I'd brought in – in which Harborough had mixed his developing stuff. Skrimshaw didn't touch his drink at first. He was talking about something or other – talking a lot. All of a sudden he picked up a glass, and drank what was in it straight off. And then, the next instant, we all saw he'd picked up the wrong glass and drunk the hypo!"

"What happened then?" I asked.

"I scarcely know. I remember that Harborough swore and that I screamed. Skrimshaw clutched at his throat.

Then he made to run out of the tent. He fell down. And it didn't seem a minute before he was dead, lying there at our feet. It was – but then I was frightened, too frightened to realize. And just then Mr. Beecher and a man who was with him came up to the tents."

"Mr. Beecher?" I said. "You knew him?"

"He'd looked in at the tents sometimes too, of a Saturday or Sunday night. I knew the other man by sight – I'd seen him once or twice, on the Levels – but I didn't know his name. And I didn't hear it mentioned at the time I'm talking about."

"Well, what happened when these two came?"

"Harborough told them what Skrimshaw had done – picked up the wrong glass. They talked a bit – at least, Beecher and Harborough did. The other man just stared at Skrimshaw's dead body and said nothing. Then Harborough told me to go into the other tent. I went – I was frightened. After some time he came to me and told me to change my things – I'd been in a land-girl's clothes that I kept there. I asked him what we were going to do. He said I was to ask no questions, but to do as he said and then to pack my things, all the things I had there, in my suitcase, and wait till he was ready, because we were going away."

"And you did all this?"

"Yes – I daren't do otherwise. I was afraid."

"What was going on in the other tent at this time? Do you know?"

"No – I couldn't see into it, of course. After some time, when I'd changed and had packed my suitcase, Harborough came for me. He was carrying a walking-stick which I'd noticed in Skrimshaw's hand, and also the small case which Skrimshaw had in his hand when he came to the tents. He told me to come away, and we set off towards Marbourne Levels."

"Were the other men, Beecher and the man you didn't know, there when you left?"

"Yes, in the other tent."

"Had anything been done with the dead man up to then?"

"Not that I know of. I think the body was still there in the other tent."

"Well, where did you and Harborough go?"

"I told you – we went off across Marbourne Levels, towards Marbourne Ferry. It was nearly dark then. Harborough said we must wait somewhere until it got quite dark, and we sat in a wood near the creek for some time. When it was really dark we left the wood and walked down by the water's side until we were near the Cod and Lobster Inn. Harborough made me wait there, on the edge of the creek; he said he'd go down by the inn and get a boat and come back for me. He wasn't long away; he came back, on the water, with a boat that he said he'd taken from the inn landing-stage. I got in, and he rowed us across the creek, to a point farther up on the opposite side. He fastened up the boat under some trees, and we left it. After we'd walked a short distance I noticed that he'd forgotten the stick. He said he'd left it in the boat on purpose. He still had the case. We walked across the promontory until we got to the outskirts of Kingsport, and there we got into a tram and came into the town. I came back here; he said he was going to an hotel. And that's all I know."

"But I suppose you saw him after that night?" I asked.

"Yes – up to the time he went across to France," she answered. "He left me money – and money for my travelling expenses to join him there. I suppose," she added, "I suppose it is really true that he's dead?"

I told her that there was no doubt on that point, and after asking her a few more questions and ascertaining that she still had sufficient funds for her present necessities, and that she intended to remain where she was for the time being, we went away, conscious that half our problem had been solved.

Chapter Twenty-seven

THE SOLITARY OCCUPANT

I T WAS STILL EARLY in the evening when we left the shabby little house and the mean street, and as we had no wish to join Chippendale until after dark we went into the principal part of Kingsport and got dinner at one of the hotels. And over dinner, and for a time afterwards, we discussed the information we had acquired from Celia Morris.

I have just said that we had half solved the problem. We knew now how and where Skrimshaw met his fate. But there were certain points about which we could not speak with certainty. One Chaney immediately raised. Was Skrimshaw really poisoned by accident, or did Harborough, by a sort of sleight-of-hand trick, substitute the glass containing the developing stuff for Skrimshaw's glass of whisky? When we remembered that Harborough certainly knew that Skrimshaw had two thousand pounds in his little suitcase, and that it was quite possible that he also knew that Skrimshaw was carrying fifty thousand pounds' worth of bearer bonds (or, if not the exact amount, that Skrimshaw had certain valuable securities on him, he, Skrimshaw, having in all probability asked Harborough's advice at the bank as to the disposal of such things), it seemed more than likely that Harborough seized an opportunity. Celia Morris might think the poisoning accidental, but Harborough was the sort of man who would be swift to act, and would act craftily. Again, as Chaney pointed out, Harborough, perhaps, had asked Skrimshaw to drop in at the tents that night, the design being already in his mind. Altogether, it seemed extremely likely that Harborough, whether acting on a sudden impulse or as the outcome of deliberate and planned intention, did poison Skrimshaw with intent to possess himself of the money Skrimshaw carried.

But now came another problem – what share had Beecher and Merrick in this? From all that we knew up to then Merrick must have been the man who accompanied Beecher to the tents. Was their visit a planned and arranged one, or was it accidental? We came to the conclusion that it was purely accidental. The probability was that Beecher and Merrick, after having supper at Sandside Farm, had set out for a stroll across the Levels, perhaps to look at the land of which Merrick had just become tenant. They dropped in on Harborough as casual callers will. But what did they find? A frightened girl, a man lying dead on the flooring of the tent, and Harborough inspecting the contents of a small suitcase packed with pound-notes! Beecher, as far as we knew him, was not the man to let an opportunity of that sort escape him. Beecher, in all probability, had in one minute assumed control of the situation. Skrimshaw was dead – there was the money and securities he had left behind him: two thousand pounds in cash; fifty thousand in easily negotiated securities. Very well! Who cared two pence that Skrimshaw was dead? But as regards the money, it was going to be a matter of share and share alike. Probably – all these things came to a question of probability – the actual financial arrangements were made between Harborough and Beecher, Merrick coming in as a person to be squared and the girl as one safely under Harborough's control.

And now the question was – where was Beecher, as the sole survivor of the principal partnership, and were we likely to get at him through Merrick? What we had seen – what Chaney and I had seen – of Sandside Farm that morning inclined us to the belief that though Merrick had not yet come into full residence there – *i.e.*, had not brought his farm stock nor his household furniture to the place – he, or some one, lived or had lived in the house. Merrick, at any rate, as a witness of what had occurred at the tents on the night of Skrimshaw's death, had got to be found – and so, as the evening wore into dusk, we left Kingsport and set off for Marbourne Levels, to join Chippendale and ascertain if he had seen or heard anything.

Driving our car to a part of the Levels from which we could most conveniently approach Sandside Farm unseen, we made our way towards the place at which I had made tryst with Chippendale. It was now well past ten o'clock, a fine summer night, lighted by a full moon, set high above the south-east horizon. And when we came out on top of the sandhills above the farmstead the view before us was one which, had it not been for our pressing business, I should have lingered to look at and admire. There before us, silvered in the rays of the moon, lay the broad stretch of one of the many irregularly shaped creeks of Wrenchester Harbour, running far inland between its densely wooded shores; on the farther side of the creek the moonlight glinted on village spires and the shining roofs of isolated farmsteads; on ours it lay on the long, curving stretch of sand and turned its yellow to whiteness. And at one point, immediately beneath us, and near Sandside Farm, there was a blot on that expanse of white where a boat had been drawn up at the edge of the lapping tide.

A sudden exclamation from Chaney drew my attention from this picture of land and sea under a full moon. Turning sharply on him, I saw that he was pointing to the house.

"A light!" he said. "Not a strong one, but there! Look!"

I looked in the direction in which he was pointing. There was certainly a light in one of the lower rooms of the house I thought in the room through the window of which we had peered that morning, and in which we had seen some signs of recent occupancy. It was certainly a poor light – the sort of light you would get from a cheap lamp or a couple of candles. And it was stationary.

There was nothing to be seen of Chippendale. Everything was very silent. You could hear the waves lapping gently on the sands, less gently on a group of rocks that projected into the sea on our left, and through the rank grass that pushed its spiky vegetation through the loosely knit sand a slight breeze shivered. In the midst of this silence, remembering the arrangement I had made with Chippendale, I gave a low whistle. No answer came to this signal, but a minute or two later a figure appeared from a clump of bushes lower down the sandhills, waved a beckoning hand, and disappeared again.

We made our way down the slope until we came close to the bushes. Then, without seeing him, we heard Chippendale's voice, speaking in cautious tones.

"Come in here!"

We crept, one by one, into the shelter of the bushes. There was Chippendale, and he gave us a warning motion of his hand.

"There's somebody about down there – at the house," he whispered. "A man! Have you noticed a boat lying out there on the beach?

He came in that, about half an hour ago. I saw him coming from where I was lying hid, up there at the top. Saw him a good way off across the creek at first. He came from the other side. When he got here he pulled the boat up a bit, and then went up to the house. You've noticed the light? There wasn't any light there at all in the house until he came."

"What sort of man is he?" asked Chaney. "What build, I mean?"

"He seemed to be a big, thickset chap," replied Chippendale. "Of course, in this light I couldn't make him out very clearly."

"It's most likely Merrick," said Chaney. "He's the tenant, anyhow. Bailiss, you know Merrick – what sort of man is he?"

"I don't know Merrick," replied Bailiss. "Never seen him."

"Never seen him?" exclaimed Chaney. "But – you asked him, so you told me, if it was true that Beecher spent that Thursday night with him, at this place!"

"Yes," answered Bailiss. "But it was over the telephone. There's a telephone here at Sandside Farm."

This seemed to set Chaney on a new train of thought.

"Um!" he muttered, after a moment's silence. "A queer business! Well, come, now, Bailiss, you're in a position to know all or most of the gossip of the countryside – you've heard, no doubt, that a man named Merrick had taken this place?"

"I've never heard anything about any Merrick beyond what came from Beecher through you," replied Bailiss. "You told me that Beecher told you in Paris that he'd spent that Thursday evening and night with his friend John Merrick, the new tenant of Sandside Farm, and asked me to find out if Merrick could corroborate this? Well, Sandside Farm is on the telephone – the previous tenant had it installed – so I rang up Merrick. He confirmed what Beecher said – namely, that Beecher spent the evening and night there and was never out of his sight or reach from the moment he came to the moment he left. The odd thing about it," concluded Bailiss, with a reflective shake of his head, "the odd thing was that I seemed to recognize Merrick's voice as one that was familiar, but I'm sure I've never met him."

Chaney looked more thoughtful than ever at that. Presently he pointed to the lighted window beneath us.

"There's no blind or curtain to that room," he remarked. "If you could get down there unseen, Chippendale, and look in –"

But there I interrupted my partner's instructions.

"No, Chaney," I said. "I'd better go. But you may be quite sure that, whoever the man is who is here, he's here for no good purpose, and he may show fight if interrupted in whatever he's doing. And more to the purpose, he may no doubt be armed."

"Well," replied Chaney, in his most matter-of-fact tones, "so are we. Three of us, at any rate. I don't know if you are, Bailiss?"

"I am!" said Bailiss. "But I didn't know you were. Fact?"

"We've each got a little something in a hip-pocket," retorted Chaney indifferently. "And we can all three hit a reasonable mark. All right, Camberwell – go down and see what's going on. We'll come a bit closer, certainly."

I made my way down to that side of the lonely house on which the light burned, and eventually got near the blind-less and curtain-less window. It was a difficult task that I had undertaken, for there was no cover of any sort in front of the window itself, no bush or wall or anything behind which I could conceal myself, and if I wanted to see into the lighted room I should have to run the risk of being seen at once by its occupants. But the thing had to be done, and I should have to take the chance, uncertain as it was.

I got to that window by dropping on hands and knees at the corner of the house and creeping along in that painful attitude until I was actually beneath the window-sill. There, crouching among a crop of nettles that sprang out of a bed of unpleasantly sharp stones, I waited a minute or two, listening. But I heard nothing whatever – except the murmuring of the waves on the beach below the house. Everything in the house itself seemed very still. Glancing above the window-sill, however, I noticed that the woodwork of the casement was thick and substantial, and, in addition, that it was well-fitting; it was unlikely, therefore, that any sound could escape – any sound, that is, of ordinary conversation. But, then, what likelihood was there of my overhearing any conversation? The man, as far as I knew, was alone. Still, there might have been somebody in the house when he came; might have been somebody there, indeed, when we made our previous inspection of it. It was a big, rambling place, and a dozen men could have hidden in it.

Very slowly, inch by inch, I lifted my head at last, until my eyes rose to the level of the bottom of the window. And in an instant I realized that I could look with impunity. There was a man in the room into which I was looking, and he was fast asleep before the fire. There he sat, in the one easy-chair which the place boasted, his legs stretched out to the blaze, his hands clasped across his waistcoat, his head dropping to his chest; probably, had the window been less well-fitting, I should have heard him snoring.

Knowing, from his attitude, that the man was very soundly asleep, and that there was no danger of his waking just then, I made a careful inspection of him. From his general appearance and clothing I came to the conclusion that he was a rather better sort of farm-labourer, dressed, for that occasion, in his Sunday best. That he had come there prepared to stay for the night seemed evident from the fact that on the table in the centre of the room (from which he had already cleared away the things which we had seen lying there in confusion at our previous visit) stood a basket of provisions, flanked by one of those stone jars in which the folk of those parts are wont to carry ale – to be precise, a gallon jar. And near it, still half full of amber-tinted fluid, stood a glass, and by the glass the man's tobacco-pipe, which he had evidently laid down before dropping off to sleep. The first question that rose to my mind after watching this man for a few minutes was – was he the only occupant of the house? But that was a question to which, of course, I could get not answer, and presently I turned and went slowly back to the others.

Seeing me walking so slowly (as a matter of fact, I was thinking hard, trying to puzzle out certain things), they came to meet me. Chaney rapped out a sharp interrogation.

"Well?"

"There's a man in there," I said. "Fast asleep in a chair before the fire."

"Merrick?" demanded Chaney.

"How should I know that?" I retorted. "He looks like a labourer – in his Sunday clothes. And he's brought food and drink with him – anyhow, there's a basket of provisions and a gallon jar of beer on the table."

"He was carrying something in both hands," remarked Chippendale. "Took whatever it was from the boat."

Chaney looked at Bailiss. "You're boss, Bailiss," he said. "What do we do?"

For once in a way Bailiss showed himself prompt and decisive.

"Get inside!" he answered. "We're not going to be afraid of one man. Come on! We'll knock till we wake him."

He advanced there and then on the door of the house. While the others grouped themselves round him I stole up to the window and watched the sleeping man. He seemed to be more soundly asleep than ever – but at Bailiss's first thundering knock on the door he woke, and at the second jumped to his feet and hurried, even eagerly, from the room.

Chapter Twenty-eight

WHERE IS MERRICK?

I WAS ROUND TO the door, mingling with the others, before the man had finished turning keys and drawing bolts – he had evidently fastened himself in for the night – so there we all were, four watchful and expectant figures, when at last the door swung open. There was a fairly strong light from the open door of the room which the man had left, and it fell full on our little semicircle. And the man half started back; watching him closely, I saw that his eyes had gone straight to Bailiss's uniform. But he made no attempt to turn; indeed, after his involuntary, start he came a little nearer to the threshold, staring inquiringly.

"Mr. Merrick in?" demanded Bailiss sharply.

That question seemed to reassure the man. He lifted a hand and scratched his head, as if puzzled.

"He isn't, mister," he answered. "Leastways, not at this present. I – fact is, mister, I come here to see if so be as he was in! But he ain't."

"Who are you?" asked Bailiss.

"Name of Flint, mister – Joe Flint."

"Where are you from, Flint?"

"Applestead, mister – the other side of the water there. Where Mr. Merrick come from – at least, where he farmed, before he come here. Leastways, before he reckoned to come here. Because – as you see, mister – he's not here yet."

"Did you expect to meet him here tonight, then?" inquired Bailiss.

Flint again lifted a hand, and again scratched his head.

"Why, mister," he replied, "I don't rightly know as how I can say what I expected! I been coming over in that there boat two or three times, expecting to find Mr. Merrick, but he ain't never here. Ain't seen nor heard anything of him this many days. Don't know what to make on it, nohow, mister."

"We'll come in and talk to you," said Bailiss. "We want to know a good deal about Mr. Merrick. Now, Flint," he went on, when we had followed the man into the room in which I had seen him asleep, "this is a very serious matter, and you must give me information. I don't know if you've seen me before –"

"I knows you, sir – the Superintendent from Wrenchester," replied Flint. "Seen you in the streets there, sir, time and again."

"Very well, Flint, now tell me this – didn't Mr. Merrick take this place, Sandside Farm, some little time ago?"

"He did, sir."

"Then why isn't he here, Flint?"

"Because he ain't never entered into what they call occupancy of it, sir. He's been here time and again, and me with him, a-looking round like, to decide about things, but he ain't never moved anything, neither live nor dead stock, nor yet household furniture, Accepting these bits of things you see here, sir – just enough for him and me to sort of camp out for the night. We been here several times, him and me – just for a night. Mr. Merrick, you see, sir, he wanted to look round this here place thorough before he came in."

"But you say you haven't seen him lately, Flint? Since when?"

"It will be getting on to a fortnight, sir, that I ain't seen him. He's never come here – when I've been here a-looking for him – and he ain't been home."

"Is he a married man, Flint?"

"Mr. Merrick, sir? No, sir, he ain't. He's a widow-man; his missis, she died two year ago. And he ain't any children, neither. No, sir, hasn't no 'cumbrances at all, Mr. Merrick hasn't."

Bailiss ceased questioning Flint at this point, and Chaney turned to him.

"What sort of man is Mr. Merrick?" he asked. "Big man – little man – or what?"

"He's a littlish gentleman, sir," replied Flint. "On the small side."

"And you say you've come here with him now and then – to inspect the place before he moved in?"

"That's it, sir. Deal of things to attend to Mr. Merrick considered there'd be before he could move his stock and furniture."

"Do you know Mr. Beecher, who used to be steward on this estate, Flint? Ever seen him?"

"Oh, yes, sir, I know Mr. Beecher. Mr. Merrick, he took this here Sandside Farm from Mr. Beecher. Old friends they was, I understand."

"Well, now, Flint, just let your memory go back a bit. Do you remember Mr. Beecher coming here one night some weeks ago to see Mr. Merrick?"

"Yes, sir. Mr. Beecher and another gentleman."

"Another gentleman, eh? Who was he?"

"Couldn't say, sir, 'cause, as far as I recollect, I never heard his name mentioned. Of course, I wasn't with them – I only see them come, and see them sitting about, having their pipes and glasses, and doing their bit of business. But I come to the opinion he was one o' these lawyer gentlemen."

"Why, Flint?"

"'Cause he had papers with him, sir – papers for Mr. Merrick to sign."

"Did you see Mr. Merrick sign them yourself?"

"I did, sir, some of them. They fetched me in to put my fist to one or two of them – what they called witnessing, sir."

"Well, this lawyer gentleman, now, Flint. What was he like?"

"Big, heavy man, sir – bigger than what you are. Clean-shaven gentleman, sir."

"And you never heard his name?"

"No, sir – never heard it mentioned."

"And I suppose you didn't know him by sight?" At that Flint paused and considered matters.

"Try to remember, Flint," said Chaney. "Had you ever seen him anywhere?"

"Well, sir, it sort of runs in my mind that I might ha' seen him in Wrenchester, and if I did, sir, it would be at the court-house. I once went there, sir, some years back, to give evidence in a case from our village, and I've a notion that perhaps I did see this gentleman there. It would be there if anywhere."

"A big, heavily built man, bigger than I am," said Chaney. "Clean-shaven, eh?"

"That's him, sir," agreed Flint.

Chaney turned to me and Bailiss and whispered a name:

"*Clayning!*"

With that whisper all sorts of recollections and ideas leapt into my mind. *Clayning!* Clayning was the last person ever seen with Skrimshaw in Wrenchester. Clayning was away from Wrenchester on that critical Thursday night. Clayning was family solicitor to the Garsdale family. Clayning it was who produced the will in which Harry Garsdale left everything to Beecher; the will which purported to be signed by Harry Garsdale and witnessed by Skrimshaw and another of Clayning's clerks. Clayning! Had he, then, with Beecher, been at the bottom of all this mystery and crime? But Chaney was asking Flint more questions.

"Were you and Mr. Merrick stopping the night here, in this house, on that occasion, Flint?" he inquired.

"That night, sir? Oh, yes, we were here for two or three nights that time." replied Flint "Might be two, might be three."

"Very well. Then you can remember if those two men, Mr. Beecher and the other man – the lawyer gentleman, as you call him – stayed here too that night? Did they?"

"They did, sir – both of them."

Bailiss looked round. I guessed what he was thinking, and voiced it for him.

"Where's the sleeping accommodation, Flint?" I asked.

"There's a shakedown or two upstairs, sir," Flint answered. "They had that; Mr. Merrick and I slept down here on these chairs."

Chaney went on.

"Now just let your mind go back, Flint, to that evening," he said. "I want to know this. After they would sign those papers what did these two men do? Did they stop in this house all the time, or did they go out?"

"They went out, sir," replied Flint. "They were out a couple of hours, and then came back. It was dark then."

"And they stayed here till next morning?"

"Yes, sir."

"And went away as they'd come?"

"As far as I know, sir. I didn't see them go – I was in the farm-buildings." Chaney drew Bailiss and me aside.

"If you remember, neither Beecher nor Clayning were at their own homes that night," he said. "I don't think there's a doubt that Clayning is the man Flint has been telling us of. And now the thing to do is to show Clayning to Flint, and see if he can identify him as the man who came here with Beecher."

"We must take Flint to Wrenchester then, now," remarked Bailiss. "It won't do to let him out of our sight till we've solved that matter."

Flint, matters being explained to him as far as we considered necessary, made no objection to accompanying us. Presently we all set out across the Levels to where we had left our car, and so returned to Wrenchester, where Flint was given proper accommodation for the night. And next morning, by ten o'clock, we had him posted at a place in the High Street whence he would get a good look at Clayning when that gentleman came to his office.

Clayning came just after ten o'clock, driving along the street in his car. I was posted with Flint in a convenient position, and of set purpose I had not told him what was expected of him; all Flint knew was that for some purpose not explained to him he was to keep a general look-out on the street. And it was Flint, of his own motion, who first saw and pointed out Clayning.

"That's the gentleman I told you about, sir," he exclaimed suddenly, pointing into the street from the window in which we were concealed. "That big gentleman there, in the blue car."

"Certain, Flint?" I asked.

"I would know him anywhere, sir. No mistaking him. That's the man as came with Mr. Beecher and brought the papers."

I took Flint back to Bailiss's office, where he and Chaney were awaiting us. And when Flint had been sworn to secrecy and duly disposed of until he was wanted again, Bailiss, Chaney, and I began to consult.

"There's no doubt," said Bailiss, "that Clayning's mixed up in this business – with Beecher, and at one time with Harborough. The thing is, to what extent? Looks to me as if there's been something fishy about that Garsdale will, and as if Clayning and Beecher had been in league with Harborough about Skrimshaw and his money and the bonds. And did Skrimshaw die by accident, as that girl said, or was he intentionally poisoned by Harborough? The events of that Thursday night –"

Chaney made a gesture which seemed to suggest that for the moment he wanted to get at a plainer issue.

"The thing I want to know about at present," he said, "is – where is this man Merrick? For Merrick was probably in the know about what had happened when Skrimshaw died, or, if he wasn't, he possibly suspected Beecher and Clayning and accused them – and has been put out of the way."

"Or sent out of the way, Chaney," I suggested. "That he's disappeared is certain. And I want to make a suggestion which seems to me a very practical one – or, rather, two suggestions. One is that a more searching and thorough examination of Sandside Farm should be made than we have given it up to now, and the other is that from now onwards a strict watch should be kept on Clayning's movements. For we want Beecher – and Clayning probably knows where Beecher is."

Chaney backed me up in that; eventually we settled that the four of us – Bailiss, Chaney, Chippendale, and myself – should revisit Sandside Farm again that night, after dark.

In the meantime two of Bailiss's most trusted plain-clothes men should, all unknown to him, keep an eye on Clayning's in-goings and out-goings.

Chapter Twenty-nine

THE SILENT ROOM

WE APPROACHED SANDSIDE FARM that night from a different base, leaving our car at a convenient spot in a turning on the road between Marbourne village and Marbourne Ferry, and making for our objective across the Levels by the path which led past Piperscombe at the point whereat Harborough had set up his tents. By this route we came out nearer the farm itself, and under cover of certain of its outlying buildings. The night, like the previous one, was magnificent; a full moon, shining in a clear sky, lit up land and sea; the scene, as we saw it from the edge of the Levels, was one of great peace and beauty. But as we came out on the cliffs and looked down on the long stretch of sand and the glitter of the creek beyond we were aware of these facts, the recognition of which pulled us up, sent us sharply to cover, and made us keep there, watching and waiting till we knew more of what was going on.

To begin with, there was once more a light in the house, and it was in the room in which I had found Flint fast asleep the night before. Secondly, down on the beach, close to where Flint's boat still laid, drawn high above the surf-line, there was another boat, in which we could plainly discover the figures of two men. And thirdly, and most important, out on the creek, half-way between our and the opposite shore, lay at anchor a yacht, the white-painted timbers of which gleamed brightly in the moon's unclouded radiance. There were a good many yachts about those creeks, as Bailiss observed, but this was none of them; they were small affairs, sail-driven; this was a steam-yacht of some considerable size. And along its shapely sides ran a long line of lighted portholes.

From the angle of the wall behind which we had taken shelter we stared at this unexpected sight in a silence eventually broken by Bailiss, who made precisely the remark which I expected him to make.

"What's this all mean?" he muttered. "A yacht – and that boat?"

"And the men in the boat, and the light in the house," I said, meaning to be sarcastic. "It means, Bailiss, that somebody has come ashore from the yacht to visit Sandside Farm, and is in the house now. And I think somebody must be Beecher, and that we have some stiff work before us."

"Beecher!" he exclaimed. "What makes you think that?"

"I think it because I have a habit of putting two and two together," I replied. "However, that's neither here nor there. I do think it. And I propose to do what I did last night – go down and have a look through that lighted window. For there is somebody in that house – and it's not Flint this time!"

"Be careful about those chaps in the boat, Camberwell," said Chaney. "If you can get to the window without being seen by them–"

"I'll manage it," I answered. "But you others – get down as near as you can to the house unobserved. And be ready with – what you've got in your pockets." Bailiss showed some indecision at that point.

"I don't know if this is wise, Chaney," he said. "There may be more than one man in the house this time, and we see two men yonder in the boat and that yacht pretty close inshore. If there's likely to be a scrap we would better get help."

"Where from?" I asked. "The village policeman at Marbourne, Bailiss? That's half an hour away, and Wrenchester's still farther. We're four men, and we're all well armed – Chaney, Chippendale, and I are, anyway, and I suppose you –"

"I can look after myself, thank you," he retorted, a little sulkily. "But four men –"

Just then I heard footsteps coming along on the Levels behind us, and presently there emerged from the bushes a man who, coming nearer, showed himself as one of the two whom Bailiss had detailed to watch Clayning. Chaney motioned him into our hiding-place, and, lifting a hand, pointed to the men in the boat. The man took the hint and whispered.

"Clayning's slipped us, Superintendent," he said. "We watched him from his office to his house this afternoon, and as well as we could keep an eye on that till after it got nearly dark. Then he came out and went off in his car – and of course we had no car. He took the Marbourne road – we made sure of that. And as you'd told me where you'd be tonight, I got a car and came on here to tell you."

"Pity you hadn't had a car handy when you were watching him at his house!" muttered Chaney. "What did you expect of a man that keeps a car always waiting?" He turned to me. "Get on with it, Camberwell – let's know what's going on in that lighted room."

I lost no more time. Already I had an idea, gained from the information just received from the plain-clothes man. And choosing my ground carefully, and availing myself of all the shadow I could, I made my way down to the house and to the window from which the light shone. As for the men in the boat, they had their backs turned on me, and saw nothing. And presently I was crouching beneath the window-sill, listening, waiting.

I let a minute or two go by; then I raised my head, and looked eagerly into the room. The two men before me were too busily engaged to turn their attention to the window. At once I saw Beecher. Beecher stood at the side of the table (from which all the untidiness we had noticed on our first inspection of the place had been cleared), busily engaged in packing into a strong leather bag a number of small packages of what looked to me like banknotes. And beyond him, in a far corner of the room, was a big man on his knees before an old oak chest. The lid – a heavy one – of this chest was thrown up against the wall; the man's broad shoulders and head were bent over the chest itself; he was taking from the cavity bundles similar in appearance to those which Beecher was handling, and as he withdrew them was laying them on the floor beside him. All of a sudden, as, emboldened by what I saw, I lifted my head a little higher, he turned round towards Beecher, and I recognized him. And he was the man I thought he would be – Clayning.

I dropped my head for the moment, but in a minute or two ventured to raise it to its former level. Beecher was still busily engaged in packing the small bundles into his bag – and I was now convinced that those bundles were, as to some of them, English banknotes, as to others, foreign. And Clayning was still busy at the old chest in the corner. Suddenly he half turned, flinging some loose papers on the table, and I saw his lips move as if making some remark to his companion. He turned again to the chest, as if to pull down and close the heavy lid, and as he did so, and before I could realize what was happening before my very eyes, Beecher, with an incredibly rapid movement, drew a revolver from his pocket, and, thrusting its barrel close to the unsuspecting man's bent back, pulled the trigger. And Clayning, shot through the heart, fell heavily across the still open chest.

Once more I dropped into the nettles – only to spring to my feet and run away towards the other three, who, already close to the house, quickened their cautious advance at the sound of the shot. I scarcely knew my own voice as I hurried out my words.

"Clayning!" I heard myself saying. "That's Clayning – Beecher's shot him! Right through the heart – he must be dead. They were –"

Chaney came to the helm there.

"Steady, Camberwell!" he said, gripping my arm. "Now! Beecher's in there? And Clayning was with him? And Beecher's shot Clayning? The door, then! He'll be coming out. Get your revolvers ready – and do as I do."

He pushed us – me, at any rate – before him to the doorway close by, which, being on the moonlit side of the house, was so situated that whoever emerged from it would at once see whatever confronted him, and he formed us into a sort of ring in front of it.

"When you hear him coming..." whispered Chaney.

But Beecher did not come. Two or three minutes passed. Above the lapping of the tide, stealing slowly up the creek, I heard my own heart thumping. But the expected drawing of a bolt, turning of a key, opening of the door before which we were carefully grouped – these did not break the prevalent stillness. Then, suddenly, somewhere above us, in the upper regions of the old house, a window was thrown open, and two sharp, piercing blasts of a whistle went screaming across sand and sea.

"He's spotted us!" exclaimed Chaney, dropping the arm that held his revolver. "Now we're in for it! Look to those fellows in the boat – they're coming. And –"

Before he could say more a shot from the upper window rang out, and Bailiss, who stood fully exposed in the moonlight, uttered a stifled cry, twisted round, and went down on one knee. Another, and the plain-clothes man, who, at the first report, had edged away towards the safety of the out-buildings, threw up his arms, and, plunging forward, clawed at the earth and lay still. In the same moment, catching sight of a figure at the window above us, I raised my revolver and fired. The figure disappeared into the darkness of the place in which it stood, and no answering shot came back.

We dragged Bailiss under the wall of the house, and turned to face the two men who at the blast of the whistle had come running from the boat. They were now within twenty yards of us, and there stopped, irresolute, evidently waiting further signals or orders from the open window above us. But none came, and, Chaney firing two shots from his revolver at them, they turned and hurried back towards the beach. We gave our attention to Bailiss then – he had been shot through the right shoulder, and his tunic was becoming soaked with blood.

Still, it might be only a flesh wound, whereas, though we were not yet sure of it, the unfortunate plain-clothes man seemed to be dead; he lay out there in the moonlight, anyway, as motionless as the pebbles among which he had collapsed, never having stirred since he fell. I was about to run across to him when a sharp exclamation from Chippendale checked me.

"The yacht!" he said. "Boat coming from it."

That was true enough. A boat had put off from the yacht, and was being pulled ashore at a rapid rate. There were several men in it, and the moment they touched the beach they sprang out and made for the two men Chaney had driven off. For a minute or two they appeared to consult it seemed to me, from the way their faces were turned towards the farmstead that they were waiting for some signal from its occupant. But, none coming, they presently spread out and began to advance on us.

"Wait till they get fairly near, and then fire all together," commanded Chaney. "If that doesn't send them off again, and they come closer, pick out your man from left to right as we stand here, and make sure. Careful, now – they're coming on!"

Bailiss, propped against the wall of the house, and groaning now and then with the pain of his wound, asked for his revolver, which I had taken when he fell.

"I can use this left hand," he faltered. "It'll be one more. And there are only three of you against a mob of them. Let me have it."

I gave him the revolver, and with another groan he settled himself in his place, and managed to level it.

"Take them from the left – your left," said Chaney. "If they've no firearms –"

The next instant we knew that these fellows, whether they had firearms or not, were certainly armed. Suddenly the moonlight glittered on what looked to me like old-fashioned cutlasses – swords of some description, anyway. They were going to rush us! And at that Chaney hesitated no longer.

"Mark your men – left to right!" he exclaimed. "And as soon as you've fired, fire again, and keep on firing. Wait – wait – a bit closer . . . now!"

The advancing assailants were within fifteen yards of us then; close enough for me to see, in the bright moonlight, that they were a formidable-looking lot, and that if they closed in on us with their cold steel we should have little or no chance against them. But with the *crack, crack, crack* of our revolvers (or, to be exact, automatic pistols – Chaney's, mine, and Chippendale's at any rate, whatever Bailiss's was) the situation changed. One man went down and lay still as the neighbouring rocks; two others collapsed and rolled about in agony; screams or yells of anger came from others. And suddenly what was left turned, fled, and presently began to pack it into the two boats. Five minutes later the boats were being pulled swiftly towards the yacht. Without waiting to see if they would return, we began to reckon up our position and see where we stood. Bailiss, as I have said, had a flesh wound in the shoulder, and now that we had time to see to him Chippendale set to work to patch him up till we could get him to a doctor. But the plain-clothes man was dead enough, and so was one of our assailants; as to the other two, one had a bullet through his left arm, and the other had been shot through the knee – a sufficient list of casualties for an engagement the possibility of which we had never even suspected half an hour ago.

But what of Beecher? From the moment I had fired point-blank at the figure seen in the open window just above me we had not heard a sound from the house. And now, nothing coming from the yacht, which, indeed, showed signs of getting under way. We broke in, Chaney and I, and proceeded warily to search for the murderer of Clayning. Clayning's dead body lay where it had fallen, in the room wherein I had watched Clayning and Beecher counting the packets of notes. On the table stood the bag into which Beecher had packed and arranged those packets; its mouth was open, and a casual glance inside showed that, as I had guessed when watching through the window, the packets were of banknotes of various countries, and probably represented a vast amount of money. That was no time for inquiry or speculation, but the thought flashed on me that Beecher and Clayning had in all likelihood converted everything they could lay hands on, the

Garsdale estates, the money shared with Harborough, into cash, and were escaping with it to – but who knows where?

Still . . . there was Beecher. Silently we made our way up the stairs of the old house, and into the room from which Beecher had blown the whistle. There was a great patch of moonlight on the floor, and Beecher, arms extended and very still, lay stretched, a black blot, across it. And I suddenly realized that for the first time in my life I had killed a man, and, leaving Chaney to look closer, I went downstairs again and into the sharp night air. Everything was very silent there, but somewhere overhead sea-birds were calling.

THE END

Please see over for further Golden Age detective fiction...

Visit Oleander to view all titles and sign up to our Newsletter

Murder on May Morning
Max Dalman

The Hymn Tune Mystery
George A. Birmingham

The Middle of Things
JS Fletcher

The Essex Murders
Vernon Loder

The Boat Race Murder
R. E. Swartwout

Who Killed Alfred Snowe?
J. S. Fletcher

Murder at the College
Victor L. Whitechurch

*The Yorkshire
Moorland Mystery*
J. S. Fletcher

Fatality in Fleet Street
Christopher St. John Sprigg

The Doctor of Pimlico
William Le Queux

The Charing Cross Mystery
J. S. Fletcher

Free Golden Age Mystery

Fatality in Fleet Street ePub
& PDF **FREE** when you sign
up for our infrequent
Newsletter.

ND - #0117 - 290524 - C0 - 203/127/14 - PB - 9781915475015 - Matt Lamination